three TRICKS

HIDDEN EMPIRE 2

ELIZABETH KNIGHT

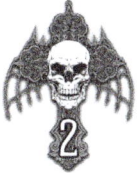

Copyright 2021 © Elizabeth Knight

All rights reserved.

This is a work of fiction. Names, characters, places, and incidents are either the product of the author's imagination or are used fictitiously, and any resemblance to actual persons living or dead, business establishments, events, or locales is entirely coincidental.

All rights reserved. No part of this book may be used to reproduce, scan, or be distributed in any printed or electronic form in any manner whatsoever without written permission of the author, except in the case of brief quotations for articles or reviews. Please do not participate in or encourage piracy of copyrighted materials.

Knight, Elizabeth

Three Tricks

Editing: Ms. K Editing & Leavens Editing

Cover artist: Dazed Designs

Formatting: Creative Wonder Publishing

Contents

Dedication	V
1. Dax	1
2. Dax	8
3. Dax	14
4. Dax	20
5. Eagle	28
6. Dax	35
7. Weston	42
8. Dax	46
9. Dax	53
10. Dax	60
11. Dax	67
12. Dax	73
13. Sprocket	80
14. Dax	85
15. Dax	92
16. Dax	98
17. Void	105
18. Eagle	113

19.	Dax	119
20.	Cognac	125
21.	Dax	132
22.	Weston	140
23.	Dax	146
24.	Dax	152
25.	Dax	160
26.	Dax	168
27.	Dax	176
28.	Dax	183
29.	Dax	190
30.	Picasso	196
31.	Dax	202
32.	Dax	208
33.	Dax	216
About Author		223
Also By		224

Chapter One

Dax

T HE FEELING OF BEING watched is what woke me.

Slowly as I could, I stretched out, reaching for the gun I kept in a holster in my headboard, but it wasn't there. Taking a breath, I stilled, listening to what was around me to see if that would give me a clue as to where I was. A strong set of arms wrapped around my middle, pulling me back against their chest. The rasp of beard nuzzled into my neck followed by a kiss that had me truly relaxing, remembering where I was.

"Sprocket, you're lucky I didn't have a gun near me, or I would have shot you," I muttered, cracking an eye open. "Didn't your mother ever teach you not to stare?"

There he was, sitting in the lone armchair in Eagle's room, wearing only a pair of pajama pants. His golden blond hair was loose and fell around his shoulders, setting off his green eyes, which were trained on me. Leaning forward, he rested his elbows on his knees as he smiled. "Well, little rebel, they might have if I'd ever had a mom around to teach me shit like that."

"Would someone like to explain to me why you're in *my* room, Sprocket?" Eagle grumbled as he shifted me closer, wrapping himself around me like an anaconda. "Did the rule of no one coming in here suddenly disappear?"

Sprocket just grinned as he gave me a wink. "No, but I thought it might be a good idea to check on her leg. Bullet wounds can easily get infected."

"Bullshit. I've been shot a few times and never had you checking on me to make sure I'm alright," Eagle said, lifting himself up on one elbow to peer over me at Sprocket.

Sprocket shrugged. "You're not as hot as she is in just underwear and a tank top."

"God, don't tell me Cognac is rubbing off on you, because that shit reasoning was just awful," I groaned, pretending to gag as I sat up.

Clearly, Sprocket decided we'd had enough sleep, even though we went to bed at four in the morning. That was normal for me, but these babies were all going to be dragging ass if they stayed up any later. So I sent them to bed. Eagle had his own plans, tossing me over his shoulder and plopping me in bed here with him.

"Dare I even ask what time it is?" I muttered, walking into the bathroom.

"Depends, do you have a gun or any sharp object handy? Actually, I take that back. I've seen what you can do with a butter knife, so I'm going to wait until I can see your hands before I give you that answer," Sprocket stated, making me shake my head.

"That tells me it's way too fucking early to be awake," I muttered, looking at myself in the mirror.

My short pastel pink hair looked like I stuck my finger in a light socket and there were bags under my eyes, setting off their silver-blue coloring. Thankfully, I hadn't had on any makeup last night or I would have been even scarier. The shittiest part of getting shot and needing stitches was having to figure out how to shower without getting them wet the first few days. So this morning I settled for washing my face and pits in the sink, then borrowing Eagle's toothbrush, knowing it would probably piss him off.

Speaking of the devil, Eagle joined me and headed over to the toilet to take care of business without a care in the world that I was still in here. Leaning against the counter, I crossed my arms and enjoyed the view of him in all his buck-naked glory. Glancing in the mirror, I can see tattooed across his whole muscular chest the Phantom Saints MC logo, a skull shrouded in torn fabric with a cross behind it. His skin had a rich olive tone that made him even more attractive to study. His dark brown hair was cut close on the sides but long on the top, and right now it was all disheveled and part of it hung in his face. Eagle met and held my gaze as I appreciated his "I woke up like this" look and I couldn't miss the heat that churned in his chocolate-colored eyes. That is until he saw what was in my hand.

"For fuck's sake, Dax! Why the hell would you use my toothbrush?!"

Smirking at him, I gave the whole thing one good lick before I deep throated it, then placed it back in its spot. "Just checking to see where our boundaries were, since you feel so comfortable pissing in front of me."

Eagle frowned and stalked over to me and gripped my neck, holding me firmly against the wall. "You damn well know you used that before I even came in here, little hellcat. You might be the infamous Two Tricks, but here, in this house, I'm the president."

"Bad move, Prez," Sprocket called from the bedroom.

Completely agreeing with the road captain, I gripped Eagle's wrist, softly stroking down his hand and arm until I felt him relax ever so slightly. Then, I swiftly gripped his thumb and pulled it back, twisting his wrist the wrong way and slamming him into the counter.

"It seems that this is going to be an area where we disagree because you're still not *my* president. I believe we agreed to be in a partnership, and correct me if I'm wrong, but to me, that means we are equal." I let him go and placed a kiss on his cheek. "Think about it and let me know, okay? I can always back out of the deal since we haven't made any solid arrangements."

Back in the bedroom, Sprocket was still in the armchair, and I could see the humor dancing in his eyes as I grabbed the bag of clothes that Tilly had gotten for me. Setting it on the bed, I pulled out what I wanted to wear, removed the tags, scattering them on the still unmade bed, and headed out to find coffee. I might be growing attached to these men more than I would like to admit but I was never going to be someone they could push around. I'd made my mark in this world through my own blood, sweat, and tears for the sole purpose of being free to live my life my way.

Sprocket followed me out of the room and into the kitchen, where I found Wes pouring himself a cup of coffee. Spotting me right away and guessing where I was headed, he held out the mug to me, which I accepted greedily. I hopped up onto the counter next to the coffee maker, knowing I was going to need another cup and was going to fight off anyone who thought they could take the last bit.

"I warned him not to wake you up, but it seems I didn't need to worry since he's still alive," Wes commented, as he leaned on the counter next to me, his hip touching my thigh.

The cutoff tank that Wes was wearing showed off his muscular tattooed arms and upper body in the most delicious way, not to mention the gray sweatpants. As always, his short hair was styled and slicked back from his face, showing off his angular jaw and rich brown eyes. I was still wrapping my head around the fact that I was now able to show him just how much I appreciated his manliness. Sure, we'd finally fucked but that didn't mean I knew where things were going from there. I hadn't ever thought it was a possibility, and now that it was, I didn't know how to move forward.

Taking a sip, I glared at Sprocket over the rim of my mug. "He didn't wake me up per se. He just creepily stared at me until my spidey senses warned me someone was in the room. I'd say he's incredibly lucky to be alive."

"How long did it take her to notice?" Wes asked.

"From a dead sleep to looking for a weapon—three minutes," Sprocket answered. "Pretty impressive after only getting three and a half hours of sleep."

Hearing this, I did some quick math in my head to figure out what time it was currently and growled as I slammed my coffee cup down on the counter. "Why the *fuck* would you wake us after only three hours of sleep! It's seven a.m.! Are you trying to make me kill you?"

"Far from it. We have a lot to do—dealing with the Mad Dogs and the De León Cartel, on top of running the day-to-day of the Phantom Saints and the Hidden Empire. You might have built your empire to run without you needing to be quite so hands-on, but with Wes here, too, I'm thinking that changes a few things," Sprocket reasoned.

"Don't you try to use logic. I'm far too stabby for that first thing in the morning," I snapped, grabbing my coffee cup and gulping more of the scalding liquid down.

"Little demon, you are stabby all the time. I don't think the early hour has anything to do with it," Void drawled as he entered the kitchen, wearing only a pair of jeans that hung low on his hips.

God, these men were trying to kill me with all this naked skin going around. Void was what I picture a modern Viking would look like, with a subtle British accent. He was massive not only in height but in bulk, which was fitting for the enforcer of their crew. His vibe was sexy intimidation and I fucking loved it, with half his head shaved, and the other, loose curly blond hair that brushed his shoulder. Not to mention, the word *oblivion* tattooed above one of his icy-blue eyes, finishing off the picture. The best part was that I had him wrapped around my finger like a big ol' teddy bear.

"Just the way you like me, right, Voidykins?" I grinned, pleased that he understood me so well.

Void walked over and wedged himself in between my legs. "Yes, little demon, the stabbier the better in my eyes... as long as we can play together. I feel like that would be a good time."

"I agree, that does sound like lots of fun. Something tells me that will probably happen sooner than later with a war on our hands," I mused, letting my hand trail down his muscular chest.

Weston shifted next to me to put his hand around my hips, holding me to his side. Wes wasn't insecure about a lot of things, but this I understood. He told me he loved me, and I freaked out on him, yet still fucked his brains out. Then, one thing led to another, and we haven't had a chance to talk since—not to mention adding Harper into the mix.

Dropping my hand, I looked up at Wes. "You seen Harper yet?"

"No, she locked herself in the room last night and refused to talk to me, so I thought it was best to let her be. You need to be the one to explain things. You dropped a huge bomb on her. Finding out that your best friend isn't who she thought she was, is not something you can just brush past, you know. This is going to take some time, and it might be better to find her somewhere else that's safe to stay. Being around all this might be too much, too fast," Wes reasoned.

He was always better at the people shit than I was, and when it came to Harper, I couldn't lose her. She is the only other person who still knew the real Dax before all this "Two Tricks" shit started. Harper became best friends with the Dax that I'd hidden away a long time ago, and I'd always tried to protect her from this part of my life. That is, until she got held hostage in her own home at gunpoint by a rival MC gang, the Mad Dogs. Sure, I'd managed to save her life and get her out of there in one piece, but she's been living behind rose-colored glasses for too long. Last night, I'd ripped them off and stomped them under my heel. I let out a heavy sigh and rested my head on Void's chest, wanting to avoid this whole thing. Give me a man to torture or someone to hunt down and kill, that would be far simpler than dealing with this emotional fallout.

"Why don't I make breakfast? How do pancakes sound?" Wes offered, running his hand up my back. "I'll even see if I can find some chocolate chips. You both love that shit."

I peeked over at him and nodded my head in agreement.

"Slow your roll there, Westly, this is Eagle's kitchen, and he hasn't given you permission to use it yet," Picasso said as he joined us. "If you want to risk it, by all means help yourself, but I can't be sure what might happen."

This caused me to snap straight up and growl at Picasso. "Anyone fucking touches him, I'll kill you... with a butter knife, so it's nice and slow."

"Easy, rebel, no one is going to mess with Wes. We already figured things out while you and Picasso were out. We just haven't had a chance to fill him in yet," Sprocket interjected, defusing the situation. "Besides, Picasso's just being a prick. Nothing new there."

I narrowed my eyes at the vice president of the Phantom Saints, holding his deep brown eyes so much like his brother's. "Don't fuck this up when we've finally started to like each other, Picasso."

"Wouldn't dream of it, spitfire. You saved my life. It belongs to you now," he reasoned, as he sat down at the counter with a smirk on his face. "Guess that makes me your personal prick now."

Groaning, I rolled my eyes. All of them needed to stop taking lessons from Cognac. Their pickup lines were getting awful.

Chapter Two

Dax

As Wes gathered what he needed for pancakes, I refilled my coffee mug and headed out into the living room. I didn't like feeling trapped with all of them cutting off my exit, even if we did have a truce of sorts between us now. Just as I got snuggled into the corner of the couch, a hand dangled a cell phone and my smartwatch in front of my face. Snatching them, I glanced up to see my personal prick grinning down at me.

"Oh, I get my watch back now?" I sassed. "What if I use it to call all of the Hidden Empire down on you guys?"

Picasso rested his arm on the back of the couch and leaned over it, so we were practically nose to nose. "You won't."

"Such confidence." I smirked. "It's foolish to think you've tamed me because I decided to work with the Phantom Saints."

He laughed. "Spitfire, there is no way I think you're tamed or even that it could possibly happen. You like us too much to kill us off, well, for now, anyway."

I narrowed my gaze at him but I didn't really have a comeback, which told me more than I wanted to know about how right he might be. "I guess we'll have to see how long that lasts."

Unlocking my phone, I ignored him until he left, leaving me to deal with all the messages, emails, and voicemails I had on my phone. Thankfully, it was fully charged so I didn't have to worry about it dying on me as I started to catch up since I didn't have time yesterday. All the voicemails from Wes I ignored and deleted without listening to, but there were a few unknown numbers that I didn't recognize. That alone set me on guard because this number was only given out to a few select people I trusted or worked directly under me. I hit the playback button and lifted it to my ear.

"Hello, this is Tim Pepperidge from Capital Bank, and I'm calling in regard to the bank account that you had us monitoring. It seems that the owner had removed all the money and closed out the account. It doesn't seem that they opened another but simply had it cashed out... in all cash. I hope this information is of use to you, and as always, we greatly value your business, Miss Blackmore."

"Son of a bitch!" I shouted, garnering everyone's attention, even causing Cognac to thunder down the stairs in only a towel.

"What? Is something wrong? Are we in trouble?" Cognac demanded, marching right up to me.

I was a little too dazed at the sight of his copper skin and muscles still slightly damp to register what he'd just said. "Hmm?"

"*Loba*, I know I'm pretty to look at, but I need you to answer me." Cognac chuckled with a smirk and a knowing look.

"It's nothing you need to worry about. It's personal," I answered, waving him off. "You're not *that* attractive, so don't let it get to your head."

"Sure, says the woman who was left speechless by seeing me in a towel," Cognac teased as he turned to walk back upstairs, letting the towel drop so I got a great show of his ass the whole way up.

Groaning, I flopped back on the couch so I was now staring up at the ceiling. It was just safer that way. My thoughts drifted back to the message that I'd just listened to, and I checked to see when they'd called. Of course, it was a day after I'd been taken, proving what I'd already guessed. Kimber, my brother's white-trash widow, was running and she took all of Devin's life insurance money that had been locked in a trust with her. I'd pulled all the strings I could to make sure that the money couldn't be taken out of the account easily. She had to jump through a shit ton of hoops, and somehow, she'd managed it. Or one of her new masters had more influence than I did, which left the De León Cartel. I swear to God, that woman would forever be a thorn in my side. This is what I get for letting the bitch live for the sake of sentimentality.

Wes appeared in my line of sight with what looked like a tray in his hands. "Harper might let you in if you have food."

Rolling off the couch, I hopped up and took the tray from him. It had two plates of fluffy pancakes, eggs, and chocolate milk—everything the two of us loved. "I'm kind of impressed you remember things like this."

"Dax, if you think I haven't been memorizing all your favorite things since the day I met you, then you're not as smart as I thought you were. I wasn't the one who said fuck feelings and refused to let anyone in after Devin died," Wes scolded me as he caught my shoulder and led me to the stairs. "Now, go fix things with the one person who knows you as well as I do."

"So bossy now that we've fucked," I grumbled, earning a swat on the ass. "Hey!"

Wes just rolled his eyes at me. With a cocked brow, he pointed in the direction that I needed to go.

Muttering to myself, I walked up to the second floor and stopped in front of the door that had temporarily been my room. Taking a deep breath, I knew that Harper wasn't going to answer the door, so I did the only thing I could think of—I kicked it open.

"What the actual fuck, Dax?!" Harper screamed as she glared at me from the floor, having fallen out of the bed.

"Um... I brought breakfast..."

Picking herself off the floor, she dusted off her ass and stomped up to me, reaching for the tray. "Thank you, now leave."

I twisted to the side, sweeping the tray out of her grasp and getting myself further into the room. Ignoring her growl of irritation, I sat on the bed and wiggled my ass further onto it before setting the tray down carefully. "As you can clearly see, this is food enough for two people. That would be you and me, in case you were wondering."

"Dax, I don't want to talk to you right now. I'm furious with you. Can't you understand that?"

"Are we talking about the level of mad like when I got paint all over the dress you needed for our final, or when I got us arrested in Mexico on spring break for taking that Maserati for a joyride?" I asked, recounting the two times I've seen her pissed at me.

"How about next-level pissed, because I just found out my best friend for the past ten years has lied to me about everything and kept a secret identity because she is a *crime lord*? Oh, yes, and let's not forget the fact that I was held captive in my own house at gunpoint because they were trying to use me against said lying bitch ass of a friend."

Hanging my head, I took the knife from the tray and started poking at the pancakes. "Yeah, that sounds like a douchebag move that would give you every right to be upset."

"You think?!"

Glancing up at Harper, I took in the hurt and betrayal reflecting back to me in her deep blue eyes with bags under them. Her blond hair was piled up on her head in a sad messy bun that was hanging off to one side, while she wore an oversized t-shirt. The Harper I knew never would let herself look like that. She was silk pajamas all the way. Being in the fashion industry, she took her appearance very seriously no matter what time of the day it was. This was yet another sign telling me just how not okay my bestie was with this whole situation.

"Would you at least sit down and let me explain how it all started? If you still decide that you hate me after knowing all the information, then I'll make sure you get somewhere safe and I'll leave you be, to live your life," I offered, silently begging to let her give me this chance.

"Will knowing this get me killed, because I really don't need any more experiences like last night?" Harper questioned, crossing her arms.

"I swear on my brother's grave that you will never again be in that kind of danger because of me," I promised, holding her gaze so she knew how serious I was.

She searched my face for a moment, then let out a huff and came to sit across from me. "Did Weston make all this?"

"We both know I sure as fuck didn't." I grinned as Harper's lips twitched, trying to hold back her own smile. "Can I eat my eggs first? You know there's no point in eating them once they're cold."

"I'm not cruel, Dax. Eat your eggs, then you better get your lying ass talking."

The tension in the room was thick as we ate in silence, making me beg for her to be mad at me instead of this wave of mistrust coming off her. Popping the last bit of eggs into my mouth, I gulped down the delicious choccy-milk and settled against the headboard. The only person who knew the full story that I was about to tell Harper was Wes, and that's because he lived it with me.

"The whole thing started eight years ago, when Devin got sent to prison for taking the fall for his president, the leader of the Blackjax MC. While he was in jail, the MC abandoned him to his fate, and he turned to a rival drug ring for protection. When he got out and tried to return to his life with the Blackjax MC, they turned him away. It didn't matter that he took the fall or was married to the president's daughter. The offense of working with this drug ring was too great for them to let him return, so he and Kimber left. In order to make ends meet, he kept working for the rival drug ring. A few months later, Devin was killed in a drug deal gone wrong when the customer didn't like the product he was pushing. It had nothing to do with Devin. He was low level and peddled whatever he was given."

"You'd told me it was drug related but I thought he OD'd. I didn't know he was dealing," Harper said. "Is this why you didn't let anyone come to his funeral?"

"I was pissed at Devin for ever getting involved with an MC, let alone becoming a dealer. Every time we talked, it was all that we fought about, and, of course, you know that I refused to go to his wedding to the she-devil. To this day, I don't understand what he was thinking. Devin was all heart and no brains, making him gullible and foolish. Kimber was just as upset as I was, but for an extremely different reason. She was used to being treated like a princess and now she was cast out with no support. I just recently learned that she talked my brother into using me as a bartering tool to get back at the

Blackjax. Joke's on them, I'm the one who fucking destroyed them."

Harper leaned forward, catching my eye. "How? How did you go from the Dax I've always known, to one that could kill so easily? I watched you, Dax. It didn't bother you one bit to kill them. Even now, you're not upset about it. I bet you didn't even have trouble sleeping."

"Simple, you don't fuck with my family, Harper," I snarled, reliving the moment when I found out Harper was in danger. "After losing half my soul, no matter how mad I was at Devin, it destroyed me. I wasn't willing to do what it took to keep my family safe, I just looked down at him for not making something of himself. What the hell kind of sister am I that I didn't even bother to help him when he lost everything? No, I had to make things right, and in order to do that, I needed to toughen the fuck up. With Weston's help, I took over the drug ring and used it as the foundation to build the Hidden Empire. In the world of crime, women are seen as objects, pawns to be used to gain favors or manipulate with whatever blackmail we find while on our backs in their beds. So, I created the persona of Two Tricks. At first, I used a figurehead, a puppet if you will, then as I grew, I got rid of anyone who knew the truth. To keep people off my scent, I worked my way up the ranks like any other member, proving myself loyal and invaluable during the light of day, then pulled the strings of the whole operation at night. The Blackjax were the first to be wiped out and the declaration was made that Two Tricks didn't work with biker gangs—ever."

The feelings from back then, as I struggled to change into the woman I've become now, were fresh in my mind. The fights I got into, the hazing, and the bodies I've buried for others tying me to the organization, just as I'd ordered. It was brutal and I had to fight tooth and nail for all the respect I've earned, but it was so worth it when I was the one that people feared. Just uttering my name could make men pee themselves, knowing that I was ruthless and bloodthirsty when I needed to be.

"Harper, the life that I live isn't pretty and I wanted to do all that I could to keep you out of it. You are the last bit of who I used to be, and I was selfish wanting to keep that safe, tucked away where no one could find it. My only weaknesses are you and Weston, and I will never regret doing whatever I have to in order to keep you safe. I am sorry that I got you pulled into this, but I won't apologize for what I had to do to keep you safe. Lying to you, keeping you in the dark, let you live freely around me under my protection. Now that someone's dared to fuck with that, it means people are gonna die by my hand until you're safe once again."

Chapter Three

Dax

Harper didn't respond right away to my declaration, instead, she just blinked at me with her mouth hanging open. "Wait... are you saying that you're going to kill even more people because of me?"

"No, I'm going to kill more people because they fucked with my family. Harper, this is the reality of my world that I didn't want you to know anything about. It's dark, bloody, and not very pretty," I said bluntly, trying to get her to see why I didn't tell her.

"Fine, I can accept that's why you kept me in the dark. I'm not forgiving you by any means, but I can understand why you did it," Harper relented. "So what happens now?"

I reached out and grabbed her hand, holding it with both of mine and looked her dead in the eye. "Harper, I *will* keep you safe. No matter what it takes. Do you believe that?"

"Yes. If I know anything at all about you, it's that you don't give your word lightly."

"The plan is to find you someplace safe and out of danger. I haven't found where that's going to be yet. Are you okay being here until then? If not, I do have a friend here that might be able to take you in, so you're not in the center of the storm," I offered.

"Worried I might be a cockblock with all this fine ass running around?" Harper teased, showing me a glimmer that my best friend might forgive me yet.

"If you want to try, go for it. They seem to be under the illusion that I'm theirs," I groaned, flopping back on the bed. "I never wanted anything serious from one guy, and now, I've suddenly acquired six."

"Wait? Are you saying that you and Weston finally expressed your undying love for each other? Why the fuck didn't you tell me this right away?" Harper screeched, all but flipping the tray over in her excitement.

We both scrambled for it, clutching the glasses of chocolate milk, lest we commit a sin we couldn't come back from. Carefully, we set everything on the floor before Harper tackled me in a bear hug, squeezing the life out of me. "Tell me everything! I need to know every detail!"

"I'm not sure you want *every* detail—"

"O M G, you fucked him too, didn't you? Oh, now I'm majorly fucking pissed at you for holding out on me," she yelled, hitting me with a pillow. "Start talking or I swear to God, I will use the super-secret weapon."

I shoved her off me and put her into a wrestling lock on her stomach. "You fucking tell anyone about that shit, and I take back everything I ever said about you, Harper. I will feed you to the wolves myself."

"Okay, I give, I give, uncle!"

Satisfied that she wasn't going to turn on me, I let her loose. "I couldn't tell you about Wes because I would have had to explain where I was and what happened. He was helping me escape... unsuccessfully, I might add. One thing led to another, and we fucked... a few times."

"Nope," Harper said, popping the "p" and wagging a finger at me. "That's not gonna fly. You owe me, and I want *all* the details."

I glared at her but gave in, knowing this is the shit she lived for. "Remember that you asked for this, alright?"

She nodded enthusiastically, clutching the pillow like an excited little kid, as I delved into the whole saga of how I ended up here, escaped, got caught, and showed up back at my house with Picasso.

"Girl, that shit's like straight out of a book! It's every girl's dark fantasy to be kidnapped by sexy bikers to then soothe their beastly natures, only to make them into the perfect men to keep you well fucked and smothered in love!" Harper cackled, rolling on the bed, until she sat back up with a pout on her lips. "Why do you get all the fun? I'm surrounded by Ken dolls who only care about looks and money. They might be hot to look at, but the moment they start talking, they prove how dumb they are."

"Contrary to your fantasies, I don't recommend going the kidnapping route. This scenario is not the typical outcome," I cautioned her, needing to make sure that she wouldn't do something stupid.

She cocked her head to the side, giving me a calculating look. "What you really mean is that I can't defend myself like you can, that I'm too vulnerable. I've known you for too long not to be able to read between the lines when you say shit like that, especially now that I know the whole story. You've always been majorly overprotective when we go out. I joke about you being my bodyguard but in a way you really are, aren't you?"

"If you're asking me if I've intervened to keep the fuck nuggets away from you, then the answer is of fucking course," I admitted with a shrug.

Not loving where this conversation was going, I decided that we needed to change things up. Slipping off the bed, I tossed a pair of pants from her bag at her. "Come on, I want to introduce you to Tilly. I think you'll hit it off."

"Is this who you're trying to pawn me off on so you can have the bedroom back for happy fun times with Westie?" Harper asked as she got dressed.

I just glared at her over my shoulder, knowing she was enjoying teasing me far too much. "Want me to introduce you to the others properly? Last night was kind of a clusterfuck."

"Absolutely, Wes might have my stamp of approval but the verdict's out on the others."

Heading back downstairs, with her hot on my heels, I found all the men sitting or standing around the counter talking. When they heard us coming, they quickly shut up and watched Harper, cautiously waiting to see if she was going to have another meltdown.

"Harper, these are the leaders of the Phantom Saints MC. Guys, this is Harper, my best friend and soul sister, that is to be treated like a lady or I'll have to chop off your dicks, okay?" I shared, giving them an evil grin, daring them to test me.

Eagle walked around the counter and held out his hand to Harper. "Name's Eagle, I'm the president of the club. If you need anything or have problems with any of my men, you let me or my brother, Picasso, whom I think you already met, know."

"Yes, thank you, I appreciate that. I'm a little out of my depth with all this," Harper said, waving her hands in every direction. "Are there any rules I should know about being here?"

"Nope, because if anyone fucking touches you, I'll gut them," I growled.

Sprocket reached out and pulled me against him where he was sitting. "Easy, little rebel, we'll make it known that she's off-limits with your wrath as the punishment. That should be more than enough to keep her safe and allow her to be anywhere she wants to be." I grunted but relaxed into him. "I'm Sprocket, by the way. It's nice to meet you, Harper."

Cognac leaned on the counter and waved, giving Harper a sultry grin. "Cognac's the name, and if you have any tips for getting my *loba* to retract her claws, I would be forever grateful."

"Oh Lord, girl, that man is trouble." Harper laughed, shaking her head. "Sorry, chicks before dicks and all that."

"Worth a shot. I'll wear her down eventually," He grinned, turning to give me a wink. "The hunt is half the fun, isn't it, *loba*?"

"Ignore him, he was dropped on his head as a child. Thank goodness he's pretty to look at," I shot back, flipping him the bird.

Void stood from his seat and walked up to Harper. I could see her gulp as she looked up at him, ready for him to say something to her. "My little demon sees you as family, that makes you our family as well. That being said, we will not be giving her up no matter how you feel about us."

My jaw dropped at his declaration. "What the hell was that?!"

"Did you want me to lie to her?" Void asked, as he faced me with a questioning brow. "Isn't that what started your fight in the first place? We will protect her, but my first priority is you, little demon, even if you end up getting mad at me for keeping you safe. Weston also understands the rules and agrees."

Rubbing my face with both hands, I stepped away from Sprocket, only for him to clamp his hands on my hips and lock his legs around mine. "Sorry, little rebel, but you're not running away that easily. We're going to need to have this conversation at some point, no matter how much you want to avoid it. Us men have said our piece and figured things out. Now, it's your turn to hear us out."

"Seriously, you guys, we have so many more important things to worry about than this. Like the fact the Mad Dogs are making moves against me, and their leader thinks he owns me or some shit," I grumbled, trying to struggle out of Sprocket's hold.

Shocking the hell out of me, I felt teeth biting into the muscle between my shoulder and neck, ceasing my struggles instantly. Sprocket let out a pleased hum as he licked my skin before he released me and turned me to face him. "I get that you've been going at this alone for a long time, but that shit changes as of right now. You have all of us behind you. I wasn't kidding when I said we would be your knights, and one of the jobs of a knight is to protect their queen. The fierceness you feel toward Harper is exactly how we feel about you," He explained, booping me on the nose. "Now, we don't have to talk about it right now, but it will happen by the end of today, even if we have to make Void strap you down."

Harper let out a bark of laughter. "Yeah, sorry, boys, that's not a threat. She'd enjoy that far too much."

Snapping my head around, I scowled. "Traitor! Whose side are you on?"

"Babe, you know I love you and I want only the best for you. Well, this right here took me all of five minutes to figure out was exactly what you need," Harper stated, hands on her hips. "I've never seen you act like this with anyone other than myself or Wes. You would have dropped Sprocket where he sat if you didn't want to be stopped, showing me the opposite of what's coming out of your mouth."

I opened and closed my mouth, trying to come up with some sort of comeback to prove her wrong, but I couldn't and that irritated me even more.

"Holy shit, is she speechless?" Picasso asked, smirking at me.

"Why don't you come a little closer and find out," I said through clenched teeth.

"Nah, I'm good over here where it's safe," Picasso answered, resting his chin on his hand.

At this, Harper lost it and started laughing so hard she had to clutch her stomach. "They've known you for, what a week, and already they've got your number, girlfriend? Oh yeah, they get my gold seal of approval. If you fuck this up, you'll never find men like them again. Clearly, the problem you had was trying to find one man who could handle you. Looks like it takes five burly bikers and one tattooed genius to do the job."

All the guys looked far too pleased with her praise, irritating me even more. "Whatever. Harper and I are going to see Tilly. I think the faster I can get her away from you lot, the better. It seems there's a traitor in the midst, pretending to be my best friend."

"Don't be a sore loser. It's not cute on you," Harper teased.

Sprocket let me go as I darted forward, grabbed Harper's hand, and dashed out the front door like the doors of hell were opening.

"Have fun, be safe, make good choices!" Cognac called after us.

Chapter Four

Dax

When we made it to Tilly's house, I marched right up the steps and hit the doorbell a few more times than was necessary, but I was still processing the fact that everyone was ganging up on me. Harper leaned against the porch railing, watching me with a self-satisfied look, as we waited for someone to answer the door.

"Who the fuck are you?" a voice snarled as the front door opened.

Standing in the doorway was a tall bald man, covered in Japanese traditional tattoos, and I mean covered. Even his head sported a bright green dragon with bared teeth, which would make most people cringe at the sight. I, on the other hand, was super impressed with the level of skill and craftsmanship of his artist.

"Hi! I'm Dax, is Tilly around?" I answered, off-handedly as I kept scoping out his tats.

"It's fucking eight in the morning, where else would she be? How did you get here and how do you know my wife?"

His icy tone caused me to finally meet his gaze. "Ah, you must be, Gator."

"Babe, what's going on?" Tilly called, as she walked up behind her husband, wrapping her arms around his naked torso, and peeking over his shoulder. "Dax! They let you out of your cage?"

"You really think those assholes could keep a girl like me down for long?" I huffed. "Eagle might be a hard-ass, but it's amazing what happens when he's trying to get in your pants."

"T, who is this chick?" Gator asked, not taking his eyes off me for a second, as if he expected me to do something crazy.

Tilly chuckled and slipped out in front of him. "Gator, meet Dax, the soon-to-be old lady of the Phantom Saints leadership. Dax, this is my other husband, Gator. He was out of town the last time you came over." Her gaze drifted over to Harper then back to me. "You didn't say anything about having a girlfriend too, you slut."

Harper walked up behind me and wrapped her arms around my neck. "Tootsie, are you keeping me a secret? I'm so hurt," she said in a sickeningly sappy voice, before laughing. "Oh, for Dax to be so lucky to land the likes of me. No, I'm her best friend and I'm looking for a place to hide out while a rival MC is coming after me to get to her."

Both Tilly and Gator looked shocked at Harper's declaration. "Ah, why don't you come in? This doesn't sound like the type of thing to talk about on the porch," Tilly suggested, shoving Gator into the house.

"Wait a minute, you're Dax, Two Tricks' enforcer?" Gator blurted, finally connecting the dots. "Don't tell me those idiots convinced you to make a deal with them to get Tricks on board."

Tilly sighed and waved her arms to herd us deeper into the house toward the kitchen. "This conversation's going to need coffee. It's way too goddamn early for this."

"Yeah, sorry about the early drop in, the guys are fucked in the head and think being up with the sun is a good thing," I muttered as I plopped down at the kitchen table.

Mutt, Tilly's second husband, walked into the kitchen, toweling off his hair. "Teetee, did I hear the doo—"

He halted when he saw us sitting at the table and I gave him a little wave. "Morning!"

"So, you did survive your face off with Void. Gotta say I'm impressed." Mutt grinned before walking up to Tilly and kissing her on the cheek. "You have a girls' day planned or something?"

Tilly smiled and squished his face with her hands before planting a kiss on his lips. "This is why I love you, ya mangy Mutt. Dax was just about to tell us what prompted this visit and I'm gonna make more coffee, since I'm assuming, you ladies, would want some?"

"You are a fucking angel," I said with a wink.

"I think caffeine is the only way I'm going to make it through this day," Harper grumbled. "Seems that the tiny one has been holding out on me about the dark side of her life."

"Yeah, I'm not sticking around for girl talk," Gator stated, as he headed out of the kitchen.

"Wait! I'm gonna need to ask a favor and you all have to be on board with it," I called, halting Gator in his tracks.

He peered at me over his shoulder, narrowing his gaze at me. "Why don't I like the sound of that?"

"Full disclosure, The Mad Dogs and the De León Cartel are coming for me. They tried to kidnap Harper to use as leverage. Obviously, I got her out of that situation, but I need a safe place for her to stay until I can find something better suited," I shared. "Oh, and I might want to mention that I'm not just Tricks' enforcer—"

"What does that mean?" Gator demanded, narrowing his eyes.

"Ah, well you see... I am Two Tricks."

The three of them gawked at me, but so far, the information was going over better than expected.

"You gotta be shitting me." Tilly laughed. "Why the fuck am I not more surprised? Guess it only makes sense. There's no way anyone else could get those five idiots wrapped around their finger." She paused and then her eyes widened. "Holy shit, do they know they kidnapped the one person they were trying to make a deal with?"

Now it was my turn to laugh, seeing her come full circle with what me being Two Tricks meant. "Apparently, we're supposed to have a *talk* about it at some point today."

"Which is how we ended up on your doorstep so early in the day. Dax's level of emotional avoidance is top notch," Harper added.

"You keep saying shit like that and I'll leave you out in the wild for someone to come find you," I threatened.

"Why us?" Mutt asked, leaning against the counter, frowning at me.

Great, now I've pissed off the cheerful one of the two of them. I hate having to play nicey-nice.

"We can make it work in the guys' house, but that would put her right at ground zero for plans to attack both parties. If something were to happen again, I want her to have as much plausible deniability as she can. Tilly is a fellow badass bitch, who won't be easy to mess with or fool, and you two are married to her. Therefore, in my brain, it makes you good people. And my guys also agreed she'd be safe here," I answered.

"Your guys, hmm?" Harper whispered, jabbing me with her elbow. "Does everyone in a motorcycle gang have multiple partners?"

Tilly glanced at both her men before answering. "I wouldn't say it's typical, or even normal, but you don't join an MC if you're prone to following the rules. Gator and I didn't plan on me falling in love with Mutt, or the two of them becoming as close as brothers, but it did and we're happy."

"God, seeing Dax with those men fawning all over her, and now you with your hunky duo, makes me think the rest of the world is missing out," Harper said wistfully. "I get it though. If you don't want to be saddled with me since we don't know each other at all, I'll manage at the house with them."

"Let Mutt and I talk it over with Eagle and the others before we give you our answer. If I'm going to put my family in danger, I need to know the whole situation," Gator announced, leaving the possibility open. "It's just temporary, right?"

I nodded. "I'm going to reach out to my contacts to get her to one of my safehouses with some bodyguards. It would only be a few days, or less, depending on how fast I can get things moving."

Gator grunted and exited the kitchen, followed by the sound of the front door.

"Twenty bucks he's going to talk to them now," Tilly challenged, wagging her brows at me.

"Pfft, it's stupid to take a bet when I already know the answer to that is yes." I snorted.

"Wise move." Mutt chuckled. "I would avoid any bets with her in the future, she's wicked crafty."

"Babe, don't you have work or something to get to?" Tilly asked, frowning at her husband.

He smiled up at her then stood. "Looks like that's my signal to leave." Giving us a salute and Tilly a quick kiss, he headed out.

"Now that we have the house to ourselves, what do you want to do?" Tilly asked, handing Harper and I mugs of coffee.

I tapped my fingers on the mug as I thought. "The guys want to have some big conversation about our feelings and where do we see this relationship going type thing. So, I'm game for anything that keeps me from dealing with that any time soon."

"Any good beaches around here? I could go for some R 'n R after what I've been through," Harper suggested.

"Hmm, that could work." Tilly grinned. "How do you feel about getting smuggled out of here?"

Leaning forward, I returned her grin with my own. "You're talking my language. What do you have in mind?"

"So one of my jobs is to bring parts that need to be worked on by Sprocket and his team here. I head out every Wednesday, and typically while I'm out in LA, I do some shopping since out here in bumfuck we don't have much variety. So really, all you need to do is hide out in the bed of my truck until we get past all the surveillance and we're home free."

"Yeah, but they know we're here with you. Wouldn't it be odd to have you just leave us?" Harper asked.

Tilly frowned and slumped forward on the table. "Well fuck."

"Guys, we're counting on the fact that they will even notice Tilly leaving. Diversion anyone?" I explained pulling my phone out and hit Brian's number.

"Dax, what's wrong?" Brian answered on the second ring.

Harper snorted at his alarm. "Nothing's wrong except that I'm hiding out with some goddamn morning people."

"They're still alive?"

"For now. They keep giving me coffee and food," I said, shaking my head at how well this man knew me. "Look, I need you to do something for me. Tricks is calling a meeting for some major news and wants to share it personally and picked out this crazy location. I'm gonna give you the coordinates, and I need you to send someone to do a flyby to make sure the area is safe. You know what, the location from what I heard is pretty extensive so send two guys up in helicopters to scout it out. Keep this between us for now. Once we get the details settled, we'll be announcing it to the Empire."

"Sure thing, boss. Is this about the De León Cartel?" Brian questioned.

"That's part of it, but a lot more is going on than you know. I promise that all your questions will be answered when that meeting happens. Text me when the guys are in the air, so I know it's getting done."

"Will do," Brian answered then hung up.

Tilly and Harper looked at me with shocked expressions as I texted Brian where to send the pilots. I wasn't sure why that kept happening, it wasn't like I was acting any different.

"You can get two helicopters in the air like that?" Harper asked, snapping her fingers.

"That's what you call a diversion? Goddamn, woman, you're going to create utter chaos when they fly over," Tilly blurted.

I cocked my head to the side as I frowned at them. "It's not that big of a deal, guys. I've come up with way more involved ideas. No one gets shot or stabbed in this situation, just a little flyby and chaos."

"The fact that you can't see the crazy you just said is kind of impressive. How have you been able to hide this from me all these years?" Harper demanded.

"If you think that's crazy talk, then I need to get you away from here as fast as possible," I said, sitting back in my chair and sipping on my coffee. "As for hiding it from you, well, I've become somewhat of a master after hiding it from the world for six years."

Tilly let out a huff of laughter. "Tad bit on the dramatic side there, don't you think, Daxie?"

"Still doesn't make it untrue. I got the shit beat out of me many times until I learned to be this scary. That didn't happen overnight. I took lessons from anyone who would take pity on me, until I could beat them. Then when I started to get more blood on my hands from friends and foes, people left me alone, knowing they'd lose a body part. Some still saw the outward appearance of a tiny female though." I shrugged, as I remembered working through the pain of losing my brother by working my body to its limit.

"What happened to those guys?" Harper hedged; her eyes wide with rapt interest.

"Let's say that a black ace of spades playing card shoved into their dead mouth made it known I wasn't going to tolerate being fucked with anymore. That's when I made myself the enforcer. Everyone was scared shitless of me and I could keep tabs on everything happening in my empire."

Tilly let out a low, impressed whistle. "What do you think's gonna happen when they find out you've been Tricks all along?"

"Is hoping for a fruit basket too much?" I smirked.

My phone chimed, letting me know that the choppers were in the air. "Well, if we're gonna do this, then I think it's best if we pack whatever we want to take with us. They'll be over us in about a half hour."

"Harper, I think you'd be able to fit into one of my suits. Dax on the other hand..." Tilly said, glancing down at my itty-bitties.

"Yeah, yeah, not all of us can be blessed with the need for boulder holders like the two of you," I muttered, crossing my arms over my chest. "Just remember that I get to wear all the backless, strapless clothes you guys can't," I stated, sticking out my tongue.

"Thanks, Tilly, I'd be happy to wear whatever you've got to share." Harper smiled, ignoring me entirely. "Should we make any food to take with us?"

"Why would we need to do that?" I questioned. "We'll just get food at the beach, oh and something alcoholic! Did you know they make adult popsicles now?!"

"God, why does that sound amazing? Okay, Harper, come with me to pick out a suit, then we'll pack the truck and be ready to roll out when the choppers get here," Tilly exclaimed with an excited clap of her hands.

It didn't take us too long to grab everything we needed, toss it in the back of the truck and snap the back bed cover over it so no one would notice. Tilly even had a cooler for us to keep our popsicles frozen when we picked them up. Just as we piled into the truck, I got a heads-up that the flyby would be happening any moment. I made sure they were going to circle the area a few times, but not directly over the compound. The *wump, wump, wump,* sound of the helicopter could be heard overhead, and Tilly started up the truck.

"Just drive like nothing is going on and once we're out of the gate, pedal to the metal," I instructed, as I hunkered down low in the back bench seat with Harper.

She rolled down the windows and turned up "Bohemian Rhapsody" as we made our way to the main drag of the compound. Everyone from the clubhouse and the garage were rushing out into the center, guns at the ready, letting us take the roundabout way with them none the wiser. When we reached the front gate, all it took was a shout and a wave from Tilly, and we were free and on our way to the beach.

Chapter Five

Eagle

"Y OU KNOW SHE'S NOT going to come back unless one of us drags her kicking and screaming, right?" Weston stated from his seat at the counter.

As much as the man pissed me off for wiggling his way into my little hellcat's heart before I could, I knew he spoke the truth. "Let's give her some time and she might reconsider."

Weston scoffed. "That woman has three moods—sleepy, stabby, and stubborn. If she's decided against doing something, there is no way to convince her otherwise. Just you wait and see, there's going to be some ridiculous diversion that will aid in her escape from the compound."

"We're not keeping her trapped here anymore," Cognac pointed out, a confused look on his face.

I love the man like a brother, and for all he could talk any woman who isn't Dax into his bed, he didn't really understand the way a woman's mind worked. Does anyone though?

"It doesn't matter. She told me she sees us as smothering because we care about her. Dax doesn't like to lean on people, and the only reason Harper and Wes get away with it is because they have been grandfathered in from before her brother died," Sprocket explained.

Now there was a man who could get into anyone's head. Watching him work his magic on Dax has been equally interesting and frustrating. It's almost as if the two of them have their own language and can read between the lines of what's really coming out of their mouths. So far, all I've been able to do consistently is piss her the fuck off... well, maybe not as bad as Picasso. If the two of them have been able to bury the hatchet, then there's hope for her and me to find our footing—if we don't kill each other first.

"Isn't Wednesday when Tilly goes into LA to get the parts for Sprocket?" Picasso mused, rubbing his chin. "All we have to do is keep a look out for her truck and then we'll know if she leaves."

"Nah, my little demon will do something with more flair to it. That's far too simple and you already figured it out. She's fooled a whole criminal empire for years. Sneaking out of here will be a cakewalk. The real question is, do we let her go, and or do we tail her?" Void asked.

Weston grinned. "Well, since Bob Ross gave her back her phone and smartwatch, I'll be able to track her with those, as long as she takes them with her."

"Why wouldn't she just ditch them, if she's that desperate to get away from us?" Picasso challenged, glaring at Wes.

Wes sighed and shook his head. "You just don't get her at all, do you? It's not about being away from you physically, it's emotional distance she wants. Besides, she has Harper with her and the last thing she would ever do is put her in danger again. If I can track Dax, then I'll also know where Harper is. If something goes down and she sends the S.O. S. signal, I'll be able to get to them. Do you trust this Tilly woman?"

"Yeah, she'll be good for Dax. Tilly's enough of a rebel to play along but won't jeopardize the Saints safety. Besides that, her husbands are men we trust completely," Sprocket said as a knock sounded on the front door. "My money's on that being Gator. No way he'll believe Dax at face value, too paranoid for that."

Void wandered over to the door and sure enough, there he was. Gator's face told me all I needed to know. Dax had told him who she was, and he wasn't gonna be happy with me.

"Come on in. We were just talking about your wife." Void smirked, as he stepped to the side.

Gator growled at Void. "Back off, she's already told you she wants nothing to do with you."

"Water under the bridge, my brother. You've already had the pleasure of meeting the little demon who holds my heart." Void laughed.

"You still have one? I thought you sold it to Lucifer himself," Gator snarled, as he brushed past my enforcer and right up to me. "What the fuck you playing at, Pres? I got some looney chick in my house saying she's Two Tricks and asking us to babysit her bimbo bestie."

We all froze at his words, and I could see Void's hackles rise at the trash that Gator was spilling. Gator had been with us since the beginning and I trusted him to be our scout for business ventures and other MCs that were struggling to take over, growing our numbers. I valued that he'd always been a straight shooter with me. He'd told me not to mess with Tricks and move on, which is why I did it when he was gone. The downside to Gator was he didn't know when to back off.

"Clearly, you didn't say any of that to her face since you're still in one piece without a mark on you," I stated, crossing my arms. "That little hellcat doesn't do well when people insult her or her family. As for what she said to you—it's all true. That pink-haired pint-sized badass is the one and only Two Tricks, also known as Dax, the enforcer."

"You went and goddamn did it, didn't you? That asinine plan to kidnap and use her as leverage to get what you wanted!" Gator snapped, his face starting to turn red.

I dropped my arms and stepped right up into Gator's face, fury blazing in my veins. "You might be my friend, but you better watch your mouth, before I cut out your tongue. I'm the president, not you, so you don't get to make the calls to keep this crew alive and prosperous." Gator's jaw clenched as if he was fighting back words. "You got something to say? Get it off your chest, man. Fucking challenge me for all I care. I will destroy you and you know it."

That seemed to break him from his silence. "You brought a goddamn motherfucking war to our doorstep that we had nothing to do with! That bitch of yours is going to ruin us because you had a good fuck and let that woman lead you around by your cock! Since when do we let women dictate what we do in the club? She walks into my house like she's the boss bitch and you put that crown on her fucking head."

My fist collided with his face, knocking him to the ground, where I pounced on him, landing blow after blow. "No one fucking talks like that about her. I'll fucking kill you!"

Eventually, I was wrestled off him and dragged a few feet away, with Void's arm around my throat. Picasso had Gator by the throat, shouting at him but the rage rushing through me was all I could hear. I was zeroed in on the man who dared to say that shit about my woman. Whatever Gator was still saying didn't get any nicer, since Picasso pulled his gun and aimed it right at Gator's forehead. My hearing snapped back into focus as I struggled against Void's hold.

"You would fucking kill me, just like that, over a woman? A member of your crew, a *brother* that's been with you since the beginning? You know Mutt and Tilly will never forgive you if you do this," Gator challenged.

"In a motherfucking heartbeat. No one speaks about our woman like that. No one!" Picasso roared, spit flying into Gator's face.

Then, like a flip of a switch, Gator sagged and lifted his hands in surrender. "Alright then."

Picasso froze, looking at the others with wide confused eyes. "Alright then, what?"

"I accept that Dax is who you say she is—that she's queen of the castle, and ruler of the Hidden Empire," Gator stated, holding Picasso's gaze.

Sprocket stepped up beside Picasso. "What the fuck was all that then? Were you testing us?"

"Yes, I had to know you were serious. There have been many women coming in and out of your lives. I had to know this one was different." Gator sighed, yanking Picasso's hand off and taking a step back. "The fact that you were going to kill me without hesitation, and the rest of you were going to let him, said it all."

Cognac took this moment to laugh his ass off. "Goddamn you, Gator, don't you think there was a better way to figure that out, where you didn't end up looking like ground meat?"

"Not on the way over here from my house, no," Gator said, using his shirt to wipe at the blood dripping from his nose and split lip. "God, Tilly's gonna be pissed."

"Well good thing Dax is going to talk her into sneaking out for the day, so you've got some time," Wes said, walking up to Gator. "Weston, second to Tricks and also one of Dax's men."

Gator raised a brow at this but shook his hand. "They let you live?"

"Seeing as Dax would, at a minimum, cut off their dicks if they hurt me, it was the wise choice," Wes stated, a cocky grin on his face.

"Don't let East fool you. We'll still kick his ass if he fucks things up for us," Picasso muttered. "Now enough of this bullshit, are you going to look after her friend, Gator?"

Gator walked into the kitchen and grabbed a dish towel off the stove and an ice pack out of the freezer. "Like I would let a woman who clearly can't protect herself stay with you bastards. The pixie said it would only be for a few days so I don't see why we can't play host. Tilly doesn't have any solid female friends and if she's hit it off with your woman that makes the world a better place for us."

"Does this mean you're finally gonna let go of the one time I drunkenly hit on T at the barbecue three years ago?" Void scowled at Gator.

"We're cool, man. We've been cool. She came clean and told me it was a dare anyway. I just liked busting your balls about it is all." Gator smiled as they exchanged knuckle bumps.

Wes walked over and leaned against the wall near me. "You sure having Tilly and Dax be friends is a good idea?"

"You gonna stop them?" I asked, giving him side-eye. "I piss her off enough as it is. I'm not looking for more trouble."

Wes grunted. "Seems you're smarter than I gave you credit for."

"If she's not gonna talk to us today, then it seems we best deal with business as usual until she makes her way back home," Sprocket spoke up. "I got bikes to fix, and I think it's the best plan to take a look over everyone's ride to make sure we're ready for when shit hits the fan."

"It's been two days since I've checked in with our people. Who the hell knows what chaos is happening? Let's hope Dax doesn't hide out for too long or else the Empire is gonna get worried and that's never a good thing," Wes added, pushing off the wall and heading upstairs.

Just as we were all going to head out of the house, the warning system on our phones went off, alerting us to someone approaching. I hit the speed dial for Rooster in the security room.

"What the hell is going on?" I demanded.

"I don't know, Pres. Nothing is showing up," Rooster blurted, as alerts sounded off in the background, along with people yelling trying to find out what had tripped the system.

Stepping out on the porch, I heard the distant sound of a helicopter. "Do we have anything to watch the sky?"

"Who would be coming at us like that? The Mad Dogs don't have that kind of pull. Hell, no one has that kind of equipment," Rooster snapped. "It seems that they're flying low enough to get caught by the motion sensor to the far east of the property. What do you want us to do?"

The sound of the chopper got louder, until I noticed that another was coming from the south as well. "There are two of them for fuck's sake. We need shooters on the roof. We need to ground them any way we can."

Men started to pour out of the clubhouse, guns drawn and pointed at the air, ready for them to pass overhead... only it never happened. "Rooster, can you tell where they are?" I yelled into the phone.

"Pres, I told you we don't have any way to keep track of something in the sky. The only reason we even knew about them was because they flew way lower than they should have been."

It clicked. This was my little hellcat's diversion.

"Call everyone off, it's not an attack, just a cat sneaking out the back door," I muttered.

"What?" Rooster shot back. "I don't get it."

"The only person who would have that kind of pull around here is Two Tricks, and we happen to be playing a game of chicken right now. We aren't in any danger, Tricks is just flexing to show us what she can do," I explained.

"Whatever you say, but everyone's gonna demand an explanation, Pres," Rooster said before he hung up.

"You gotta hand it to her, she keeps things interesting." Sprocket chuckled as he passed me down the steps. "Could she be more perfect?"

Chapter Six

Dax

"WHAT DO YOU SAY about going to Santa Monica? Then we can play at the pier as well as lay out?" Tilly asked.

"Oh my God, yes! It's been ages since I've been out there!" Harper exclaimed, pinning me with a hopeful look.

I rolled my eyes. "Whatever you guys want to do is fine."

The beach was never something that I really loved but I knew Harper did. I was far too pale and burned no matter what I did or how much SPF one thousand I put on. We'd already stopped in a town along the way where I picked up a simple bikini for the day, and they thankfully took electronic pay, since I only had my phone. If anyone from the Empire caught me, they would think I've lost my mind acting all soft, but for Harper I would do anything to help keep our friendship intact. If that meant getting roasted in the sun then I'm fucking doing it.

"Wherever we end up, I need a drink, preferably a margarita," Tilly stated. "Why is it so goddamn hot this summer? It hasn't rained in like two months."

"We can't have it all, even if they say California is paradise," Harper chuckled.

I glanced at the rearview mirror and noticed a nondescript tan Ford Taurus was still following us. We'd picked up it up once we left the town twenty minutes ago and I didn't like how it always seemed to linger a few cars back. Granted, there weren't many exits out here until we got closer to the more metropolitan area, but it still gave me a nagging feeling.

"Hey, can we stop somewhere along the way? I just want to get a few personal items from one of my buildings," I called up to the front.

Of course, being the smallest, I took the back bench seat so Harper could have the leg room.

"Sure, where is it?" Tilly asked, watching me in the mirror.

"Near Saugus in the warehouse district," I shared. "Once we get closer, I'll direct you. It's pretty off the beaten path."

"Where else would a self-respecting criminal mastermind put their building? Next to a Walmart?" Tilly joked, giving me a wink.

As we exited off for Santa Clarita the Taurus continued on, setting me a little more at ease, but I still wasn't convinced we were out of the woods just yet. We wove our way around the city as I gave directions, purposely making it more difficult than it needed to be—just in case they switched cars on me. That, and I didn't want Tilly to be able to tell anyone about this location if she was ever taken or tortured.

"You sneaky bitch, this is right next to the railway," Tilly said, giving me a knowing look as we pulled up to a battered warehouse with no signage. "How very convenient for you and your business."

"Location, location, location." I grinned. "You two wait here. I'll be just a sec."

Popping open the small jump door, I escaped into the blazing sun reflecting off all the metal roofs as I made my way through the parking lot. There were only three cars parked outside, letting me know that Carol was working the front desk and would let me in. I knew this location had gotten a few new faces that didn't know me yet and would have made things more challenging. I got up to the door, which I knew would be locked, and hit the speaker button.

It crackled a few times before a voice that sounded like gravel answered. "If you're delivering, you're late, go around back."

I couldn't help but grin, Carol hated nothing more than tardiness. One of the many reasons she still worked for me at seventy years old. "Carol, it's Dax, I need to grab a few things out of the office."

"Oh, hello, sweetie, let me buzz you in." Seconds later the door buzzed, and I entered.

The inside of the office area reeked of cigarettes, since I let Carol smoke inside—seeing as she was too old to be walking out back fifty times a day for her fix. We never had inspections since I paid everyone off, so it's not like anyone was gonna know about it. When I rounded the corner, I found her standing next to her desk, flapping her hand at me. She looked as if she could be anyone's grandmother, short permed white hair, wearing khaki slacks, a god-awful floral print shirt, with a cream sweater over it, and a Kleenex tucked up her sleeve.

"Come here and give me a hug. It's been ages since you've been by," Carol wheezed. As I hugged her, she squeezed my head against her boobs like she was trying to smother me. "What can I do you for?" she asked once I was freed.

"Shit's about to hit the fan, Carol. I've got the De Leon Cartel and the Mad Dogs after me, wanting to take over my turf," I answered honestly. "You might want to think about taking a trip to go see your daughter in Portland for a bit. We'll be able to manage this place with one of the others."

"The fucking hell you will. This is my goddamn warehouse and I've been looking after it for forty years! For fuck's sake, Dax, it's why you kept me on when you took over the smuggling ring who started it," Carol groused. "My daughter's a total cunt as it is. Staying with her would kill me just as fast as sitting right here doing my job, making sure we get what we need in and out."

I leaned in and kissed her on the cheek. "This is why you're the best, Carol. Don't you let anyone tell you differently."

"I'd shoot the little shit right in the kneecap if I caught wind of that talk going on around here."

"Man, why couldn't you have been my mom? I feel like I would have been way more successful with your kind of attitude." I smirked.

Carol tweaked my nose. "Sweetie, you're the spitting image of me when I was your age. Now go get what you need and give 'em hell."

Flashing her a bright smile, I headed off to the back office that Weston and I would work out of if we needed to be on location for a deal or something. Placing my hand on the scanner first, then inputting my ten-digit passcode, the door snicked open. The office wasn't fancy, just like the rest of the building, but its outward appearance was deceiving. Why waste your time looking around a space that looked like it was from the sixties with sagging, yellowed ceiling tiles from water damage. There was a large inspirational poster, a desk, filing cabinets, and a credenza to fill the space. Heading over to the filing cabinet, I pulled the whole thing back, revealing a gun and supply rack filled with everything I could possibly need.

We used it to showcase our merchandise, but since I know the boss, I decided to borrow a few things, as well as grab some cash. Grabbing a small duffle, I tossed in some boxes of nine mil ammo, two extra clips already loaded, and two of my favorite Smith & Wesson M&P Shield 380s. I put on the holster that tucked into my shorts on my lower back that also had a spot for a tactical knife. My money was on the fact that Tilly knew how to use a gun as well, so I packed with both of us in mind. Feeling better now that I had trusty backup, I grabbed a few of my calling cards just to remind everyone who was really in charge and headed back out front.

"Carol, you better still be alive when this is over or I'm gonna let your daughter bury you back in Kansas where that prick of a husband you killed off is," I hollered as I blew her a kiss.

"Fuck you, Dax. I hope you choke on a dick before you get an orgasm!" Carol shot back, making me laugh all the way back out to the car.

Harper and Tilly both gave me an odd look as I hopped back into the truck. "What's so funny?" Harper asked, twisting in her seat.

"Oh, just the sassy office lady. She's the mother I wish I had growing up," I explained. Digging in the duffle, I grabbed a Springfield 911 out along with an inside waistband holster like the one I was wearing. "You strike me as a Springfield type of gal, T. I loaded one in the chamber ready to go, so mind the safety."

"What the *fuck*, Dax!" Harper shrieked, jerking away from the thing like it would bite her. "You made us drive over here so you could get guns?!"

Tilly took the gun without hesitation and double-checked the safety before she holstered it, giving me a nod of approval. "Nice choice."

"How are you so chill with this, Tilly?" Harper demanded.

Before she could answer, I cut in, leveling Harper with a stern look. "Ah, I hate to break it to you, but I never go anywhere without a weapon if I can help it. It's the reality of my life. I've made some people very angry with the job that I do and that's without a cartel on my ass. Now I find out there's also another MC after me and potentially you? Yeah, sorry, babe, but I'm gonna make sure I'm packing, that's for damn sure."

"What she said," Tilly agreed with a shrug. "Being in a one-percenter MC isn't all fun and games. We deal in a lot of shit that could get me killed. Gator made sure I could defend myself if I needed to. Thankfully, I've only ever shot paper but I'm ready if the need arises."

Harper sagged in her seat, covering her face with her hands. "I can't. I can't do this, guys. For Christ's sake, I'm a fashion designer, not some secret agent or crime lord. I wasn't built for shit like this."

"That's exactly why you're not getting a gun," I chirped. "Alright, we're only forty-five minutes from the pier, just forget we even stopped here and carry on with business as usual."

Harper stayed silent and sulked in her seat as we got back onto the highway for the last leg of our journey.

"Holy fuck, it's only eleven o'clock and it's already this busy?" Tilly grumbled, as we walked down the hill past all the street performers and teenagers running around.

"It's still the middle of summer. Where did you think people were going to hang out?" Harper asked, knocking into Tilly with her shoulder. "Lighten up and just pretend you're a tourist instead of a local."

I caught wind of the sweet sugary deep-fried goodness. "I'm gonna need me a funnel cake, that's for damn sure."

"Leave it to you to be more focused on the food than finding a spot on the beach that isn't overrun with children," Harper said, grabbing my hand and dragging me down the steps to the beach. "You can come back to get your cardiac arrest later."

As much as I hated to admit it, the feel of the sand under my feet and the ocean breeze was amazing. I could have done without the scorching sun, but it would make it worth going into the water that never got above sixty-five degrees. The waves weren't very high but there were still the idiots who thought they were cool enough to make it happen and get lucky with the ladies when they got back to shore. I couldn't remember the last time I'd been out here, until I caught sight of the bicycle snow cone vendor peddling down the boardwalk.

"Dax, come on, we need to hurry before he gets too far away!" Devin yelled as we raced. "Last one there has to eat the grape flavor!" His blond curly hair kept falling into his eyes since he wouldn't let our foster mom take him to get it cut. He looked over his shoulder, grinning at me as we ran. Because I was seven seconds older, I let him win. Little did he know that I'd tricked him into thinking I hated grape flavored things, just for this reason. No matter what, I was going to win.

Mary had surprised us that morning, telling us that we were going to the beach. Devin and I had never been. We'd swum in pools before, but never the ocean. It was also the last home that Devin and I really had. Mary had been diagnosed with cancer and finally gotten to the point she couldn't take care of us any longer. This was our last hurrah before she had us pack up our things and a social worker came to pick us up. Devin cried for a week after that, and it caused the other kids in the group home to pick on him. That was until I gave Connor, the leader of the pack, a black eye and a fat lip.

This beach held one of the last happy memories I had as a child—one I'd hadn't thought of in years. I should have known then that I couldn't abandon Devin; he'd never been able to stick up for himself. Now here I was alone, with him buried in the ground, because I was too selfish and wanted my own life. I watched Harper as she scoured the beach for the best spot, ready to claim it the moment she found it, further resolving my need to protect her. This wouldn't be another instance of not being able to come back here with my family. Not this time.

Chapter Seven

Weston

I GAVE UP TRYING to work off just the laptop they'd given me and headed out of the house toward the garage. When I entered the space, all three bays were open, letting the breeze flow through, making it slightly less of an oven. Scanning the place, I saw four guys working on bikes and one other welding something, causing sparks to fly around him, not at all worried that he was only wearing leather gloves and a wifebeater for protection. When he saw me and flipped up the welding hood, I all but groaned seeing it was Sprocket—talk about giving a guy a complex.

"What's up, Westie?" he called, setting down the torch.

"I need to head back to my house and get supplies. Dax got a little sidetracked with saving Harper and all, and I don't have any wheels," I explained, as I walked over and hitched a hip to sit on the edge of the worktable. "You guys don't happen to have a spare vehicle around, do you?"

Sprocket grinned at me, cocking a brow. "You don't want to borrow Harper's? I'm sure she'd let you use it."

"Yeah, I'm not getting into that fucking clown car. I have no idea how Picasso managed it."

"Guess I can't blame you on that. How much stuff are you needing to grab?" he asked, pulling off the gloves and welding helmet.

"Nothing too crazy, but I figured while I'm there I would gather her stuff as well. Unless you guys are planning to move into our place, then I'll just pack an overnight bag," I probed, even though I could guess the answer.

"Now see, this is the kind of thing that would be helpful to know if our woman didn't run off to the beach." Sprocket chuckled. "I would pack more than an overnight bag, even if we decided to move into your house. This is the safer option until we know what the next move is going to be. I don't doubt that we'll be going back and forth for things, but this is a better command center."

"I wouldn't be too sure about that. You haven't seen the kind of shit that Dax comes up with. Sometimes I think she's watched one too many James Bond movies with all the hidden tricks and traps she's had put in," I shared, knowing that they didn't have a clue what they were signing up for with Dax. "Although I agree, for the immediate future, staying together here will be easier, at least until we get Harper situated."

"Do you know what our little rebel has planned for that?"

I scratched my jaw, grimacing at the stubble since I haven't shaved in a few days. "There are a few groups that I know she'll want to reach out to. I just need to find out who is in the area or finished with a job that I can pull them from. Personally, I know who I would pick, but Dax doesn't always get along with them and I'm not sure how she would feel about putting Harper's life in their hands."

Sprocket frowned at that. "Why would she work with people that she doesn't trust, that seems out of character?"

"They're assassins. The best in the business except when it came to killing her," I explained, smiling to myself. "After they watched her for a week or so, they decided that Dax was too perfect of a psycho to kill. They tried to get her to leave the Hidden Empire and join their team. When she turned them down, they worked out a deal to work together—she would send them on jobs and supply them with whatever they needed."

"I feel like that would make her like them even more—"

"Yeah, up until they asked if Harper was single."

"Oh fuck! They must know who Harper is from stalking her for the hit." Sprocket laughed. "Now I get why she would be pissy with them, since she never wanted Harper to know about this life, let alone date an assassin."

"Three of them to be exact," I corrected. "They wanted a deal like we have with Dax. Something about less loose ends to clean up if things didn't go well."

"They didn't tell Dax that, right?"

"Yeah, not their smartest move, but in fairness to them, they really hadn't known Dax very long," I reasoned. "Yet, who better to keep Harper alive than the ones who'd most likely be given the job or know who else took the job? If the best killers in the States are guarding her, then it makes it a whole hell of a lot easier. Not to mention they are more paranoid than Dax is, which I didn't think was possible."

"It sounds like you're on the right track. We'll back you up on this, so I would get in touch. What do you think they would want in return for doing the job?" Sprocket asked as he walked over to his tool chest and grabbed a set of keys, tossing them to me. "I doubt they would do it out of the goodness of their hearts."

Catching the keys, I gave him a sly smile. "I don't know about that. Even though it's been three years, they keep tabs on Harper's relationship status. If they didn't *need* Dax so bad, my money would be on them already having made a move on her."

"Well, if that isn't the case, let us know what they want and we'll help if we can. Harper is family and we do whatever it takes for them. Those keys are to my Defender. It should give you enough space to bring back what you need. It's parked in the garage near the clubhouse. The fob should open the door for you to get in." Sprocket nodded as he headed back to what he was working on. "Don't you dare fucking get a scratch on it or I'll put a scratch in you. I restored that thing myself."

"No problem, I don't drive like Dax," I tossed over my shoulder as I left.

Out of all the guys, I could see Sprocket and I becoming friends for real. The others... the jury was still out, but for Dax, I was willing to do just about anything to keep her.

Chapter Eight

Dax

"NOW THAT WE'VE FOUND our spot and marked it—like the alpha bitches that we are—can I go get my deep-fried treasure?" I begged Harper as she slathered herself with suntan lotion.

Harper peered over her glasses at me. "Only if you promise to bring me back one of those lemonades with vodka in it."

"They don't come with vodka—"

"Oh, so you're telling me that the great and mighty Two Tricks can't manage to get booze put into a carnival drink?"

Okay, so clearly Harper hadn't moved on from our little stop along the way. I should have seen this coming.

"As the queen wishes, her humble servant will make it happen." I bowed dramatically. "Tilly, do you want anything?"

"Hell yes. I want one of those Japadogs. I don't care which one, I've heard they're all good. Oh, and I'll totally take a vodka lemonade too." She grinned.

"You know what, on second thought, maybe you guys should get this shit yourself. I'm not a pack mule," I teased, as I started to walk back to the pier.

I watched the beach as I walked, knowing that I was acting like a paranoid freak, but I knew better than to ignore my gut. That car earlier had been following us, I know it. When there is one... another is soon to follow. What I didn't know is who the mastermind was behind the tail and if it was for me or Harper. The double-edged sword of rescuing her was I proved that she was important. If it were anyone else, I would have let them die. Still, this didn't seem like a move that the Mad Dogs would make, leaving the cartel, which had much deeper pockets. Convinced that I didn't see anyone lurking and watching the girls as I left, I let myself relax ever so slightly.

The pier was full of people running about, so I decided to start with the drinks first since this would be a two-step process. It didn't take long for me to get the lemonade. I got the largest size I could get with the special cup that allowed refills. Then I made my way over to the Mexican restaurant that had a bar on the patio and sat down.

"Yeah, I'm gonna need to see some ID for you to sit there, kid," the middle-aged bartender said as he scowled at me.

Squinting up at him, I slid the drink to the side and out of the way. "I'm sorry, are you talking to me?"

"Look, you might be able to fake your way into getting those tattoos and piercings, but I'm not going to serve a minor," the man stated, crossing his arms.

"I'm thirty fucking years old, dude, and I own the shop where I got these tattoos done, thank you very much," I snarled. Then, when I saw I was attracting attention from the rest of the people eating, I took a deep breath. "It would seem we started off on the wrong foot. Hi, I was hoping to get six shots of vodka. If you need an ID, I would be happy to show you one. If you could manage to ask nicely for it."

The man didn't seem at all impressed with my show of restraint. "You plan to drink all those shots?"

"What I do with them once I've paid for them is none of your concern, sir."

"No, you're going to put them in those cups and who the hell knows what you'll do with them then. I'm not going to be responsible for seeing on the news some kid gets kidnapped by some pink-haired tattooed freak."

Now why the fuck did he need to make it personal?

Lunging forward, I grabbed his button-down shirt and yanked him so he crashed into the bar and bent at the waist. I pulled out my dagger and slammed it into the bar right between his thumb and pointer finger. "Listen up, asshat, I wasn't looking for trouble but then you had to go and piss me off. Now say what you want about my appearance, I couldn't give a flying fuck, but now you're saying I might kidnap someone? That just crosses the line. So here's what you're going to do—put the goddamn shots in the lemonade, ring me up, and don't open your mouth to speak another word. If you should choose to ignore me, then I'll take your tongue out so you don't ever spout shit like that again. Peachy?"

"Someone's gonna call the cops and you'll be arrested if you lay a finger on me," he grunted.

"You think so? Let's see." I leaned back and looked around, seeing people with phones out, filming what was happening. "It's alright, folks. I'm an undercover cop and this bastard was trying to sell me drugs under the table. Make sure if you feel sick, dizzy, or have memory lapses that you get to a hospital to make sure you haven't been drugged."

People gasped and some even got up and left the restaurant, terror written on their faces, but no one made a move to stop me. Good thing they'd been blasting the news about the major crackdown on drug trafficking along the beach.

"Hmm, guess that plan didn't work out for you, now did it? For the inconvenience and damage control I'm going to have to do, I'll be taking those shots free of charge," I explained, shoving him back. "Make sure it's Grey Goose and not that well off-brand shit."

Now white as a sheet, and far less sure of himself, he grabbed the bottle of Grey Goose as I popped the lids to the drinks. He put far more than two shots worth in, but I wasn't going to complain, all the better to deal with this kind of bullshit. Securing the lids once again, I hopped off the stool and left one of my ace of spades calling cards with a flaming skull in the middle of the bar.

"Here's a tip for you, don't judge a person by their appearance, because they might be a bigger fucking threat than you think they are. When the cops do come to collect, give them that card and they'll know what to do."

As I left the bar, I scrolled through my contacts until I reached the right one. "Santa Monica police department, is this an emergency?"

"Hello, this is Dax. Is Jacquie available?" I asked.

"Hold one moment while I patch you through to the chief."

I rolled my eyes at the peppy hold music. Whoever called the police for a good reason? It should be hard rock or even some depressing violin shit, not something you would expect at a little kid's birthday party.

"Dax! What's up girl?" Jacqueline answered. "You ready to get that drink to celebrate my promotion?"

"Soon, I promise, but I need a small favor. Can you send two of my guys over to the pier to pick up a bartender from Mariasol? I might have accused him of trying to sell me drugs when he tried to refuse service based on the fact that I might kidnap someone."

Jacquie laughed. "Now you definitely owe me a drink, but yeah, I can do that. I'm sure once we get him down to the station, they'll find some dirt on him to teach him a lesson."

"And this is why you got the job, because you live to fight injustice," I proclaimed loudly, "How about next week? I need to fill you and Michele in on some shit that's going down."

"You good, Dax?"

"That's TBD. I'll tell you what I can when we get together. Kiss the kids and tell Hank hi for me," I said, ending the call and shoving the phone in my back pocket.

Thankfully, the rest of the trip was uneventful, and I made it back to the beach with all our goodies, only to halt in my tracks when I spotted three identical Greek gods of hotness hanging around Harper.

"Weston better not have fucking done what I think he did," I muttered as I sped up my approach. "I'm gonna kill him with my bare hands when I get back."

He knew better then to ask these cocky fuckwads for a favor, especially when it came to Harper. Now I was going to have to try and kill three of the best assassins I've ever worked with or had the displeasure of knowing. Refilling their position would be a bitch, but I wasn't about to let them get their claws into my best friend.

"Finally, you're back!" Harper called, waving and grinning ear to ear. "Look, some of your friends found us."

Glaring at them, I handed out the food and drinks that I had worked so very hard to get and now couldn't enjoy. "Well, if it isn't the Wright brothers. What the fuck do you think you're doing here?"

"Oh, Dax, you're always so warm and welcoming," Jaxson replied, batting lashes that woman would kill for, at me.

I had to hand it to them, they made an impressive vision in their swim trunks, golden skin, tattoos, chiseled jawline, and matching crew cuts. They were identical in every way but for their eye color, giving you a chance to figure out who the fuck you were talking to.

"Dax!" Harper snapped. I could tell by the pout on her lips that she wanted me to shut the hell up so she could work her magic on them. Little did she know that they had been panting after her like a dog in heat for the past three years.

"So sorry, how have you been? Killed anyone lately?" I asked, flashing a bright smile.

Magnus, the self-proclaimed oldest by ten minutes, glowered at me. "There's no need to be rude, Dax, especially when you're asking for favors that could cost us quite the payday."

Ghost—given name Casper—bent over Harper's shoulder and took a long pull from her straw, his eyebrows snapping up. "Holy shit, you trying to make a Molotov cocktail with that much vodka going on? That could get an elephant drunk."

"What, can't handle your liquor, Ghost? Hate to break it to you, but real women can drink," I sassed.

Tilly let out a little giggle as she sat eating her hotdog and sipping her lemonade, enjoying the front-row seat to this spectacle. I get it, who in their right mind would fight with men like them, when they looked like that and could kill you in half a heartbeat? Luckily they liked little old me enough not to make my best friend cry with my death, because it sure wasn't my winning personality that was doing it. On second thought, it could be the supplies I got for them too—

"Enough, all of you," Harper snapped, as she stood from her beach chair. "Tell me what the hell is going on right now, because I've had about all the secrets and alter egos I can handle."

The boys lined up in front of her like some synchronized swimming move with the same blinding smile on their faces.

"I'm Magnus Wright."

"Jaxson Wright."

"Casper—but everyone calls me Ghost. We're assassins," Ghost answered, laying it all out there.

Harper blinked at them a few times before she turned to me. "Are they serious right now?"

"Unfortunately." I shrugged. "You said you didn't want any secrets. This is what happens when you meet new people who call themselves my friends."

As her legs started to go out, both Jaxson and I moved to help her, but he got there first. Slowly, he lowered her back to her chair and handed her the lemonade. "Ah, I think this will help."

Robotically, she took a long sip, still watching the brothers with wide eyes. They shifted, waiting for her to give them a verdict on what she thought about the situation.

"Why are you here? You said Dax needed something from you guys?"

Magnus rubbed the back of his neck as he glanced over at me, and I nodded in agreement. My feelings aside, this was the smartest choice to keep her safe.

"Weston called us and explained your situation. So, if you're willing, we would like to be your bodyguards," Magnus ventured, bracing himself for her answer.

Harper started laughing hard enough to make her cry. "Weston wants three assassins to keep me safe? Wouldn't you guys be the ones they contact to kill me? I might be a blonde, but I'm not that dumb to believe you would pass up a profit for a no-name fashion designer who happens to be best friends with Two Tricks."

I flinched as she told them who I really was. We'd danced around that answer for years and now they finally knew the truth.

Ghost squatted down in front of her and placed his hands on her knees. "We already turned down the job, Harper, before Weston asked us for our help, if I'm being honest. Not because it wasn't a profitable job, but because it was you. I know this doesn't make any sense but you're just gonna have to believe me when I say the last thing we want, is you to be dead."

"Hey, I have an idea," Tilly piped up. "Why not let them spend the day with us and you can get to know them and decide when we pack things up?"

"I guess..." Harper answered, looking slightly lost at all this news.

Grinning, I grabbed Tilly where she sat and wrapped her head up in a hug. "This is why I keep you around Tilly-Billy. As for you, boys, this will be a test to make sure you can treat my best friend the way she deserves. Otherwise, I'll just shoot you."

"Dax, haven't we told you before not to threaten us with a good time? Man, the chance for us to really have a go at you on equal footing would be *amazing!*" Jaxson said with a grin.

"Yeah, it's official, you four are weird as fuck," Tilly said, pointing at us, still sipping on her lemonade.

So much for a relaxing afternoon now that these goons were going to be around.

Chapter Nine

Dax

MUCH TO MY AMAZEMENT, the day turned out to be pretty fun. The guys were on their best behavior, trying to impress Harper by winning all the stupid carnival games and each getting her a prize. They even treated us to dinner—not at the Mexican restaurant though, since I advised them that would be a bad idea.

"What do you mean you had a man arrested?" Tilly laughed. "You can do that? Damn!"

"Fuck, if anyone else pulled a knife on a guy, they'd be the one carted away in handcuffs," Jaxson agreed with a whistle. "That's a cold move, Dax, for realz."

Rolling my eyes, I let out an overdramatic sigh and turned to face them all. "The man accused me of trying to kidnap someone and getting them wasted, and you're telling me that I'm the one in the wrong here? Oh, did I mention he started out thinking I, myself, was a minor? That is a big change in assumptions, don't you think?"

"Could you blame the man? You look like an angry twelve-year-old," Magnus quipped.

"You," I snapped out my pointer finger, "are on thin ice, so you better be willing to get dessert *and* drinks."

"Woman, you have more money than all of us combined, and you're worried about paying a dinner bill?" Ghost cut in.

"How do you think the rich stay rich, Cappy?" I huffed, heading off toward the seafood restaurant we all agreed on.

Ghost stopped in his tracks, glaring at me. "Nope, no, you've come up with some weird-as-fuck nicknames for us, but that one is not gonna fly. It's not even close to my real name!"

"And Ghost is?" I shot back.

"Um, yeah, the most famous lovable ghost is Casper. Everyone knows this, that's why it stuck," he argued.

"Bro, relax, she's just trying to get under your skin and it's working. Brush it off," Magnus said, grabbing Ghost by the back of the neck and shoving him forward. "I'm fucking hungry, so stop holding up the party."

As the day went on and the sun lowered, the pier got busier, meaning that the restaurant was packed.

"How many?" the hostess asked.

"Six," I answered, slipping her a hundred-dollar bill. "First available is fine."

The young girl's eyes widened as she looked at the money, then back to me. "Ah, sure thing. Let me go check a few things and I'll be right back."

"Looks like you don't mind spending money under the right circumstances." Jaxton grinned.

Harper put her arm around my shoulders and cocked a hip. "The one thing that Dax doesn't fuck around with is food and coffee. If there is a way that she can get either faster or in a larger quantity, then she will make it happen however she can. That's something that's always been true. I just didn't know how much backing you had to make those demands."

Soon the hostess was back and waved us to follow her. "Normally this room is reserved for parties or special events, but we don't have any booked tonight so it will be just the six of you in there. I'll make sure to get a server over to you right away."

The room had two walls of glass windows looking out over the water and the activity of the pier. The restaurant was a little higher up on the hill, so we had an awesome birds-eye view. I sat in the middle with Tilly and Harper on either side, with the Wright brothers across from us. In a flash, we had bread on the table, waters filled, and a wine list presented to us by a very pretty waitress.

"I'm Taylor and I'll be taking care of you tonight. Please let me know if you need *anything* at all."

"We might need a moment to look over the menu before we can let you know," I muttered, irritated at her cheerleader vibe.

I was all for women fixing other women's crowns and having each other's backs, but chicks like this would stab you in the back faster than you could say pom-pom.

"Sure thing, I'll give you guys a chance to look things over and be back in a jiff," Taylor said with a swish of her high ponytail and left the room.

Once we ordered and got our drinks, I could tell there was a shift in the guys. "Look, Dax, we know that Harper is important to you, and you want to keep her as safe as possible. Can you honestly say that we aren't the best option for that?" Magnus pointed out.

Leaning back in my chair, I crossed my arms, giving them an evaluating look. "I'm not the one you need to convince of that, I know your skills. I might not love your personalities but you are the best I've ever seen at doing what you do." I pointed at Harper. "She's the one who has to say yes to this, because I'm not going to force her into anything."

Three pairs of eyes locked onto my best friend, hope filling their gaze, as they all but begged for her to say yes.

"I don't even know you guys, not really. Sure, we had fun today, but how can I trust that you'll risk your life to save mine? Dax has proven time and time again that she, while not always honest, has my best interests at heart," Harper stated. "If I come with you, how long would it be? I have a business to run and client orders to make. I can't just give all that up at the drop of a hat."

Now it was my turn to step into this conversation, as much as it killed me inside to do it. "Harper, you can rebuild your business, but you can't do that if you're dead."

"How bad can things be if we're here spending the day on the beach like nothing's wrong?!" she snapped, glaring at me. "This doesn't make any sense. You talk about how I'm a walking target but here I am out to dinner like any other day."

Ghost reached across the table and took her hand that was clenched around her knife. "Angel, you've been safe all day because the four of us have been with you, and you're in a public spot like this with security and police running around. Being out in the open, in a public place, is sometimes safer than hiding away in a safehouse. Dax is right though, you have to be alive to make your hard work count. So you don't want to lose clients, hell, we could just burn your shop down so you get the insurance money and the excuse for why you're not working."

I had to stifle my laughter at the look of horror written on Harper's face. "That's an option to you?!"

"Ah..."

Ghost didn't have a chance to save himself as our waitress and another server entered the room ladened with trays of our food. There was something about this other server that I didn't like, but I couldn't put my finger on it. He refused to look me in the eye as he handed me the plate without so much as a warning it would be hot. As he turned, I noticed a bulge that looked oddly gun-shaped on his ankle, making me tense. Then I heard the cocking of a gun, and sure enough, Regina George was standing in front of the door with a pistol aimed at the table. Taking my eyes off her was my first mistake. I had relaxed, knowing I had the guys to keep watch. Never leave a man to do a woman's work.

"Dax Rose Blackmore, Two Tricks' enforcer, correct?" Psycho Barbie asked, cocking her head to the side. "Mr. De León has been looking for you."

Well, that clears up who's been after me.

"Is that so? He could have called, emailed, or even sent a text. Why the hostile takeover?" I asked, leaning forward and resting my chin on one hand, so I could have better access to my gun.

"I didn't say he wanted to talk. No, he just wants your head on a platter—something about killing his son. I don't know all the details. I was just given the hit," she rattled on.

This is the problem with being too self-confident, it makes you stupid. Quick as a flash, I kicked back my chair, pulled my gun, fired, and twisted to do the same to the other server, who tossed his tray at my head. Ducking, I grabbed Harper's arm and yanked her out of her chair, tossing her toward Tilly as I advanced. This idiot hadn't thought far enough ahead to need his gun, but when spring-loaded forearm sheaths ripped through his shirt, I figured out why.

"Get them the fuck out of here, Magnus, I've got this handled," I ordered, not bothering to glance back. "Don't you let her get a fucking scratch or else you'll know firsthand what it means to have the wrath of Two Tricks' enforcer on your ass."

The hitman and I squared off as I blocked him from going after the others. I knew I didn't have much time, but I needed to get something out of this asshole. "How many of you are there? No way you could pull a job off like this on the fly. You've been watching us all day." All I got for an answer was a smile. "You want to play hardball I see. Guess I'll just have to take you with me then."

Shooting the guy in the leg, he grunted but didn't fall as I hoped, but it still gave me enough time to stash my gun and rush him. I kicked out his good leg, causing him to slam to the ground on his back, giving me the right angle to stomp on his wrist, causing him to release one of his knives. Scooping up the knife, I used it to cut the tendons in his wrists so he couldn't use them against me. Banging came from the still locked door to the rest of the restaurant, since like the smart boys they were, the Wright brothers had taken the girls out the rear fire exit. Grabbing two handfuls of the hitman's shirt, I started to drag him to the door. I heard him try and call for help like the victim he was pretending to be.

Dropping him, I grabbed his throat and plugged his nose until he opened his mouth, and I could pry it open. "Goddamn it! They already cut out your motherfucking tongue. You're useless!"

As anger flooded my body, I took the knife and dragged it across his neck, leaving him to splutter in his own blood as he died. Rushing out the back door, I swore as people looked at me like I was a crazy person since I was covered in blood.

"Please, you have to help us! They were trying to kill us. They need an ambulance. Someone was shot and another was stabbed. They've gone crazy!" I sobbed hysterically, pointing back the way I came.

Out of the crowd, Jaxson appeared with a large beach towel, which he draped over me and tucked me into his side leading me away. "The others are in the car. We just need to get you there. Are you still armed?"

"Yes, I only shot off two rounds and I have backup clips plus my knife," I answered. "Jax, they cut out his tongue. I couldn't get anything from him so keep your eyes peeled."

"Our Hummer is bulletproof. They're both safe in the car. We just need to get there in one piece," Jaxson assured me. "I should have known the private room was too good to be true, and I'm still really fucking hungry."

We ducked behind some of the buildings, in a back alley out of the crowd, and I used the towel to wipe off the blood as best I could. "You have to take her and go. This is no longer up for discussion. I don't give a fuck if she never speaks to me again, I need her alive."

Jaxson met my gaze, searching my expression. "Do you trust us to keep her alive through this?"

"I don't have another option," I stated, seconds before I put my gun to his head. "Know that if anything happens to her, you make her cry, you treat her wrong, and I find out about it, you will die by my hand. It will not be fast, it will not be pleasant, and you will beg until your voice runs out. Have I made myself clear?"

Jaxson flashed me a devious smile. "I knew we would win you over. Harper will be treated like the queen she is, wrapped in bubble wrap for safekeeping. There will never be a woman in all the world who is going to be safer or more cherished than, Harper Lynn Person, in our care."

"Do you have Tilly's keys?" I asked, dropping my gun. Jaxson lifted a hand and let the keys dangle from his finger. Snatching them, I turned and headed off. "Meet up at the rest stop near where the Five and Fourteen branch off. Tilly's got to come back with me."

Getting back to the car, I hit the speed dial and waited for him to pick up.

"Dax—"

"I am motherfucking pissed at you for calling them, but we will talk about that when I get back. There was another hit, this time from the cartel. Diego is looking for me. I need you to field the police while I head back. I need to take the back routes, so I'm not followed."

Not giving Wes a chance to answer me, I hung up on him and turned the key and slammed on the gas pedal. It's always easier to tell when someone is following you when you're going hella fucking fast.

Chapter Ten

Dax

As would be typical to living in or around the LA area, the traffic was from hell, and I didn't have my car or bike that I could risk with my normal stunts. So I had to be slightly more careful as I sped out of the city and back toward the open lands and mountains. It worried me slightly, that after only a week, I was already growing a little more attached to the quieter setting and slower pace. The sun had fully set when I arrived at the rest area to find Tilly sitting at one of the picnic tables, scrolling on her phone. I threw the car into park and ran out, looking around the place.

"Where the fuck are the brothers and Harper?" I demanded.

"They left twenty minutes ago and told me to sit tight until you got here," she answered, getting up and heading over to the truck. "I called my guys to have them meet us at the twenty-four-hour diner that's near the compound. I'm hungry as fuck after all that excitement and sun."

I groaned, knowing that meant my guys would be coming with and they would be pissed when Wes told them what happened. He might not like all the guys, but he would be honest because he would want them to do that for him. "Any chance I can talk you out of doing that?"

"Nope, you've avoided your men long enough," Tilly said, getting into the driver's seat. "I think it's about time you guys had that conversation you've been avoiding. Harper is as safe as she's gonna get and you have a target painted on your little pink head. If today didn't prove that you need backup, then I don't know what else will."

Muttering to myself, I got back into the truck and pouted—I'm not proud of it, but it happened. It was another thirty minutes to the diner, and I could already see the lot of them waiting next to their bikes, not at all pleased.

"Do I still have a lot of blood on me?" I asked, flipping down the visor. "I should've cleaned up at the rest stop."

Tilly grabbed a gray hoodie and tossed it at me. "Put that on and just make sure you wash your face and hands when you walk in... if they let you stay."

"They better, I don't do heart-to-heart conversations like this well, let alone while hungry," I grumbled, as I yanked the sweatshirt on.

"Good luck, and let's hope they don't ground you so we can still play together later this week." Tilly grinned, giving me a wink then got out of the truck.

As soon as my feet hit the pavement, I was swooped up into a crushing hug with the rasp of beard on my neck, as Void nuzzled me only to jerk his head back. "I smell blood. Are you hurt, little demon?"

"No, I'm fine. It's not mine. There's nothing to worry about," I explained, as he carried me over to the others. "You can put me down."

"If I do that then you'll run away from us again," Void stated, his grip tightening slightly to prove I wasn't going anywhere.

Eagle's face was stony as we approached, telling me just how mad he must be right now. "What the hell were you thinking, dragging Harper and Tilly along? You could have gotten them killed!"

"You don't think I know that?!" I growled, punching Void in the chest to let me go, which he ignored. "We were at Santa Monica Pier for Christ's sake. I didn't think we could get any safer than that. How was I supposed to know that they would expend so much manpower on this? I did the best I could. I'm armed. I made sure Tilly had a gun and I spent the day with three assassins."

Void snarled at this, while the others tensed, except for Weston and Sprocket.

"Calm down, they only have the hots for Harper. This is their dream situation, which apparently, two of you handed to them on a silver platter," I accused.

Weston just crossed his arms and scowled. "Yeah, and if I hadn't, then think of the mess you would have been in, trying to keep both girls safe while dealing with two low-level assassins. Just so you know, you owe Jaqueline way more than a night out with drinks after the mess she cleaned up."

"I got her the goddamn job. Cleaning up after me was part of the deal," I snapped. "I get that you're all pissed that I put them in danger, well guess what, no one is more upset about it than I am, so lay the fuck off."

Sprocket darted forward, gripping my jaw in an uncharacteristic show of dominance. "You're not hearing a word we're saying, little rebel. It's not just Tilly and Harper we were worried about getting shot or killed—it was you. Dax, you may not be willing to admit that we are all tied together with something deeper than an alliance, but we all have. You, my pink haired vixen, are ours, and we are yours, whether you like it or not. So don't go around putting your life in danger because it belongs to us and us alone."

I wanted to fight him on that, to prove that I wasn't going to be owned by them. For most of my life, I've never needed anyone and what they were offering sounded too good to be true. I couldn't just let my walls come crashing down—they had been built for a reason and kept my heart safe after losing half of it. How could I get them to understand that I wasn't whole? They wanted something from me I didn't know if I could give—

"Come on, let's feed our *loba.* You know she doesn't act rationally when she's hungry," Cognac spoke, breaking the tension and the near panic attack that I was about to have. Then he met my gaze with his own. "Don't think this is just going to blow over. We will come back to this once food has reached your stomach."

It would seem that the others agreed with him, as Void proceeded to carry me into the diner.

"Hello, boys, your booth is free in the back corner," the woman behind the counter called, waving in the booth's direction. "I'll come over in a sec."

Void finally set me down, only to ensure that I was put smack dab in the middle of the large round booth.

"Would you calm down if I promised not to run away? I really need to wash up before I put anything near my mouth. Who knows what cooties that guy had." I shivered just thinking about it.

Cognac slung his arm over my shoulder. "I'll keep an eye on her. We'll be right back."

"Seriously, you don't trust me enough to use the bathroom?"

"*Loba*, you of all people should know that trust is earned, and you haven't been proving yourself very trustworthy," Cognac countered, as he steered me to the back corner. "Besides, the bathrooms here are a one-person situation, just think of all the fun we could have."

I glowered up at him but didn't fight as he held the door open for me and we both entered. Stripping off the sweatshirt, I tossed it right at his face but he caught it with a grin. "Why so salty?"

"Oh, I don't know, maybe sending my best friend off with three assassins, having to kill a man and get it covered up, or the fact that you guys are treating me like a prisoner again," I snapped, yanking off my tank top so I was only in the black-and-white skull bikini top.

Blood had splattered all over my chest and soaked into the tank top, leaving residue behind on my skin. I washed out the top the best I could before I pumped soap onto it and used it as a washcloth. Much to my surprise, Cognac stayed silent and just watched me with hooded eyes as I cleaned myself up.

"You're being creepy," I stated, glancing at him out of the corner of my eye.

With a chuckle, he pushed off the door and walked up behind me so I could look at him in the mirror. "Change your mind on letting me touch you yet?"

Of course he would be more concerned about getting into my pants than anything else. Tell a man like Cognac that he can't play with the kitty and suddenly he turns into a man that will do anything to change your mind.

"Really, that's what you're going to ask me right now, as I clean the blood of a man I killed off my body?"

He stepped closer, until I could feel his body heat on my back, but still not touching. "*Loba*, do you have any idea how hot that is? What man wouldn't be turned the fuck on by the feral beauty of a woman protecting herself at all costs?" I felt pressure along my holster as he ran a finger over the handle of the gun there. Then he lowered his head so his breath played along my damp skin as he spoke, "A strong woman refuses to be the victim. They become the hunter, like the she-wolf I know you are."

Dropping the shirt, I turned and grabbed the back of his head, yanking him down until his lips crashed into mine. He wanted feral; I'd give him feral.

Without missing a beat, he wedged his leg in between mine and lifted me up so I was now sitting on the counter with my bikini top in my hands. I hadn't even noticed him untying it as he ravaged my mouth, each of us fighting to rule the kiss but being outsmarted by the other. My hand dug into the back of his neck as he cupped my breasts in his, massaging them as he stepped closer. Jerking back, I broke the kiss and stared at him with his puffy lips and lust-filled eyes trained on me.

"Don't think you've won just because we're about to fuck in a diner bathroom," I announced. "Sex is a need, and after a good fight, I like to fuck. Don't think this makes you anything more than convenient."

"You sure do know how to sweep a man off his feet, but duly noted, *loba*, I've been warned," Cognac said, as he leaned back and yanked off his shirt, dropping it to the floor. "We doing this down and dirty or do you want some foreplay?"

"What did I say about thinking you were special?"

"Rough and tumble it is." Cognac shrugged and scooped me up, yanking off my shorts that I'd unbuttoned. "Do I need a rain jacket?"

Dragging down the zipper of his jeans, I then shifted my bikini bottom to the side and sank down on him. "Nah, I got that shit tied up years ago. Kids will never be a thing for me. Now get to work."

Cognac slammed me up against the tile wall of the bathroom and started to thrust into me without a second's hesitation. "Too bad, I think a little hellion like you running around would be kind of epic."

"Shut the fuck up," I growled as I twisted one of his nipples, making him hiss.

Shifting me, so one hand was now in my hair, gripping tightly, he stepped away from the wall and yanked back exposing my front. Then he dipped down and latched onto one of my nipples, circling it with his tongue, only to bite it a moment later once it had peaked.

"Son of a bitch," I gasped, clawing into his back.

He moaned around my nipple as he gave it a tug, causing me to once again dig my nails into his flesh. With the added pain, he sped up pistoning into me with sexy grunts and growls as he worked. It would seem my glorious Latin lover enjoyed a little pain with his pleasure, something that I was very willing to oblige. Lifting one hand, I grabbed his throat and squeezed with my nails, shoving him away from my breast. He didn't go without a fight, making me question whether I had a nipple left after I removed him. Keeping track of his pulse, I tightened my grip, watching as his eyes alight with the challenge. Would he be able to finish in time before he passed out? Guess we were about to find out.

Releasing my hair, he grasped my hips and all but lifted me off of him, only to thrust in his full length, time after time, slamming me down. I could feel him bottoming out, and I loved the thud echoing deep inside of me, followed by a flash of pain reminding me that I was still alive. The build to the finish was hurtling down the tunnel, pulling moans out of my own mouth as I let my eyes go unfocused, reveling in the feeling that only rough sex could give you. Cognac started to slow slightly, his movements less sure, more erratic, telling me he was close as well. Bearing down, I swirled my hips and rocked against him, filled to the brim with his cock, and squeezed him with my muscles all but drawing his finish out of him. I could feel the hot cum filling me as he dropped to his knees, cradling me to his chest as his heart beat wildly and he started to gasp for the small amount of air I was allowing him.

I tilted my head so my lips caressed his ear. "You didn't finish the job—"

Suddenly, I was being tossed up, my hand yanked from his throat and once again I was plastered to the bathroom wall. Two fingers slid into me as a mouth descended on my clit, all but sucking my soul from my body as he pumped those fingers. It had taken him all but three seconds to find my G-spot and work me up into a frenzy. Now it was impossible to keep my appreciation for his work to myself, as I writhed and moaned, the sound reverberating off the white walls.

"Oh God yes, just like that! Don't you fucking move from that spot, or I will stab you in the eye," I threatened, as I toed up to the edge of the cliff, ready to fall with just the right nudge.

That nudge came in the form of someone hitting me with a Mac truck as he bit down on my clit. I screamed as I came, my whole body vibrating and twitching as if I was possessed, but he wasn't done with me yet. Somehow, he managed to pull out two more orgasms back-to-back, leaving me a sweaty panting mess as I flopped into his lap. I rested my head on his shoulder as he wrapped me up in a ball nestled against his chest.

"Since I don't know your body, I could only give you three, but just think what fun we could have once we get to know each other a bit more."

Chapter Eleven

Dax

Once again dressed, we walked out of the bathroom and back to the table. The guys shifted so I could be locked in the corner, soothing their fear of me running away again. I glanced over at Tilly, and she just gave me a thumbs up and grinned. Welp, that sure clears up how far they could hear me from the bathroom. It's a good thing that I wasn't shy about sex or else I would have been a puddle of embarrassment.

"Feeling better?" Picasso asked as he slid a menu over to me.

"Much, thank you for asking." I smiled, then chugged down the glass of water.

The waitress that had greeted us when we came in arrived at the table with her order pad out and pen poised. "Before we get started, am I going to find any nasty surprises in the bathroom? I run a clean place around here and I let a lot of things slide, but I'm not cleaning up after nothing kinky."

"Nah, Nelly, you'd never know we were in there," Cognac shared, giving me a wink.

"Glad to hear it. I'd hate to toss you boys out after so many years of being such loyal customers," Nelly stated, then turned to Sprocket. "What'll it be, sugarplum?"

Something about hearing her using a pet name like that on Sprocket raised my hackles. I had to grit my teeth together so I didn't lash out, since I've been screaming from the heavens that these men aren't mine.

"Patty melt for me with pepper jack," Sprocket answered, adding a few more things, but I wasn't really listening.

No, my eyes were on this woman whose age I couldn't quite guess. She was pretty enough with her black hair pulled back, thick arched brows, and bright green eyes. Nelly was fit, but the uniform she was wearing did nothing to flatter her figure... but that could be on purpose. Diners in general seemed to attract an odd sort of clientele, not to mention the sign said open twenty-four hours. Everything about her was blunt and to the point, but there was something in the odd, slightly southern lilt to her speech that made me think she had a soft spot for these men.

"Little demon, turn off the death glare for a moment so she can live long enough to get your order," Void whispered into my ear, snapping me back into the here and now.

"Any day now, Rainbow Bright," Nelly demanded. "We've got a good salad with some lite dressing if you're not sure what to order."

I went for the gun on the small of my back, but both Void and Eagle wrapped their arms around me, trapping me in their hold.

"She'll have the bacon burger, no tomato. Really—as in don't even try to put it on then take it off again. She'll know and make you remake the whole thing. Side of onion rings with ranch and BBQ sauce, and a strawberry milkshake with all the whipped cream you can put on it," Weston rattled off, sensing that Nelly needed to move along.

Nelly blinked at Weston, then flicked her gaze to me then over to Cognac. "Sure thing..."

With that, she left, apparently having gotten everyone's order before mine. Feeling that it was safe, Void and Eagle relaxed but didn't remove their arms from me, just let them rest on my hips, each grabbing an ass cheek.

"So, I take it you don't like tomatoes," Sprocket mused, holding back a smirk.

"How can that be? I saw you eating pizza," Picasso interjected.

I let out a huff, knowing that this wouldn't make sense to them because no one seemed to understand my pain. "Pizza sauce isn't chunky."

"So ketchup is okay?" he pressed.

"It's purée, so yes. If there are any kind of chunks of tomato, I'll pick it out if I can, but raw tomato is a no-go. There's essence of tomato left behind. You can't get rid of that shit no matter what you do, so it's better to just burn it and try again," I explained.

This made them all chuckle at my expense.

"Little rebel, you never cease to amaze me at what hill you are willing to die on... essence of tomato. God, that is priceless." Sprocket laughed, slouching back in his seat.

"Oh yeah, sugarplum, like you don't have something you hate to eat?" I snapped, crossing my arms and jutting my chin.

"Nope," he answered, popping the "p." "When you've gone hungry and had to eat out of trash cans, you learn not to be picky."

Well, that's one way to end an argument.

Nelly came back over with all the drinks and refilled the waters. "You boys haven't been around much lately, too distracted with other things?"

Why did this woman want to die? This is the second chick that has tried to start shit with me tonight and my already short fuse of dealing with bullshit is all but nonexistent at the moment.

"Where are our manners?" Eagle spoke up. "Nelly, this is our girlfriend Dax, and her boyfriend Weston. They recently came to live with us, and we've been taking some time to get things sorted, combining our lives and all."

Damn that man, he put me right in the perfect position that I couldn't yell at him. If I pissed this woman off, not only would she feel like she won but she most likely would fuck with my food. I could only handle one meal getting fucked up, not two.

"*Ours,* as in all of you?" Nelly asked, brows furrowed. "Wait, did you say she already has a boyfriend? I mean, I should have guessed, seeing that he could order for her but... this is for real? You all live together and everything?"

"We are still working out the details," I added. "You know, since Weston and I have a house in the city, as well as jobs and all that. Who knows, this might not last all that long, but hey who wouldn't give it a try for five men who look like these guys?"

Eagle tightened his arm around me, pulling me into his lap. "Yes, we have lots to talk about, which is why we came to neutral ground to figure it all out."

"How the fuck is this neutral when it's your place, and this woman is eye fucking you all the time?!" I snapped, before I realized that I'd just outed myself for being jealous.

Eagle chuckled as he raised a hand to grip my chin and turn me to him. It didn't take a rocket scientist to figure out where this was going, and I had two options. Let him stake his claim or make a scene... His lips melded to mine before his tongue flicked out, asking to deepen the kiss. This was when I decided to play the upper hand and bit down on his lower lip hard, then sucked it into my mouth to lick the blood off before releasing him. I sat back, giving him a smug look as his eyes smoldered with desire and irritation at one-upping him. I heard Nelly huff and walk away from our table. I just hoped she wouldn't fuck with my food or else I was going to shoot her in the leg. I wasn't *that* petty.

"Little hellcat, there is no need to be jealous over Nelly, she's like family. We've been coming to this diner for years and nothing has happened between us," Eagle assured me.

"Now, can we talk about you moving in with us, officially?" Void asked, pulling me from Eagle's lap onto his own.

I shifted, so I was now straddling him, nose to nose. "Why the fuck would I move in with you after we've known each other for a week, and our whole foundation is built upon you kidnapping me? You get this makes no sense, right?"

"This is not only connected to the fact that we want you to be ours in every way possible, instead look at this like Two Tricks would," Void started, covering my mouth with his hand when I started to speak. "No, you're going to listen to all the facts, *then* you can shoot them all to hell if you want."

I relaxed and licked the underside of his hand like the two-year-old that I sometimes acted like. Void just grunted and pulled his hand away, wiping it off on his jeans.

"You're lucky you're fucking cute," Void growled. "Alright, so both the Mad Dogs and the De León Cartel are after you. It's safe to say they have been tailing you for some time if they knew about Harper. Uh-uh, no interrupting." I pouted but settled back to listen. "Yes, they could have followed her home that night from your house, but they'd already sent the pizza guy to your house to kidnap her, and you hadn't seen her in a week. They picked that night because you were back from our compound, making me guess they think it would be much harder to get you there. Granted, I don't have a clue the scope of your Hidden Empire, but I guess that's why you call it hidden. If you have a better plan that will keep everyone involved safe, then I'm all ears, but from where I'm looking, we need a central location. Weston even went back to your place and collected a bunch of stuff to bring here."

I turned to look at Wes with a questioning brow.

"Yeah, shortcake, he's telling the truth. I needed my equipment. I couldn't work on the shit they were letting me use," Wes said to confirm. "I also brought along some of your stuff as well. Nothing major, just things I knew you'd miss."

"Why weren't we dating a long time ago? You make the best kind of wife." I winked, blowing him a kiss.

He grinned and rested his head on a hand, leaning on the table. "You're gonna need to blame yourself for that one. I would have made a move forever ago if I didn't think you'd run for the hills."

"Anyway," Eagle cut in. "Having a 'home base' isn't the worst idea and from what Picasso and Wes tell me, your place can't fit all of us."

I contemplated this a moment, knowing that what Void and Eagle said did have merit. "If—and I'm not saying yes—we do this, I will need to be able to come and go as I need to. I have the tattoo shop and all the other moving parts of the empire to run. I decided to do an announcement and come clean about the fact that I'm Tricks. Things will move a lot faster if I don't have to do the whole dog and pony show and I can just order things to happen. You lot tend to smother me about everything, and I'm used to being the top dog and calling the shots on how things go."

"This is where learning to compromise might come in handy," Sprocket shared. "The same could be said for us as well. The five of us have learned how to work together but adding in you and Wes will take a little adjusting. Having open and honest conversations like this one will help things in the long run, not running off to the beach to avoid doing the hard work."

Twisting back around, I shifted to sit on my own so I could see them all. "Hard work I have no problem with, I've done it all my life. It's just this emotional bullshit I can't wrap my head around. You want honesty, then here is one big-ass-heaping scoop for you all. I never thought I would be alive long enough to have deep relationships, a husband, kids, the whole family thing. Once my twin, Devin, died, I felt like my future did too. It's just pure luck and stubborn-ass determination on Weston's part that I'm still around."

"What it sounds like to me is that you just didn't want to get attached to people because you didn't want them to hurt when you died, like you did when Devin passed. I get that, believe it or not. When I was twelve, my mom and sisters were killed when we snuck out of Mexico. The coyote, who my father paid to get us out and across the border, turned on us and sold us all to traffickers, but my sisters were too little and weren't strong enough to survive being stowed away in a shipping container to Venezuela. My mother was eight months pregnant with my baby brother—they didn't make it either. I had to sit there, trapped in the dark with one jug of water to last us the two-week trip after crossing the desert and I watched them die," Cognac shared, his copper eyes locked onto mine as he spoke. "Trauma, death, and other life-altering things can happen to anyone. I thought about killing myself many times since that day, but how we choose to live after what we've lost... that is up to us."

Chapter Twelve

Dax

MY HEART ALL BUT sank to my stomach as Cognac told me his story. I could see the pain in his eyes that he hid so well from others. I'd always prided myself on being able to read people, but he had just proven to me that I hadn't had a clue what he was hiding under that bright smile. Becoming Two Tricks changed me, but that didn't mean it caused me to lose all forms of sympathy for someone who had experienced loss—just in the cases where they took from me first.

"Cognac—"

"No, *loba*, I didn't tell you that to get your pity or even to try and get sympathy sex from you later. I just wanted you to know that another person here at this table knows what it's like to lose something so dear to your heart. A few of us have even worse stories, but we all chose to live and found it was easier to do things together than on our own. Really give us a chance for you to get to know us and vice-versa, it might just surprise you," Cognac pressed.

"What? Like you want us all to go on dates and shit like that?" I laughed.

"Yes, little demon, I think that is exactly what he's saying, and I happen to agree with him. Like you said, our whole relationship has been backward and upside-down. Maybe if we rewind a little, it might help," Void suggested.

I fidgeted in my seat and was thankfully saved when a man wearing a food-splattered apron showed up with all our food.

"Hey, boys, got your grub," he announced, as he started to pass out plates. "Need anything else?"

"We're good, Jerry, thanks," Picasso answered, giving the man a salute.

If I was a betting woman—and we all know that I am—I would have to guess that Jerry is Nelly's father. They looked too much alike not to be related, but he was too old to be a brother. Jerry gave the table a onceover and nodded to himself before he headed back to the kitchen. Looking around the diner, I noticed that we were the only ones still here. Even Tilly and her men had left. I glanced down at my watch to find it was only eight-thirty, far too early for this place to be empty.

"Did you guys ask for the place to be ours tonight?" I inquired, searching the space for any hint of someone trying to kill us.

"No, well, at least I didn't ask," Eagle answered, pausing to look around the space.

Unwilling to go without food twice, I started to shove my burger into my mouth and chewed as fast as I could. Mid chewing, I pulled out my gun and laid it on the table for easy access, watching the windows for anything. When I saw the headlights, I knew it was too late.

"Guys, we got company!" I grabbed my gun, then the edge of the table and flipped it forward so it was a shield.

"Jerry, grab Nelly and get the fuck out of here!" Eagle bellowed, just before the sound of the truck engine became deafening as it smashed through the front doors.

The guys moved instantly, ducking behind the table. Void shoved me under him as the *boom* and *crash* of the impact sent glass and other shrapnel flying.

Who the fuck were these guys that they didn't give a fuck about the police getting called on them? Neither of these hits had been subtle or in places that could be easily written off. Not to mention, this was the second hit of the night unless they had another person that I didn't kill back at the restaurant. I never did get a good look at the driver of the Taurus.

The cock of a shotgun echoed in the quiet of the diner. "Come out, come out, I know you're there! I've spent all day following you and your friends, but we haven't gotten to play."

This creepy motherfucker. Too bad I needed him alive.

"Let me up, Void," I whispered harshly, elbowing him in the gut. "We can't kill this asshole. We need to find out what he knows."

Void grunted but shifted to the side so I could wiggle out and climb over the top of him to peek around the table. When I did, the middle-aged balding man with a sawed-off shotgun spotted me and pulled the trigger. Ducking behind the table once again, I rolled as a chunk of the table went flying. This asshole was shooting slug shells, making this all the more fucked up. These types of bullets have been named the deadliest thing you could put in a shotgun. I'm talking like a bullet and a pipe bomb had a baby type of fucked.

"If we can't get the guy alive without one of us getting killed in the process, you better take his psycho ass down. He's shooting slugs," I told the others.

Weston frowned and glared at me. "Why do you always have to have some of the worst of humanity come after you? Couldn't we just get normal thugs and lackeys?"

"Pfft, this is way more fun." I smirked and leaped up and over the back of the seats, landing with my back to the wall.

This was the start of the hallway to the bathrooms, but also offered protection from being seen as I planned what move to make next. I had to keep this guy's attention so he didn't go shooting up the table and taking all the guys out. I spotted the rolling dirty dish cart and grinned—oh this is gonna be fun. Diving across the open space, I shoved chairs into tables as I went, sending them crashing every which way. Then I hopped a ride on the dish express and rolled toward the kitchen and through the main section of the diner, gun at the ready to shoot this asshole right in the dick. Only he wasn't out there waiting for me like I thought he would be. I reached the counter and ditched the cart, scrambling behind the dining counter and out of sight.

"I thought you wanted to play. Don't tell me you've left already?" I yelled, trying to peek over the counter in different places to find out where baldly was.

I noticed the guys had left their safe spot with their guns drawn, spreading out to cover the dining area. Guess I couldn't have expected them to just hide out while I took care of things. They were much too macho for that. I had to hand it to Void though, he had a silencer on his gun. One point for team enforcer.

"No, I haven't left yet, I just thought it might be more fun with a friend," Baldie's voice said from the direction of the kitchen.

"Fuck," I swore. My money was on the fact that Jerry or Nelly didn't listen and leave when they should have.

Peeking back into the kitchen from the opening of the order shelf, I spotted our trigger-happy hitman and his new "friend" Nelly. Now I was left with the choice of if I really cared enough to save her or just let her become cannon fodder so I didn't have to worry about her taking my guys. Goddamn it, they would be pissed if I let her die, and I really didn't need more flak from them right now. Moving out from behind the counter, I headed for the guys.

"He has a Nelly shield for protection in the kitchen. I can only see one way in and out of there, so some of you need to cover from the counter and the rest of us will go to the main entrance," I directed. When I tried to head off, Picasso grabbed my arm.

"Look, I of all people know that you can handle yourself, but can we please not do anything to make this night worse?" he begged.

I frowned at him. "What are you talking about? This is nothing. That asswipe could've done a hell of a lot more damage to this place if he wanted to. Lucky for us, he really only wants me. I just haven't decided if it's dead or alive. The other two definitely wanted me dead, this one I'm not so sure."

"Spitfire, you do realize that you're not making any of this sound like something we shouldn't worry about, right?" Picasso groaned, rubbing his face with a hand.

"Buck up, boys, the faster we can deal with this, the faster you can yell at me about how reckless I am," I said, as I moved down the hall to the swinging kitchen doors.

Grabbing the dirty dish cart along the way, I crept my way along the wall, stopping to wait for Weston, Picasso, and Eagle to join me.

"I'm gonna shove the cart in first and then try and get around the worktable in the middle of the kitchen. I'll go left, one of you go right, and the rest try not to shoot us or get shot," I whispered, gearing up to rush the door. "Oh yeah, and don't shoot Nelly either. I'll be the only one to do that, if she deserves it."

Eagle frowned and Weston moved to stop me, but I was already in motion, using the cart as a battering ram and shoving the double door wide for us to dive through. Shots echoed in the space, the *ting* of bullets hitting metal overhead as the others laid down cover for us to get closer. The blast of the shotgun was deafening, and I had to force myself not to flinch and cover my ears. There was a reason these guns were for outdoor use only; they could burst an eardrum faster than a rock concert. I rolled onto the metal shelf running under the center counter, knocking pans and baking sheets off, adding to the chaos level of noise in an effort to hide where I was coming out from. Aiming for the hitman's leg, I shot him right in the knee cap.

"Gah!"

Three bullets used, five left, I noted when he still didn't go down or let go of Nelly. I peered up from where I was grabbing a pizza tray and chucked it, like a giant Frisbee, at his hand. It almost missed him, but I managed to get his elbow and his reflexes jerked, releasing Nelly. Diving out of my spot, I grabbed Nelly's legs and pulled them out from under her, causing her to crash to the floor, leaving the hitman open for the others to get a clear shot. In seconds, four bullets hit him right in the chest and started to bloom with blood, telling me he wasn't wearing a vest under his shirt. Ignoring Nelly, who was sobbing on the floor, I scrambled over to baldie.

"Who the fuck hired you?" I demanded, as I climbed onto his chest, shoving my thumb into one of the bullet holes. "Tell me now or I'll take the last moments of your life, giving you a taste of what hell is gonna be like."

He coughed, blood bubbling up in his mouth, telling me he'd been hit in the lung. "Diego wants you to suffer for the loss of his son. I understand that now because I wanted you dead for killing my children. At least this way, I will be with them in the afterlife."

"You cut out your own son's tongue? What the hell kind of father does that?" I demanded.

"It's a sin to lie. Without a tongue, you can't lie ever again." He gasped, trying to catch a breath that would never come now that his lungs were full of blood.

Stashing my gun back into the holster, I stabbed my pointer finger into another wound. "What about killing, isn't that an even bigger sin?"

"Not if it's ridding the world of evil..." he whispered as he slipped away, blood pooling around his whole body.

Shoving off him, I stood and wiped my bloody hands on my shorts and turned to find a sobbing Nelly wrapped around Eagle, like the snake she was, clutching his shirt. I might have brushed it off if her face wasn't nuzzled all up in his neck as well, like she belonged there.

"Aw, fuck no, that is not happening," I roared, whipping my gun out and pointing it right at her head. "Get your motherfucking hands off of what's mine you twatwaffle."

The sobbing only got louder, and she wrapped her arms tightly around his neck. I met his gaze and I saw shock on his face. "Dax, she almost died, and it doesn't mean anything to me. Let's just find her father so I can hand her off to him."

"Fuck you, Eagle," I spit. "You talk about wanting to make something work between us, but you won't do something as simple as removing a woman who is clearly into you. She's taking advantage of this moment to climb all over you, but you're too blind to see it." I dropped my gun and shook my head in disbelief. "You might be fine sharing me with the guys, but I'm sure as fuck not okay with anyone else touching what belongs to me—if you even do. So this ends one of two ways—you remove the sobbing opportunist bitch or I walk out those doors and go back to my life."

"Dax, I get you don't have the same thoughts on family that we do, but Nelly is family, nothing more. We protect and comfort our family when they've almost been killed. Are you saying you wouldn't do the same for one of your people?" Picasso argued, because heaven forbid anyone disagrees with his big brother. "This is what you wanted for your brother isn't it? To be protected when they get involved with something that they didn't do?"

"This is nothing like that!" I screamed, my whole body shaking with rage. "I can't do this. You're asking me to change into someone I'm not willing to be. I can't fix the shattered person I am. You either accept me how I am now, or I don't need any of you in my life. If you'll pick her over me, then clearly everything you said is a lie."

"Rebel, that's not what we're doing." Sprocket shifted to block my shot. "All we want to do is get her somewhere safe, then we can all leave, together, and go back home."

No, this was a clear betrayal that proved they were lying about everything. Why wouldn't they pick me over her?

Weston shoved his gun into the back of his pants and came over to me, hands raised in surrender as I shifted the gun to him. "Come on, shortcake. I think it's time we both went home."

Dropping my arm, I looked back at the five men who had almost gotten past my walls, but I'd managed to save myself at the last moment, before it was too late. It was safer this way. For it to just be me and Wes—the one man who never let me down.

Chapter Thirteen

Sprocket

WE WATCHED IN SILENCE as Dax walked out of the diner hand in hand with Weston and turned on Eagle. "What the fuck, man? You're just going to let her walk out like that?"

"Picasso, find Jerry so we can make sure that both of them get home safe," Eagle ordered, ignoring me.

Picasso peeled Nelly off of Eagle's chest and escorted her out of the disaster zone of a kitchen. I respected Eagle as our president, and only once had he made me question his judgment, until this moment. What he was doing was wrong.

He was being a stubborn prick and forcing us all to fall in line with his thinking.

"No, Enzo," I snapped. "You're making the wrong choice here and forcing us to do the same. Dax is everything we need, and you goddamn know it."

"Are you challenging me right now, Connor?" Eagle bit back. "Because if that's what's happening, now would not be the smartest time to do it."

I sighed and let my shoulders slump. "You know I'm not, but the whole reason you have a crew leadership is to protect each other from making bad choices—like this one. If Dax leaves now, she's never going to come back. That woman doesn't give second chances when she's locked her heart away, and to be honest, if we let her go, then we don't deserve her."

"She would have easily killed Nelly for what she just did. I'm a hard-ass and I've got blood on my hands, but I wouldn't kill an innocent woman because she was hugging someone. That's too far and I'm not sure that's what's best for us or the crew. A loaded gun is bound to go off at some point," Eagle argued.

Void picked up a pot and whipped it across the room at the wall, putting a dent in it. "We fucking knew what she was when we decided to kidnap her. You were the one that caught feelings first. It's not fair to change the rules on her now. I don't have any problem that she's more bloodthirsty than most of us, and the only reason I'm not just like her is because of you guys. I got kicked out of the ring because I killed too many people fighting, then you guys brought me into the crew. We all know I can lose my shit any time I get into a fight, but you guys make sure I don't get that far. Dax has never had that from someone. Wes is too fucking scared of her walking away, so he'll do whatever he has to in order to prevent that—even if it's to her detriment." Void raked his hands through his hair. "Don't make us choose between you or her, because in this moment, I'm not sure I'd stand by you."

Eagle's eyebrows shot up at this. "Are you saying you would walk out right now and never come back if I said we had to let her go?"

"Pres, why are you really freaking out about this?" Cognac asked, leaning against the counter, arms crossed with a scowl on his face. "Something shook you and it wasn't the fact that she would have shot Nelly, because we all know any of us would have been fine shooting a man who thought he could touch Dax."

Eagle looked around the kitchen and then turned to survey the dining area. "We risk a lot in our lives with what we do, but we always do it knowing we are providing for those we protect. Dax has an empire that she rules, but they aren't people to her, they are a means to an end. She can count on one hand the people she cares about and will die for. What if we never reach that point with her? Do I always have to wonder if she's going to do something that might blow back on the club? We have kids, families, and fringe people that we protect and consider valuable because they're alive. I don't think Dax considers that at all—"

I wanted to wrap my hands around Eagle's throat and shake him. "Seriously, you really don't think she gives a shit about human life? What about the fact that she saved Nelly after she was a bitch to her?"

"That was purely because she didn't want us to be upset with her, not because it mattered. If that pan had hit his hand and the gun went off, Nelly would be dead. She missed and happened to hit his elbow. Then she drops her to the floor to jam her finger in a dying guy's body, not giving a flying fuck about the bystander," Eagle listed.

Then it struck me. "You think she's going to be like your uncle, don't you?"

"Don't you dare bring that fucking bastard up," Eagle growled, getting right up in my face. "That is a line I'm not willing to let you cross, Sprocket. Leave it the fuck alone. There is no way she could ever be like that heinous man that I killed with my own fucking bare hands."

Cognac cleared his throat, drawing our attention. "Can we go stop her from trying to steal one of our bikes now and bring her home?"

The roar of an engine told us all she'd managed to get one of our bikes going and the screech of tires peeling out of the lot made us all tense, knowing she was on the road.

"Looks like we missed that chance," Void snarked.

"Nothing has changed, guys," Eagle argued.

"God, did you not listen to a word any of them have said? Are you going to be that self-righteous and force all of us to make possibly one of the biggest mistakes, because the big bad boss of the Phantom Saints is intimidated by a woman who you can't control?" Picasso spoke up as he entered the kitchen. "Nelly was pushing her all night, even after you told her that we didn't have any interest in her. Then you let her cry all over you when Dax had been attacked twice, forced to hide away her best friend, and hasn't gotten to finish a meal. I don't think Sprocket is that far off when he asked about Hannibal."

Eagle sagged and looked at Picasso with a pleading expression. "Please don't. Don't make me have to revisit what that bastard did."

"I won't... right now, but seriously, bro, you're going to need to tell her at some point if you want to make this work," Picasso warned. "Just for the record, I backed you up because you're my brother, but I gotta say, this is one of the worst moves you've made in a long time."

"Bro, you played the dead brother card. I don't see you getting out of that hole any time soon," Cognac pointed out.

Picasso nodded his head. "Yeah, I fucked up. This goddamn brother complex of mine makes me say all the stupid shit to her when she pushes back. The thing is, I know that if we can get to the point where we can fight honestly about how we're feeling about things, then we're fighting for each other and our relationship. We can't just ask her to make all the changes. We need to adjust to support her too."

I blinked at him a few times. "Wow, I think that's the most insightful thing you've ever fucking said."

He gave me a smirk and shrugged. "I listen to you, believe it or not, Sprock. Doesn't mean I'll do anything about it, but I hear you on this. I know we're just as much in the wrong as she is."

"So what happens if I don't agree that I'm in the wrong?" Eagle demanded, glaring at all of us.

"Then you can't say shit about family and crew first, because that woman is more than that to all of us. You're just being a stubborn ass who won't see it," Void announced. "There isn't a more perfect woman on this planet for the five of us—hell, even Weston fits in. I'm not going to give her up and if you tell me that I have to leave the club to have her, then that will just help to prove myself to her."

Eagle turned to Picasso. "You too, brother?"

"Eagle—this won't end well either way. I stay and resent you *or* I leave, and you resent me. How is that going to work out for any of us?" he answered.

"Alright, I might have been too hasty," Eagle bit out. "We came here tonight to try and work out how to do this, but I ended up making it worse. I trust you guys enough to listen, especially if you'd all walk out on the club over it, and no, I'm not just caving because of that. Void's right. I don't think there's another woman out here that could handle all of us. If this is going to work, I'm gonna need to learn that pushing her isn't the right move, but I don't know how else to act."

"Pres, this is why you have us," Void said. "You're also going to need to admit that what happened with Nelly wasn't right. You shouldn't have let her hang off you like that when our girl asked you to remove her."

Eagle nodded and took a deep breath and put his hand out. "So, we're all-in?"

"This will only work if we get Wes and Dax to agree as well," I interjected. "So put your damn hand down, we're not doing that."

Pushing off the counter, I headed out of the diner to where our bikes had all been knocked over. Should have guessed that she would've retaliated somehow, the question is, is this all she did. Examining all the bikes, I noticed that Eagle's and Weston's bikes were missing, and so were all the spark plugs. I couldn't help but grin at how impressive of a trick that was and how fast she did it in the dark. I noticed something on the ground and picked up a black ace of spades with a flaming skull in the middle of the card... Dax's card, claiming her hit on us... or could it be the threat of more to come?

Cognac snatched the card out of my hand and held it up to the light from the diner. "Yeah, we're fucked."

Chapter Fourteen

Dax

I HAD TO HAND it to Eagle, he had a sweet bike, even if I did hate the ape hanger handlebars. His were almost too high for me to ride comfortably, but I managed just fine and smiled the whole time, knowing how pissed he was going to be. One thing you didn't fuck with was a man's bike and I sure fucked with theirs. What would that phone call sound like? Or would they have their precious Nelly and her father take them back to the compound?

Wes and I drove at breakneck speeds back into the city. I didn't want them to be able to catch up to us and I'd learned my lesson with them the last time we made an escape. I was dropping this fucking bike off at a different location and Wes and I would head to my penthouse or as Wes called it, my love nest. Since we both agreed not to bring people back home, I decided to get a place that was all mine, and I could do what I wanted there. It kept things simple, but this would be the first time Wes would be seeing it.

We pulled into one of our warehouses, keyed in the code to open the gate and drove in. Wes hopped off his bike, opened one of the garage doors and I drove the bike inside, leaving it in perfect view of the small windows on the door. None of my people would let them in without contacting me first and I didn't plan on giving the bike back as of yet. Like I said, it was a sweet ride and with a new set of handlebars, it would be a good backup to have. These assholes needed to learn firsthand why you didn't fuck with Two Tricks, because I was just getting started. In my mind, we no longer had an alliance. Because if they didn't want me, then they didn't get what created the person I am today.

"You sure about this, Dax?" Wes asked, gripping my hips, and pulling me to his chest. "Don't get me wrong, they deserve to lose you if they can't get their heads out of their asses. I was talking more about having a third group after your head."

"They might not want to date me, but I highly doubt they want to kill me just yet. When I'm done with them, they might, but that will take a little time to set in motion," I answered, looking up at him. "You having any second thoughts?"

Wes shifted so his arms wrapped around me, and he ducked his head, kissing me like his life depended on it. "Never. You're all I've ever wanted, Dax. The day that you gave me a black eye for picking on Devin, I knew that you were the only woman for me. The fire inside you drew me to you, and I've been trapped ever since."

"You've always chosen me, haven't you," I murmured. "Please don't ever make me walk away from you like I just did to them. I was almost to the point I wasn't sure I could, but if it's between denying who I am and submitting to something I know isn't right—I'll always choose me."

"Shortcake, you think I don't know that already? You've been that way even before you lost Devin." Wes sighed and rested his head on top of mine. "Did you change when you lost Devin? Yes—just not in the way you think you have. You're not broken, Dax, you're more guarded, quicker to call people on their bullshit, and trust needs to be earned time and time again, but that isn't broken."

"Ha, that's what you see when you look at me?" I laughed. "What about the amount of people I've killed, tortured, or extorted? That has to say something about me is broken."

"Why does it have to prove that you're broken? Everything you've done is to stop others from taking advantage of those less fortunate. Every location where you have a warehouse, the crime rate drops, homeless people are cared for, and community centers are built to support families. Okay, so getting to that point was due to a fair amount of bloodshed and broken bodies, but you get my point. This is the side of the Hidden Empire that no one knows about but makes the biggest impact." He kissed the top of my head, took my hand, and intertwined our fingers. "Come on, let's get to the love nest so we can finally relax. Today has been a little more eventful than I was expecting, and I have some things to fill you in on."

"Nothing major, right? Because if it is, then I'm gonna need you to keep that to yourself until tomorrow. I've hit my limit of fucks to give about things other than cookie dough ice cream and watching *Big Bang Theory*." I groaned, following after him.

"Guess I'll be filling you in on things tomorrow then." Wes grinned at me.

"Wait, is it something that we can let slide?"

"It will be fine, trust me. The Empire is as much my baby as it is yours."

Wes mounted his bike and I slid in right behind him, wrapping my arms around him and resting my head on his back. I could hear the slow steady rhythm of his heartbeat and it set me at ease the whole way to the high-rise in the heart of the city. We pulled into my parking spot then headed into the lobby, so I could grab my spare key fob that I always made sure they had on hand. I never knew when or how I was going to show up here, so it was helpful to have a backup plan so I could actually get into the place.

"Ms. Rose, good evening," Sebastian, the model they hired for the front desk, greeted. "One moment and I'll grab your key."

"Did you have to pay extra in the HOA for him?" Wes teased, knowing that pretty boys were not my thing.

"Here you are, and your maid was by yesterday, so everything should be stocked and ready for you," Sebastian informed me with a blinding white smile.

"Thanks, Bas. Oh and if anyone comes here looking for me, you know what to do right?" I asked.

He clutched his chest like I'd wounded him, "How could you think I've forgotten that you don't exist the moment you leave with your key? Devin Rose who?"

Grabbing a bill from my phone wallet, I passed it over to him. "You're everything we pay for and more, Bas, never change."

Sebastian gave me a wink and turned back to his computer, ignoring me just like I always asked.

"You think someone would be able to find this place when you have zero ties to it and use a fake name on everything?" Wes questioned as we walked to the elevator.

"What do I always say? It's better to be alive and paranoid than dead and relaxed." I huffed.

I hit the button for the twentieth floor and settled in the corner out of the way of anyone coming or going. It was also a better vantage to shoot someone. Once the doors opened, I exited and headed right for the stairs, going up two more floors before heading down the long hall to my place.

"Do you make all your dates do this routine?" Wes laughed, as we entered the apartment.

It was a simple two-bedroom, two-bath with wood floors, lots of windows and a perfect view of the city below. I flicked on all the lights, making the place feel more welcoming. I'd had it done by an interior designer since I didn't really care what it looked like. It was a lot of gray and cream with soft pops of sage green, none of which I would have chosen for myself, but still looked nice.

"No one coming here would think you own this, that's for sure," Wes commented as he poked around. "Until they look in your closet."

"I'm making grilled cheese. Do you want one?" I called, heading into the kitchen.

Cooking wasn't my strong suit, but there were a few things I could do without fucking it up... most of the time. I grabbed everything out of the fridge and looked at the clock, noting it was past ten and the guys would be crying that they were up too late. Ugh, what did I care if they were still awake or not? They were no longer my problem. They made it clear that I was the crazy one and didn't stop me from leaving.

"You want me to make it?" Wes offered as he walked into the kitchen.

"I'm afraid if I let the food out of my sight something crazy is gonna happen again before I can eat it." I smirked as I butter the bread.

Wes stepped up beside me and started to work on his own, a comfortable silence between us. He had always been my rock, even before Devin died, making sure I was looked after and that I didn't get into more trouble than I could handle. I remember when we watched *Peter Pan*. He used to say that he was my shadow, always right behind me even if I couldn't see him. I set the bread on the pan then the cheese, ham, and then more cheese, before topping it off. Wes reached up and turned the flame down on the burner but didn't stop me from what I was doing.

"Thanks," I whispered, as I leaned on the counter, watching my sandwich.

"What if they apologize?"

"Hmm?"

"The guys. What if they come knocking on the door right now, begging to get you back?" Wes asked.

I looked over at him sitting on the counter, watching me with those intense dark brown eyes that seemed to always peer into my soul. "They won't."

"I'm not so sure about that," he countered and held up a hand. "Look, I don't agree with what happened or that they let you walk away. I'm also not saying they shouldn't get a taste of their own medicine and take a few hits, but I wouldn't be so quick to write them off completely."

"None of them stopped me," I argued. "How does that translate to, *oops, sorry we didn't agree, but stood by silently as you left because we don't have a brain to think for ourselves.*"

"You're gonna wanna flip that," Wes suggested, nodding to my sandwich.

"Ah fuck!" Thankfully, it wasn't burned, but it was definitely extra crispy that's for sure. "I swear to God, if I can't eat this sandwich in peace, I'm going to shoot someone."

Weston hopped off the counter and pulled me into his arms, wrapping me up tight. I let myself relax into him, balling the back of his shirt with my hands, desperate to cling to something that was safe.

"It's too hard to care, Wes," I murmured, feeling tears burn in my eyes, but I refused to let them fall. They didn't deserve to have me cry over them, no one did.

He didn't say anything, just held me until he shifted to dump my sandwich on the plate. Then he scooped me up and carried me back through the bedroom into the bathroom. I was set down on the edge of the massive tub that I had put in, because there was nothing better than a bubble bath when you needed time for yourself. Wes started the water and headed back out of the room. Quickly I stripped and grabbed a few bath salts and bubbles. Once it was full enough, I slipped in and turned on the jets, watching as the water turned dark red and the bubbles grew. When Wes returned, he had a tray with our food, two beers, and candy that he set down next to me. Snatching up the cheesy goodness, I moaned at the first bite, popping in a Flaming Hot Cheeto for the perfect mix. Wes joined me and winced a little at the temp but didn't say anything as I handed him his plate and beer.

"I think this is the best meal I've had in weeks." I grinned, poking him with my foot. "I'm not really that complicated, you know." Weston let out a bark of laughter at that. "What?!"

"Shortcake, I love the shit out of you, but that is so far from the truth. You are like a Chinese puzzle box that has a ticking time bomb strapped to it that will explode if it's done wrong."

I gaped at him. "No! That's not true!"

"Yeah, what happens if someone does something that upsets you?"

Goddamn it!

"Fine, I see your point there, *but*, I was talking more about the things that make me happy that are not that complicated. Food, art, music, bubble bath, my motorcycle—"

"Dax, the only people who know that stuff about you are me and Harper. You don't let anyone know you long enough to figure that stuff out. It takes time for people to notice those things. I've spent the past twenty odd years as your shadow and Harper lived with you. You don't date, the men you sleep with hardly ever see you more than twice, and even that's months in between so you don't get attached to them. Everything you do now is designed to keep people away and I'm no help, because I fucking love that I'm one of the only people who *knows* you," Wes explained.

"So, you're saying this is my fault?"

"No. That's what you're hearing, but not what I said," Wes chided. "I was trying to show you that it's not quite as easy as you think to see this side of you."

"Are you trying to get me to take them back?"

Wes slouched in the tub, staring up at the ceiling. "You could test the patience of a saint. I will stand behind whatever you want to do about them. Hell, I'll even help. All I want you to do is think about *why* you're doing it and make sure before you blow the motherfucking bridge up, that you don't want to cross it again."

I sat there munching on my Cheetos, thinking about what he'd just said. He might not be wrong, but even if I considered giving them a second chance, it wouldn't be easy.

Chapter Fifteen

Dax

I TUMBLED INTO BED, not bothering to put on pajamas since it was just Wes here with me. He'd carried the tray back into the kitchen and then came back and joined me, also in his birthday suit. Sliding right up behind me, he pulled me against him and shoved his leg in between mine. He let out a heavy sigh and all but collapsed against me, nuzzling into my neck.

"Maybe I should be talking you into never giving them a chance, then I get you all to myself," he muttered, his lips brushing along my skin.

"I have to say, I was surprised you even gave it a thought. You never struck me as the type to share."

Wes lifted his head to look down at me. "Do you really think I would let something like that stand in the way of *finally* getting to be with you? There is no way in hell something that minor would be a roadblock, and besides, I already outlasted them."

"Smug about that, are we?" I grinned and lifted my head to kiss him.

"You have no idea, but I'm more than willing to help you get an idea," he teased, as he shifted his body over me, pressing me into the mattress as he plundered my mouth.

Yeah, I know, I just had sex a few hours ago with another man, but what woman in her right mind would say no to another round after a horrible night?

Wes kneaded one of my boobs, while the other hand drifted between my legs to run his finger up and down my pussy, making me moan. I shifted my legs wide so he could fit better between them on his knees, giving him space to work his magic. There was something different about what was happening between us this time—it wasn't frantic or possessive, like most of my encounters. No, this was slow, torturous, and all about my pleasure, something I hadn't experienced in a long time, if ever. Wes released my lips, only to start kissing along my jaw and down my neck, until he reached my pulse point. He bit down on it and sucked the skin into his mouth harshly.

"Oh fuck!" I gasped as he shoved two fingers into me, causing my eyes to roll back in my head and arched off the mattress.

He didn't rush any movement of his hand, using every thrust and twitch to his advantage. Moving on from my neck, he licked my collarbone and swirled his thumb around my clit, giving me an overload of sensation. I tried to thrust down on him to speed up his pace, but he used his free hand to grasp me around my throat and with his legs resting over mine held me still.

"There are straps built into this bed," I offered, as I squirmed again and made him growl. "The frame is custom built with them in mind, just flip the top board on either end."

Wes sat back and slowly slid his hand out of me, making me cry out as he flicked the bean for good measure. "You are a wicked woman, Dax, and I wouldn't have you any other way."

Rolling off the bed, he found the straps that already had leather cuffs on them. He started with my ankles and then kissed up each leg as he crawled toward the headboard, which put his cock right in my face. So I did what any girl would and licked it like a lollipop before swallowing it down to his balls, a trick I pride myself on being able to do. Wes grunted and almost fell on me, caught off guard by my attack, but that just made me even more pleased. With my hands still free, I grabbed his ass and pulled him closer so I could get a better rhythm.

"Holy shit, Dax, you better slow down, or things will end faster than I'd like." Weston groaned as he tried to back away from me, but I grabbed his ball sac and tugged. "Okay, fuck, I guess I'll stay here."

I hummed with pleasure that he was submitting to my attention. Playfully, I ran a finger up the backside to swirl some of my spit around his asshole.

"Nope, sorry, babe, but that is exit only," he growled and grabbed my hand. "Now, if you want me to play with your asshole, then I'm more than happy to oblige."

Releasing him with a pop, I grinned up at him. "Oh, you shouldn't say things like that Westie, because I love a good ass fucking. Hell, getting double penetrated is something every woman needs in her life at least once—I prefer once a month myself."

Wes crouched down, grasping the side of my head, pulled me up to him and ravaged my mouth the released me grinning. "Seems that we'll have to find someone to play with once a month then. Maybe one of those idiots might redeem themselves enough to get visitation."

"I like the way you think. I have to admit I'm a little sad I never got to fuck Void or Sprocket. Both of them would definitely be a good time," I shared.

Wes started to kiss down my arm, then shackled one, then the other, and adjusted the leather to keep me spread eagle on the bed. He journeyed down my body until he sat back on his heels and looked at me splayed out for his pleasure. "What to do with you..."

"My hope is that eventually, I'll get fucked," I teased, shimmying my chest, trying to entice him.

"That's a given, but how much should I torture you first," he mused, tapping his chin. "I think a good edging is in order, to help you relax, of course. It has been a long day."

"Dangerous game there, Westie. You sure that's a move you want to make?"

"To have power over you for once—yeah I think I'll take that risk," he answered as he lay out on his belly and slid his hands under my ass, lifting me slightly. "Thank you for the feast I'm about to enjoy."

I started to laugh, only to have it cut off the moment his mouth landed on my pussy with one long lick of his tongue. Much to my irritation, he shifted his attention to my inner thigh, nibbling along the tender flesh venturing in closer and closer. Just then he was about to reach my clit, he moved to the other side and did the same thing again. My breathing became labored as it felt like my skin was being set on fire and the only thing that could save me was where he refused to put his mouth. When he reached the center again, his breath caressed me, cooling once it hit my drenched needy skin. Then he used a hand to spread me wide open and his tongue danced around my clit, grazing it as it swirled around the area, still not giving me enough stimulation.

"How long are you going to do this to me?" I whimpered. "I think I might actually lose my mind."

"Tell me what you want, my heart," Weston said seductively, peering up at me from between my legs.

I thrust up with my hips. "I *need* to come. Please, my shadow, let me come."

"No."

And with that simple response, he flicked my clit every which way, rapidly, but then when I felt it building, he would stop or slow down. I know I was begging now, but I had no idea if I was bartering or threatening him to finish the job. I felt a single finger enter me and move languidly in and out, lightly rubbing against my G-spot, forcing me to shudder with anticipation.

"Please, please, please," I mumbled. "What do you want? I'll do anything, please just let me come."

"Look at you, a puddle of need and want," Weston purred.

"If you don't let me come, I will stab you right in the balls, you hear me? I will do it, don't even think I won't," I growled, thrashing against the restraints. "I'm sorry, I didn't mean it, please, please just promise me that I will get to come soon."

"You want to come that badly?"

I all but let out a sob. "Yes!"

He unhooked the tie downs and flipped me over so I was now on my knees with my ass in the air and my face in the mattress. His mouth descended upon my ass, keeping that one lone finger in my pussy to keep the flames alive. The heady sensation of both holes being manipulated made me writhe, but I tried not to move too much for fear he would stop.

"Lube?"

"Nightstand," I gasped and cried out when he left me to go grab it.

Thankfully, he returned seconds later, and the cool feeling of lube landed on my ass, followed by a finger working it in. He took his time to make sure I was good and warmed up, while also making sure that my pussy was hanging on to that cliff by her fingernails. Never had someone taken it to the extreme of denying me my release, they were far too eager to hold themselves back. Not Wes, he'd been waiting years to get this moment, so I knew he was going to draw out every second he could. Finally it came time and he adjusted behind me, but I didn't know where he was going to enter and that was far more thrilling than it should be.

Wes slid home into my pussy, his arm wrapping around me as he pinched my clit between his fingers, causing me to rocket forward as I finally got to fall off the cliff into pure bliss, while he pounded into me. I bit down on the pillow as he fucked me through my orgasm that was so powerful, I thought I might black out. Wes was a god among men, and I was the lucky bitch who had him all to myself.

"That's it, my heart, scream for me. Let everyone in this place know who is owning your body right now." Wes panted as he gripped my hips and yanked me back on his dick. "This pussy is mine tonight and I will make sure that it never forgets me."

Wes all but fucked me to death and I lived for every moment of it. Just when I didn't think I could take any more, he switched to my ass. Releasing my hand, he grabbed my hair and sat me back down on him so my back was plastered to his chest. He thrust up into me as he strummed on my aching clit while his other hand pulled at my nipple. I no longer could tell what was happening to me, I just knew it was all amazing and fulfilled something deep inside of me that had nothing to do with the length of Weston's cock. Was this what having sex with someone you loved felt like?

Abandoning my nipples, he gripped my jaw and twisted my face back so he could kiss the ever-loving shit out of me as he slammed home. He was getting close, but this wasn't how I wanted things to finish. Pulling away, I turned to face him and guided his dick into my ass and worked him over myself, swirling my hips and pushing him all the way in. I wrapped my hands around his neck for leverage and bounced all up on that dick while being able to watch the pure lust and pleasure written all over his face. That was all me. I was putting that look there and I had never been prouder of that fact. When I started to falter, he wrapped me up around him and he took over again, until we both shattered as we lost ourselves to the torrent of bliss.

It took us a moment to regain our senses, sprawled out on the bed, intertwined in the most intimate way possible. He brushed back my sweaty hair, placing gentle kisses until he landed on my lips, telling me without words how he felt about me. The sensation that I thought I'd lost came flooding back into me as if a dam broke. I cupped his jaw and pulled back slightly to see his face, searching it to see if what I was feeling was being reflected back. I should have known it would be. This man was my rock, my shadow, the man who for longer than I would like to admit held my heart safe until I was ready to take it back.

"I love you, Weston. I think I've always loved you," I whispered, as I felt a tear roll down my cheek.

The awe and affection that passed over his face was the final straw and the tears started to flow. He cradled my face in his hands and started to kiss away the tears with gentle patience and held me until I calmed down.

"Dax Rose Blackmore, I love you more than you'll ever know, and I'm beyond honored to receive your love," he murmured. "Thank you for trusting me enough to love me."

We stayed wrapped up in each other for a bit, until Wes softened and slipped out of me. He left to get a washcloth and cleaned us both up, then removed the leather cuffs and settled in, curling me up into a ball and tucking me against him. With a final kiss on the back of my neck, we drifted off to sleep.

Chapter Sixteen

Dax

I N THE MORNING, I decided that it would be best to forget everything that had happened in the past week with the Phantom Saints and deal with my problems. Wes took me by the house to get my bike and stop by my gun safe to restock on ammo and the like. Then we headed out to the shipping docks, which housed our biggest warehouse that we worked out of, and my headquarters for the Hidden Empire. The security guards waved us by as we arrived. We continued through, weaving our way through all the shipping containers. Everything was loud—people yelling over engines, forklifts honking as they zipped around, and of course the massive freightliners that were getting loaded, signaling their departure. It was a world of its own and one that could turn on you if you didn't watch your surroundings.

When we pulled up to the low, white building that was ours, I parked. The moment I cut the engine, Brian was there to greet me.

"Dax, it's good to see you, boss." He grinned, making him seem slightly less intimidating.

Brian was my right-hand man when it came to enforcement issues. He was average height, but he was built like a brick house and smart as a fox. He and Jeff had both been the perfect blend of muscle and smarts—not easy to find in this line of work. Now I was going to have to find someone to replace Jeff and it wasn't something I was looking forward to.

"Anything interesting happen while I was gone?" I asked as we headed into the warehouse.

"You mean besides the fact that the De León Cartel is after you, and word on the streets is that the Mad Dogs are helping them?"

I paused and looked up at him. "I'm sorry about Jeff. I know he was like a brother to you. Have you spoken to Kate? Everything okay with the baby?"

"They had the funeral a few days ago, thanks for handling it. There was no way that Kate could have managed that with a newborn," Brian said, gripping my shoulder and giving it a quick squeeze.

Sneaking a glance at Weston, knowing he was the one who'd most likely taken care of that matter, I nodded to Brian "He died because of me. It's the least I can do to support his family. His wife will also continue to get his paychecks until that kid is eighteen. Jeff always wanted to be a dad, so I'll make sure they're provided for." Clearing my throat, I kept moving further into the space toward my office. "Send out the call to all the underlings that we will be having a meeting tonight here at ten. This is nonnegotiable. They either show up or they better hide real well where I can't find them. Wes will be informing the others, so they know we're not fucking around."

"What do you want me to tell them if they ask what it's about?" Brian asked.

I placed my hand on the scanner that locks my office and looked him dead in the eye. "Changes are coming." I shoved open my door and walked into my space.

My office was much like my tattoo shop with black, white, and red splashed around the place and some abstract art that I painted. My desk was something you would see on the set of *The Adams Family* with its Victorian flair, painted a glossy black, with white drawers and the leather chair behind it. Technically, this started out as Tricks' office, but since I'd killed off the guy who played Tricks in the beginning, I took it over and the big boss man worked from a secret location—for security purposes, of course. Now that I look back on it, I'm amazed that I kept it quiet for so many years. It probably helped that I would kill anyone who found out and tried to blackmail me about it, or if the rumors started, I would put them to rest one way or another. Being able to work in plain sight had made controlling this empire so much easier and built even more fear of Tricks himself... well, herself. Yet that era was coming to an end, and it was time for me to take my rightful place as the known leader of the Hidden Empire.

"You sure about this, Dax?" Weston asked as he sat in the chair opposite of me. "It might be risky to draw that big of a crowd when you don't know how people will react."

"Really, because they all know how I'll react?" I answered, quirking a brow at him. "If I have to clean house, I'll do it. We can't have people who aren't loyal while we're at war. Besides, I have a network far bigger than anyone in the Empire besides us knows about."

"True. Do you want me to call the entire West Coast crew out here for this meeting?"

"If they want to remain part of our Empire, then I would highly suggest our West Coast members make it to this family chat," I stated.

My grasp of the West Coast went all the way to Oregon, Washington, Arizona, Nevada and even to Alaska. My whole business was getting what you needed where you needed it and all these places served one of those purposes. Yes, Los Angeles was the largest hub, but I didn't like to flaunt my power unless I needed to—better to have people underestimate you. This is why I'm so surprised that Diego is making his move. The man owns the East Coast and has a better foothold in Mexico than I do. Sure, I was the biggest roadblock, but we were a whole continent away from each other. For him to kill his own son just to blame me, told me there was something bigger at work that I just hadn't thought of. Was he bringing another power to the rise? Did he hope that by taking me out, he could gain favor from this new player in town?

"Wes, I think we need to take a look worldwide to see who's getting restless. All this doesn't add up. Why would a cartel boss like Diego work with an MC, of all people, to get rid of me? I know his first plan was to blow us up from the inside out, making my people turn on me, but when that didn't work, he sent the Mad Dogs," I mused, tapping my fingers on the desk. "It makes perfect sense why the Mad Dogs want me. They would then get power over the Empire. I'm just not seeing Diego's reasoning."

"No problem, I'll reach out to some of my contacts and see if there are any whispers on the dark web," Wes assured me as he left the office to go work on his own.

Booting up my computer, I opened the encrypted connection to the Empire database and started reviewing transactions from the last week. Before I knew it, I was lost in the flow of information and checking on things that had been left off to Tricks to decide, that Wes wouldn't have been able to handle. There were some vendors that were only willing to work with me directly, which made sense since I fostered the connection.

"Levin, why are you holding up the shipment of PKPs? I have a buyer who is getting upset with me for backing out of the deal. Now, why would he think *I'm* the one who is backing out?" I demanded, watching Levin's face on the monitor when he answered my call.

"Why would I know, *kroshka*? I reached out to the man who take the gun to the train, but he not show. Then I try to reach you and you don't call me back. What I suppose to think, eh?" Levin groused.

Levin was in his sixties and has been my Russian arms dealer for years. He's never screwed me over before, so when I discovered this deal hadn't gone through, I was shocked.

"You know that if you can't reach me that you're supposed to contact Weston. He is my right hand, and knows all the deals we have going on," I challenged.

"Ack, *kroshka* that *durachok*," he spat, waving a dismissive hand. "He can do nothing but type on computer. No respect for the way things used to be—no, I speak to you. Why didn't you answer me? This was days ago."

"I was away on an unexpected business trip, and I wasn't in a place I could speak freely. I know how much you value your privacy."

"*Da*, then it's good you back, now we can make deal." Levin nodded and stood from his chair to grab something, making me almost seasick with all the motion.

I grabbed the energy drink from my desk and took a few gulps, rubbing my forehead, waiting for Levin to settle himself. I was surprised this video call had been going so well. He had a habit of fucking something up along the way. Levin was all but a Luddite in his hatred toward technology, but he suffered through it to keep his business running. When we first started working together, I used to have to fly out and meet him with the new client proposal, before Wes taught him how to use the laptop we got him.

"Ah, here it is!" Levin shouted, as he sat proudly in front of the screen.

He was holding up a sniper rifle that had me leaning forward to make sure I wasn't seeing things. "Where did you get that?!"

"Eh, eh, eh, not all secrets are to be shared, *kroshka*." Levin smiled. "I make you good deal if you find buyer willing to take them. I have one hundred, all modified with new technology firing chambers that is not on market. These fell off very special truck, you see."

"Yes, I want them, what's the deal?"

"See, I knew you like dis gun, maybe you want one for yourself? Start new hobby?" Levin chuckled. "Word is that trouble is coming for you, *kroshka*, and I do not want to lose best customer, eh."

"Got any other goodies I should know about?"

"You want tank? I got a one out back if you like—"

"Not quite what I was thinking. You forget we can't fight that dirty here on US soil."

"*A huy li*? Dis makes no sense," Levin mutters as he looks around his office. "If you don't want tank then what about rocket launcher?"

"Sounds like I better just stick to the rifles then, Lev." I smirk, knowing that his suggestions would only continue to be outlandish. "Hey, do the whispers say what kind of trouble is coming my way?"

Levin paused and set aside whatever he was going to show me to put his face way too close to the camera. "No, *kroshka*, but trouble that is this quiet is never good. Like wolf stalking bunny, you don't know it there till you dead."

"Well, isn't that comforting," I mumble to myself. "Who else has been hearing these sorts of things?"

"Hmm, I hear from Taaj. He told me he hear from Cheng, at the docks."

"You people are worse than a bunch of *babushkas* sitting around knitting," I tease. "How do I know you don't spill our clients?"

Levin slammed his fist on his desk. "*Blayt*, you know better than that. I would have no business if I talked about our deals, not even going to the Black Dolphin Prison would get it out of me."

"Okay, okay, calm down, Lev. I'm sorry, I shouldn't have questioned your professionalism after all these years. One can't be too careful with a wolf hiding in the shadows, as you warned."

Appeased, he settled down. "Good, now when is the new exchange for first deal, then we talk about second deal, da?"

"For the first deal, do I need to find another way to get them to Austria? This time, I plan to send someone to personally guarantee that it gets to where it needs to."

"Das is good if you can get someone to babysit the shipment on the train, then I don't have to charge more."

I nodded in agreement. He was being exceptionally fair with an issue that I didn't manage well, while being kidnapped and all. "How long have you been sitting on that inventory?"

"Too long. I need it gone so I can get new things. This deal good for us both. Now the sniper rifles, these will take much more skill to sneak them into the US, they are banned you know."

"Yes, I know, that's why they will fetch a high price, even more with the modifications," I answered, rolling my eyes. "What do you want for them?"

"A favor..."

This caught my attention. Levin never asked for favors, because that meant one of these days, I might do the same.

"What's the favor?"

"I need to get my granddaughter to America before my *balvan* of a son can sell her off to cover his debts. He is in deep to the Russian Mafia, and they want their pound of flesh. She is only sixteen, that is no life for her. She good girl, headstrong, but good girl—like you," Levin explained.

I knew his son was a bastard, but no one wants to believe they will sell their children to cover for their mistakes. "How long do I have to get her out if I agree?"

"My son has until the end of the month to make good on his debt, or they take her."

Turning, I looked at the calendar on my phone, noting it was only ten days into the month, leaving twenty-one days to get her out... if I could.

"Tell me everything you can about who your son is in debt to, as well as information on her. I'll also need a picture so if I do try and pull this off, I have what I need to get her papers out of the country. Give me a few days to think this over and see what it will take to make it happen. Right now isn't the best time for me to plan a rescue mission and deal with my own problems," I warned.

"Then you should know that she was selected by the Russian military to be an infiltrator, but I've stalled them with just giving her basic training. She is able to take care of herself and can easily play American, but this is another reason they cannot have her. Think of what could happen if they had someone like her working for them. She would be their best assassin. No one would be safe. My little *malishka* deserves to have the chance at a normal life."

Now Levin was just playing at my heartstrings. "I will give you an answer as soon as I can. Let me know when the drop will take place for the first order, and I'll have someone there."

"Da, we will speak soon, *kroshka*."

I ended the call and flopped back into my chair. What was I going to do about this situation?

Chapter Seventeen

Void

AS I SURVEYED THE aftermath of what happened at the diner in the afternoon light, I couldn't help but be more impressed with my little demon. None of us had been prepared for a truck to come crashing through the front doors. My first instinct had been to protect her, even as she was tossing back the table to keep us all safe, acting on her built-in will to survive. When she'd shared last night that she didn't think she'd live this long, I was shocked—that woman didn't know herself very well. Not just anyone could do what she's done in such a short amount of time, having no background in the criminal world.

"How sweet of you to come check on me today, Void. Are the others coming too?" Nelly asked as she sidled up to me.

I glanced down at her with disdain. She was the reason that Dax left us.

"I didn't come because of you," I corrected. "This diner is under our protection, and I wanted to get a look at the truck before it was taken away."

I walked away and toward the smashed-up black truck, ignoring the huff of irritation.

"What's that pink-haired slut got that I don't?" she snarled. "And since when do you all *share* a woman? That's just fucked up."

I whipped around and stormed up to her, grabbing her by the throat, lifting her until she was on her tippy toes. "Don't you fucking talk like that about my little demon. She is more woman than you will ever be, you spiteful bitch. Eagle has never had eyes for you and acting like some damsel in distress isn't going to do a goddamn thing for you. Our woman is strong and proud, able to take care of herself, which you saw firsthand. As a warning, if you ever talk like that in front of her, I'll let her kill you."

Her eyes went wide at my threat, and she scrambled with her hands, trying to loosen my grip on her. "Let me go, Void. You wouldn't hurt an innocent woman who's under your protection."

"Lucky for me, as of this moment, you're not under our protection. We won't be coming back here ever again, and if I see you sniffing around, causing trouble for Dax, I'll make sure that something worse than a truck through your building happens. Don't. Fuck. With. Our. Woman." Dropping her to the ground, I gave her one last glare, knowing it could make a grown man pee himself, and left to do my job.

As far as I was concerned, anything else could wait until my little demon was back by my side raising hell. Not knowing where she was or if she was safe was driving me insane and that didn't bode well for anyone who got in my way. I'd been dead serious last night when I said I'd leave the crew if it came down to it—that woman was my soulmate. The others could laugh at me for thinking it, but I knew the moment she tossed me through a sliding glass door, she was perfect. Never had a person come close to my level of crazy, and she might actually surpass it, now that I was getting to know her. I'd reached out to all my contacts, trying to figure out where she was. Eagle and Cognac were off trying to find his bike since it had a tracker on it, but I didn't think she'd make it that easy.

Ripping open the truck door that was hanging off its hinges at an odd angle, I tossed it in the bed of the truck. Then I popped open the glove compartment and found it empty, not even a fast-food napkin. I hopped up in the cab, careful not to get cut by the glass and other shrapnel that was in it, but I couldn't find a goddamn thing to give us a clue. I took a picture of the VIN to see if Cognac would be able to get any information off it. Not that it would help much if it was stolen, but it was always smart to cover our bases.

My phone vibrated in my back pocket. Seeing it was Eagle, I answered it. "You find it?"

"She locked it in a goddamn garage right in front of the window with a sign on it that reads *Thanks for the new bike*. What the fuck man? That's my fucking bike!" Eagle ranted and I could hear Cognac next to him, laughing his ass off.

"You didn't really think this would be easy after we had to walk our bikes back last night, did you?" I asked, climbing out of the truck. "Oh, by the way, we're not going back to Jerry's Diner. Nelly just made a whole scene and I had to set her straight."

"What the fuck! Anything I need to worry about?"

"Nah, I'm pretty sure she got the message."

Eagle grunted at that. "I have no doubt. You find anything helpful on the truck?"

"Not a damn thing. There's nothing, and I mean not even a French fry, under the seat," I answered, kicking a leg over my bike. "You heard from Wes at all?"

"Why would he call us? He's probably grinning ear to ear now that he has her all to himself, the bastard," Eagle grumbled. "How the hell am I supposed to get my bike back now? Cognac just talked to one of the workers and they were instructed to tell us to fuck right off."

"Sounds like a woman who got told she wasn't as important to us as she was led to believe." I sighed, running a hand through my hair. "Fixing this isn't going to be easy, and that's after we find out where she's hiding."

"Picasso called me a bit ago saying her bike is gone, but neither of them is there," Cognac yelled into the phone. "My guess is that she has another hideaway somewhere in the city."

That definitely sounded like her. My phone started to beep, letting me know another call was coming in. "Hey, I'm gonna let you go, one of my contacts is calling."

Before Eagle could answer, I switched the call over. "Speak fast."

"This is big news, Void. There's a meeting tonight at the docks and your girl made it a show-up-or-die situation. No one really knows what it's about, but speculation is that she's gonna try and take the Empire from under Tricks since all this shit has been going on. Man, people are fucking scared. Do you know what kind of war would happen if it went down between Dax and the bloodthirsty tyrant Two Tricks? I don't think there would be a city left after that," Buzz announced.

If Tricks and Dax weren't the same person I would have to agree with him, but my money will always be on my little demon to win. "Did they say what time?"

"No, apparently there is an established agreed upon time that these things happen that everyone knows about but isn't saying, although I do know it's at night," Buzz shared. "You thinking of crashing the party? Did you guys put Dax up to this?"

"Don't you worry about that," I cautioned. "You hear anything else about this, I'm your first phone call—you got me?"

"Yeah, Void, I hear you loud and clear," Buzz answered, then hung up.

I made another quick phone call to my guy in the local police and then to Ducky to come tow the truck to the scrapyard before I headed back to the compound. Looks like we had a date with the docks tonight.

Buzz ended up not being able to get me much more information about the meeting, other than all members were getting called in. I don't think anyone really knows the true hold that Dax has over the West Coast, but tonight, my money was bet on her coming out as Two Tricks. This drove my need to watch her back, more than I already craved to have her back at my side. How could my little demon think this was a good idea to do without any backup that she knew would be on her side completely? Guess that would be because motherfucking Eagle had to have a freak-out and chase her away. I looked around the kitchen and watched the others as they went through the motions of our day. No one really wanted to speak, knowing it would just start another fight like it had when Eagle wasn't keen on the idea of us going to the docks.

"What makes you think we won't get shot for just being there?" Eagle demanded. "Do we even have an alliance still?"

"Well, this would be the fastest way to find out," Cognac said.

Eagle chopped furiously at the ingredients he was using for dinner. Whenever Eagle got stressed, he cooked up a storm, and it looked like we were having a five-course meal tonight.

"I want to fix things but is this really the best way to go about it?" Eagle ventured, looking up from his work to see our response.

Sprocket sucked down the last of his beer and took a deep breath. Oh man, shit was about to get real...

"Do you though? The rest of us have been in a fog all day, trying to find some way to convince Dax that we want her to come back, but all you've done is bitch and moan. *Dax took my bike, now she won't give it back. Why won't Dax answer my phone calls? I wasn't in the wrong, she went too far. Why should I apologize? Whine, whine, moan, grumble, grumble, chop, chop.*" Pausing, he tossed the bottle into the bin, and it clanged against all the others that were in there. "All that sounds like to me, is you're still pissed at her for taking a stand and walking away. This is never going to work if you don't get your head out of your ass and deal with the fact that woman is not going to be your sidekick. Dax is a badass in the criminal world just as much as you are in the MC world. If you both can find a way to share ruling the evil empire, then I see this being one of the most unstoppable duos in history."

Eagle stood there stunned, watching Sprocket grab another beer out of the fridge and pop the top. The rest of us watched in silence, afraid to move and set off the bomb. With a slam of a knife, Eagle launched himself at Sprocket sending him stumbling back out of the kitchen into the living room. Fists flying as neither one of them were willing to back down. Sprocket gave as good as he got, if not more, being smaller and faster than our president. The sound of shattering wood brought us to our feet, and we hurried into the living room where they both landed on the coffee table, still grappling at each other.

Picasso caught my eye and nodded—it was time to end this. "I'll get Eagle."

Wading in, I slipped an arm around Eagle's neck, pulled tight and lifted slightly until I could feel him freeze. He knew I would knock his ass out if I needed to. I'd done it before, and it was never fun when he woke up. Picasso hauled Sprocket away, the man going limp as blood trickled down his face from his busted lip and the cut on his cheek. It'd been years since these two had gotten into a fight. Typically, it happened between the brothers, but even that had been some time ago.

"You good?" I asked our president.

He tapped my arm twice, signaling me he'd calmed down. Hoisting him up, I tossed him on the couch and got a look at his face—black eye, broken nose, and bruised ego aside, his eyes looked tortured. Heaving a heavy sigh, I headed to the kitchen to grab the pack of peas we kept just for this and slapped it into his hand as I sat down next to him.

"What the hell is really going on, man? You were the one that started this whole thing, bringing up the old rules and shit—what changed?" I questioned.

Eagle looked at me with his good eye, the other now swollen shut. "Two things—I can't control her, she's a loose cannon doing whatever the fuck she wants. Do you realize the power that she has as the ruler of the Hidden Empire? What happens if things go too far, and she does something we can't stand behind?"

"Yeah, I'm not buying that. Spell it out for me, man," I challenged. "What did Sprocket mean when he talked about your uncle?"

The change in his body was instant. It was as if he turned to stone and his eyes went vacant, as if he was lost in the past. "Hannibal... my mother's older brother, and his twin, Bear, the previous VP of the Blackjax. Hannibal was the man I looked up to most of my life since my father cared more about his clients than either of us boys. He was the leader of the Devils Spawn MC. They were small time and worked as support to other gangs in the area. All they wanted to do was cause trouble and wish they could be like the Hell's Angels back in the day. Picasso and I would hang around them, but we weren't allowed to do much other than simple errands, fetching shit for them. Han taught us how to shoot, how to ride, and how to take what we wanted whenever we wanted it." Eagle paused as Picasso handed him a glass of whiskey and started to clean up the coffee table, as if he couldn't sit still.

I noticed that Cognac and Sprocket were listening in on the story from the other end of the couch. This made me wonder how much Sprocket really knew. He had an odd knack of finding shit out about you that you never wanted to be found.

"When I turned sixteen, I was finally able to prospect into the MC and that's when I really learned what it was that they did. The Devils Spawn were human traffickers, dealing in flesh of all ages and selling them to the highest bidders. The first job they gave us was to babysit the merchandise before they went to auction and drug them up so they would be compliant. I did everything I could to avoid being the one who would shoot them up, but it was how they trapped you in the system. A patched in member would stand there and watch you to make sure it got done and then they would take turns with the women we knew didn't need to stay pure. Those who refused to do what they were told got shot point-blank in the head without a second thought. The Devils Spawn were lackeys to none other than the De León Cartel... that is until I ratted them out to the FBI. As family, I got a lot of leeway to pick and choose where I wanted to work in the system, but when my time ran out and I was forced to work one of the auctions, I knew it had to end."

"Hannibal escaped somehow—he was an oily bastard like that, once I got to know the real version of him. Did you know that I'm named after him? My mother's side of the family liked to use the same three family names and so I got blessed with Enzo, just like that sick fuck. He figured out that someone from the inside had blown the whistle and I still don't know how he narrowed it down to me. After that, what little control he had on the crazy that lived inside him snapped. He kidnapped Picasso, beat the shit out of him and sent me the photos, telling me that if I didn't fix this, then Picasso was dead. Of course there was no way to fix this, so I had to turn to Bear, the new president of the Blackjax, to help me out. With his help, I was able to save Picasso, but my first kill also happened to be family. I couldn't make his twin do it and all this happened because of what I'd done," Eagle explained, tossing back the last of his whiskey. "Then we learned what an MC was supposed to be like from Bear, and Picasso and I started the Phantom Saints, taking over the property that Hannibal used and the rest you all know."

"That is one fucked-up story, man," Cognac blurted, rubbing his face with his hands. "But it doesn't explain your issue with our *loba*."

"Dax has the same kind of crazy in her that Hannibal did, and I'm afraid that she could crack just like him if the right pressure is applied," Eagle answered, not looking at any of us.

Sprocket scoffed and shot to his feet. "She is nothing like that sadist! From what I can tell, Hannibal never had a heart or a conscience. The whole goddamn reason Dax became who she is, is because her heart was broken at the loss of her brother. Yeah, she destroyed the Blackjax, but she never went after the families, only the members. And even then, it was a calculated attack to end it quickly. They could have rebuilt if they wanted to, but they chose to join us or leave the MC life all together. What about that says she's some psycho crazy killer who rapes and kills people?"

I raised a hand when it looked like Sprocket was going to continue his rant and he snapped his mouth shut. Confident he wasn't going to say anything more, I turned back to Eagle. "You said two things. What's the second thing?"

Eagle looked me in the eye, his face deadly serious. "I would burn the world down for her if she asked me to, because that same kind of crazy lives deep inside me too. What I'm truly terrified about is that she'd ask me to, and the crazy would be set free from the cage I've locked it down in since the day I shot my uncle right between the eyes as he begged me to save him."

"Well, fuck."

Chapter Eighteen

Eagle

I WATCHED THE GUYS' faces as they absorbed what I'd just told them. This was a truth I never wanted to admit to myself and somehow, I ended up falling for the one woman who could turn me into what I feared most. Hannibal still haunted my dreams as he stared me down, crazed and babbling nonsense about how we could rule the world together if I let him live. He used to always tell me that he saw himself in me, and that turned my stomach. I refused to ever be like him and when I saw Dax turn her gun on Nelly, I snapped. I was transported back to those dark days, watching sobbing women and children beg to be set free, until we doped them up. I'd helped to turn children into drug addicts—yeah, I might not have given them the drugs with my own hands, but I'd helped collect the drugs we used. As much as the nightmares clung to me, they were my constant reminder of what was hiding deep in my blood, waiting for me to slip up. Then Dax entered my life and one night of her in my bed and I slept like a baby.

Did I deserve to be given that freedom? No, my life would never be on the right side of the law, but I worked hard to make sure that I kept people like my uncle out of my territory. This was the driving force behind why I chased the Mad Dogs out of California, took over their businesses and cleaned them up. Flesh would *never* be dealt if I had anything to say about it. People might not understand why I choose to live this life still, but where did a man like me go? I couldn't ever be the good guy, not really. As a result of my trauma, my desperate need to control myself and others around me became a way to cope, to make sure that nothing like that would happen in this club. How Picasso only turned into the moody asshole artist he is was beyond my understanding. Hannibal nearly beat him to death and most of the scars have been covered up by tattoos, but I still knew they were there.

"Well, fuck," Void muttered as he leaned back into the couch.

If there was ever another man who could understand what I feared, it would be him. When I found him fighting in the underground rings after he was kicked out of official fights, I saw the pain in his eyes. Cognac knew loss as well but the fire that fueled him was revenge against the cartel that stole his family from him. I'd hoped never to have to tell him this story, knowing that he'd been sold. Not through our network, but that made little difference to the person who was trafficked. These men had become brothers, bonded together by pain and anger, and the only way to keep us all sane was to make sure no one fucked with our carefully structured world—the one thing Dax would be able to blow up with a single word.

"I thought she was his enforcer for the profit or the clout. Knowing that she is the dark queen of the Empire changes everything," I stated, dropping my now thawed bag of peas.

Picasso snapped a piece of the coffee table, tossing it across the room. "You can't keep letting that asshole torture you from the grave, Eagle. It gives him too much power."

"You know that it runs in our family. Why do you think Mom wants nothing to do with us? Yeah, we all go home for Christmas, but she lives in a fantasy where we aren't the leaders of a gang and her brothers died in a tragic accident. What do you think will happen if we show up with the woman who killed her brother?" I demanded. "I think it would break her. She hides away in her perfect world, but if we shatter that, I don't think she could take it."

"Why the fuck do we have to tell her? Dax is a tattoo artist who also paints. That's what the world knows her as. Why do you have to make it out to be the worst possible situation? You're so fucking scared to turn into some Jekyll and Hyde shit, you've built this perfect fortress, not only for you but for me as well. Could you just man up for one goddamn second and see that you're pissed at yourself and not Dax or anything that happened about last night? She scares the shit out of you because she can handle the so-called crazy without losing to it. What makes you think she would even want to turn you into that person?" Picasso was now shouting at me in a way that hadn't happened since we became the leaders of the Phantom Saints. "I got to see a glimpse of the woman under the attitude and she's crying out for someone to stay by her side no matter how broken she is, and you tossed her worst fear in her face. You did exactly what you're afraid she'll do to you—see the vulnerable underbelly and go for the kill."

His words hit harder than Sprocket's fist in my face, and it finally sank in how badly I fucked up.

"I think he just got it," Cognac whispered loudly. "So does that mean we're going to the docks tonight?"

Shoving myself to my feet with a grunt, I nodded. "Let Sprocket and I clean up and we'll make a plan as we eat. Chances are this meeting isn't until the docks are closed for the night."

Cognac grinned at me like the Cheshire cat, the gleam of excitement in his eyes. "Oh, this shit's gonna be good!"

Void grunted his agreement, but I saw the smirk on his smug face. That man had no problem at all with the idea of burning down the world around us if it meant she would be safe, and I envied that. Seems I might have something to learn from my enforcer after all these years.

We pulled up to the docks around eleven. The security was gone, the shipping yard silent but for the ringing of the buoys out in the ocean. I drove past the vacant guard shack onto the docks at a low idle so we didn't attract too much attention.

If we were late, then it would be even more obvious that we shouldn't be here. Too early wasn't that much better. As we made our way further back, I spotted a warehouse that glowed in the night with cars and bikes scattered all around. Either there was another secret meeting, or this is what we were looking for. I cut the engine and the others followed, coasting our way up to the building and parked a little way from everyone else, in case we needed to get out of there in a hurry.

"You ready for this, Pres?" Sprocket asked as he stood next to me. "Because if you have any second thoughts or you need to work through your shit, then now is not the time to do this."

I clapped him on the back. "I'm good. Still got shit to work on but it's more about me than her. I owe her an apology, a huge fucking apology if I'm being honest."

"Glad to see you managed to remove your head from your ass."

"Let's just hope I'm not too late and she'll give us another chance. You guys don't deserve to be punished for what I did."

Sprocket shook his head. "It wasn't just you who let her walk out that door. None of us stopped her from doing it. Any one of us could have manned up and told you what we really thought, but we didn't."

"That won't happen again," Void announced. "I told my little demon that I wasn't going to let her go and I plan to make good on my word, no matter what I have to do to make it happen."

"What, you going to kidnap her again?" Cognac joked, laughing to himself until he saw Void's face. "Oh fuck, you would."

"Of course I fucking would. It worked the first time, didn't it?" Void answered with a shrug of his shoulders and headed off to the warehouse.

"I love that man like a brother, but sometimes he worries me," Cognac muttered as he followed.

Picasso fell in beside me as we journeyed into the demon's lair to await whatever fate she had for us. Was Picasso right about Hannibal still controlling me? It was hard to swallow that kind of truth, but I knew my brother always had my back and would never lie to me about shit like that just to get his way. Something had happened between him and Dax while he was at her house and it wasn't just the rescue mission for Harper. No, it was deeper than that. He said he'd seen behind her walls and caught a glimpse of her true self that she's locked away, much like I've done. I wonder who she would be if she'd never lost her brother? Shaking my head, I pulled myself back to the present, the time to be lost in thought was not when we were in unknown territory. For all we knew, she could have put out a hit order on us if we ever showed up here. Yeah, Buzz was a double agent and had been feeding us a lot of the information we had on the Empire over the years, but that didn't mean he'd be able to catch everything.

"Yo, is Weston around?" Cognac asked the hulking mass of muscles that stood at the door.

The guard tried to fold his arms over his chest, but he was so bulky that it didn't really work. "If you have to ask that, you don't belong here, so move along."

I took a deep breath and rolled my head to shake off some of the stiffness that was settling in after my fight with Sprocket. I squared my shoulders and stepped up. "Eagle, President to the Phantom Saints. We were told to be here and to ask for Wes when we arrived. You want him to find out that you ignored his order and mention it to Dax?"

It was an amazing thing to watch a man of his size wither at the mention of my little hellcat. "Wait here."

"Well, look who's back in the game. Way to go Pres," Cognac cheered, punching me in the shoulder.

I glared at him but didn't rise to his teasing. It's just what Cognac did, meaning all was right in our world. It didn't take long before Wes came storming out the door and got right up in my face, rage covering his face.

"What the actual fuck, Eagle? Why the hell are you here right now?" he barked, but when I tried to answer, he cut me off. "On second thought, I don't want to know. You need to leave. You're not welcome here."

"Is that order coming from you or from her?" Picasso snapped, shoving Weston to the side and out of my face. "We aren't here to cause trouble, Westley. It's clear that she's going to tell everyone about what's going on, and seeing as we are allies, we wanted to offer our services and provide backup. It's not safe for her to do this without people she can count on to have her back."

"Oh, and you think that's you assholes? I'm sorry but did you all forget the part where you told her to fuck off and that she wasn't wanted anymore? Because I sure as fuck do!" Wes shouted, grabbing Picasso's shirt, ready to lay him out on the pavement. But in the last second, Void grabbed his arm, halting the punch.

"Wes," Void warned. "Don't make us defend ourselves against you. We are in deep enough shit with her already."

Holy shit, Void just saved our asses, because I know that Picasso would have retaliated, and nothing would infuriate Dax more than Weston getting hurt.

"Just let us in. You won't even know we're there, alright?" I offered. "None of us want to cause more problems, we just need to somehow show her that we're there for her."

Wes snorted. "It's gonna take a lot more than this to do the trick."

"The groveling will come later, I assure you," Sprocket interjected. "Our goal is to keep her alive long enough to atone for our sins."

Wes gave us all a hard look and I could tell he was at war with what to do. "Keep your mouths shut, and only step in if I give you guys a signal. Dax *has* to prove that no matter what, she is and always has been the leader of the Hidden Empire. Don't fuck this up for her."

Chapter Nineteen

Dax

I took one last look at myself in the mirror, in a way I felt like I was wearing a costume with the black leather pants, black crop top, and gun holster in full view. To me it looked like a little kid was trying to dress like Lara Croft from Tomb Raider but for them to believe what I was about to tell them, looking the part was bound to help. My two favorite knives were strapped to my thighs and extra magazines for my guns were in the pouch on my lower back. I had my dual Smith & Wesson, but these were bright pink and had been a birthday gift from Weston last year and I hadn't had the chance to use them other than on the practice range. If I was going to make a statement, then why the fuck not remind them I'm a girl, and can still kill them where they stand. Slipping on my fingerless gloves, I headed back into the office and found Wes leaning on my desk holding a glass of Brandy out to me.

"It better be the good stuff." I grinned as I took it from him.

"I poured it from your secret stash, so I hope it's the good stuff," he teased, grabbing my hips, and settling me in between his legs. "It's going to be fine, most of the chatter I've been hearing is that they want you to take down Tricks' ass and rule the joint."

"That's so sweet, but what happens when they find out that we're one and the same? Are they still going to be okay with all that's gone down?" I sighed, taking the double shot all at once.

Wes kissed me on the forehead then looked down at me. "My heart, what I'm more worried about is that once you do this, *everyone* is going to know the truth. You will no longer be able to run around this world carefree, a target will now be firmly painted on your back."

"This might also draw out whoever is trying to kill me though. If they figure out that I'm Tricks, then it will either make things worse and I'll get hit even harder, or they'll see this as a huge mistake. Going after one lowly enforcer is one thing but making a move on the queen of the Hidden Empire is another. I had people as Dax, but as Two Tricks I have a whole ass motherfucking army."

"Playing devil's advocate here... but what if they already know that you're Tricks?"

"Look, Kimber might be working with them and a few other people, but the only people who *knew* before two days ago, is you. We've been so careful to keep this secret, even killing people over it, how could it have slipped?" I challenged, pushing away from him. "I can't have you going soft on me now because I'm your lover, shadow. You need to keep being the man watching my back or else I won't survive this."

"What do you think I'm doing?" Wes frowned. "This right here is me watching your back, because if you are too distracted, then you should not be coming out to them tonight. The moment you do, this turns one of two ways: they accept it with a few troublemakers or they turn on you and we end up having to wipe them out, starting again. We know that the underbosses are loyal. They've always been more loyal to you than Tricks, wanting your go-ahead as well as our fake leader. It's the grunts that are going to be the unknown, well and our partners. They don't take kindly to being lied to."

I started pacing before I chucked the glass watching it shatter on the far wall. "Why is this all going to hell now?! What's changed and why can't I figure out the missing piece of the puzzle? There is something staring me in the face, and I can't fucking see what it is because I've been so distracted by those goddamn fucking Phantom bastards. This is why I can't get emotionally attached. It makes me stupid."

"Am I just supposed to ignore all that?" Wes deadpanned.

I scowled at him over my shoulder and raked my hands through my hair. "Don't start, clearly you don't apply."

"Just checking, since I'm going soft and all."

Groaning, I marched up to him, grabbed the back of his head and yanked him down to me so I could tongue fuck his mouth, before jerking back. "Don't be the woman in this relationship, my shadow, you've been doing so well."

Wes just grinned at me and kissed me on the nose. "Better get out there before they get restless, I originally came in here to tell you that all the important people are here, and I've got Brian and Matheus working on a list of who didn't show."

"Won't that be fun to deal with tomorrow, after all this bullshit? I love a good beating after a stressful few days, it really is the best therapy," I mused as I grabbed my distressed black jean jacket with my flaming skull and ace of spades on it that Harper made me, to complete the whole look.

Tossing open the door I walked the perimeter of the warehouse until I got to the stairs that led to the foreman's platform. The clang of the metal under my boots seemed to quiet the room until it fell into silence once I reached the landing and faced the crowd of people below. It was high enough to see the whole warehouse floor, but not too high if I had to jump ship over the railing. Right under me was the emergency exit where both our bikes were stashed if it came to it. The whole building was also rigged to explode if the tide turned against us, it would leave another scar on my soul, but I refused to let them win.

Looking out, I saw at least two hundred people watching me with upturned faces, mostly men with a scattering of women. Typically, we had the good sense to stay out of shit like this, but I never turned one away if they really wanted to work for Tricks. I mean, that would have been very hypocritical of me, wouldn't it?

"Well, I'm guessing you're all curious to find out what's going on and why this meeting has been called. You know me, I'm not one to beat around the bush so here it is... I. Am. Two Tricks. Always have been, always will be," I announced, projecting my voice the best I could.

When no one reacted, I didn't quite know what to do with that. I'd been expecting them to freak out, demand answers, or start shooting, but standing there with their jaws on the floor was not at all what I pictured.

"Very funny, Dax, now tell us what the hell is really going on here," someone shouted from the crowd.

"Yeah, we were told that a war was coming that you started," another chimed in.

The crowd below started to build with chatter as they started to talk among themselves. With a sigh, I pulled out one of my guns and shot up toward the ceiling. The sound echoed through the warehouse snapping everyone's attention back to me.

"Shut the fuck up! I wasn't done talking," I snapped and climbed up so I could sit on the railing with my feet dangling over the side. "If you don't want to believe me about being Tricks, that's fine it doesn't really change how things run around here, other than I get to stop killing people who find out. As for the rumor of war, that is true... the Mad Dogs and the De León Cartel are working together to take the Hidden Empire from me. That, of course, won't fucking happen as long as I have breath in my body, but this does mean we need to step up our vigilance. You see someone around that shouldn't be or a deal feels funny to you, then Weston or I better fucking hear about it first. Sadly, Jeff was a casualty meant to bring the situation to my attention and I take full responsibility for his life being cut short."

At this information, people started shouting and jeering, fists raised in the air and anger contorting many faces.

"We demand vengeance!"

"The Empire doesn't allow such a slight to stand, we will have blood!"

"Blood for blood!"

No, this was more of what I'd been picturing to have happened when I explained that there was no Two Tricks. I let them rant for a few more minutes, glancing at the bottom of the stairs where Brian was standing guard, making sure things were clear on that end. Calmly, I crossed one leg over the other before I slipped two fingers into my mouth and let out a shrill whistle not wanting to waste another bullet. Besides, they were upset about the situation, not with me.

"If you can bet on anything, it's that I won't let this stand, no one attacks the Empire, let alone takes one of my people from me. I am already working on finding out how deep this attack goes, but I need your help. There is someone in our midst that is spilling our secrets—hell there might be more than one. We all know how I hate fucking snitches and just because I've come out with my real identity, it changes nothing about how I do what I do. I made up Tricks so that I could freely interact with all of you and keep tabs on the inner workings of the Empire. Trust and believe that I do know every single one of you by name and those who are not in this building will be dealt with—I do not bluff," I reminded them.

"Now, what do we do going forward you ask? The Empire will conduct business as usual. We are not going to let this change the fact that we are the big dogs on the playground. They want to fuck with us, then they'll end up like everyone before them... under my boot. We of the Hidden Empire, fought for our place on the top and that is where I plan to stay." I climbed on top of the railing and raised my arms above my head and bellowed, "Who's with me?!"

A gun went off, and I was knocked off balance at the impact of the bullet hitting me in the shoulder. I leaned to the left, but everything was happening too fast, another bullet found its mark in my back as I tried to grab the railing to stop my fall, but blood was running down my arm making my fingers slip. Continuing to grasp at the air, I saw Weston's terrified face as he all but jumped after me, trying to grab my hand but it was too late. I slammed into the concrete floor with a grunt as the air got knocked out of my lungs. My brain started to panic as I couldn't take in a deep breath, but I shoved it aside, forcing myself to roll over so I was on my side. Pain screamed at me as I realized I was lying on my wounded shoulder, but I needed my working arm free as I grabbed my gun out of the holster. This was the exact reason I'd worn a shoulder holster; it was the easiest to get a gun out of. The moment my hand curled around the grip, I saw someone running at me, gun drawn and determination written all over his face.

Adrenaline coursed through my body like I was hooked up to a power plant, speeding up my processing time. I shot him right between the eyes before the sound of the gun going off reached my ears. I had to get to the exit, there was no way I was going to be able to defend myself in this shape. Why? Why the fuck so was I so motherfucking cocky that I didn't wear a vest? My ego kept me from showing that weakness even when I knew I was being hunted, I wanted to believe that my people that I've watched over for the past ten years would have my back. Fucking emotions, you'd think after getting tossed to the curb by the guys, I'd have learned, but somewhere deep inside, I was still that little girl who wanted to have a family that didn't leave me.

Slowly, I crawled to the glowing red sign that was my beacon of hope. All I had to do was get out and to my bike. Then I could get back to the apartment and call the doc to come patch me up and Wes... Fuck! Weston! Was he still on the platform or had he been able to make it off without getting hit? Clenching my jaw, I sat up, all but screaming in pain, as the wound in my back felt like it was trying to steal my soul from me. My breathing wasn't getting any better either, in fact I sounded as if I was breathing in water. My breath hitched, and I coughed, blood splattering around me. No! The goddamn bullet hit my lung!

"Dax!" a voice roared.

I glanced up and there was Eagle with Void right behind him. Another cough racked my body, followed by more blood dripping down my chin. Eagle dropped and slid right up to me, grabbing my face in his hands, terror written all over his face. I could tell he was talking but somewhere along the way, my hearing had gone, leaving the world silent. I reached out, gun still in my hand, but I didn't seem to be able to let go of it. Then over his shoulder, I saw a man raise his gun in the mass of moving bodies and aim it right at Eagle's head. I shoved him to the side, pushing him to the ground as I let out bullet after bullet, filling the man's body with lead but not before he got another shot off and I was flung to the ground. Now Void was screaming at me, his hands covered in blood as he ripped off his shirt and pressed it to my wound. My eyes were getting so heavy it was hard to keep them open and moments before they shut, I saw the other Phantom Saints and Weston gathering around me.

Would this be the end to my adventures? God, I hoped not, because now it's motherfucking personal!

Chapter Twenty

Cognac

"Does it seem odd that no one is really making a big deal out of the fact that she just told them that she's Two Tricks?" Sprocket asked as we leaned against the back wall of the warehouse.

I was far too transfixed on my *loba* to think that deeply into what Sprocket was saying. There she was, leaning on the railing like the ruling queen of the Empire that she was. The attitude that dripped from her as she surveyed her people made my heart swell as much as my cock did. Her outfit sure didn't help either, catching a glimpse of her toned stomach and the flash of something pink tucked into her jacket that was also cropped. Some of her people started to get restless as she told them about the attack on her man, this was more of the reaction we'd all been watching out for, it just wasn't when we'd expected it. Her voice rang out through the space drawing me in even deeper, which was the opposite of what I should be doing.

At the sound of her whistle, I shook myself out of her spell and turned to the others. "I think we should spread out, if something goes down, we aren't much help here stuck in the back."

"He makes a good point, we are here to prove we're on her side, it would be better to spread out in teams of two so we can spot any trouble," Sprocket agreed.

"That won't work, there's five of us, idiot," Picasso snapped.

Sprocket just glanced over his shoulder and grinned. "You're forgetting someone."

We all looked back up at the platform where Weston stood against the wall, arms crossed ready to burst into action if needed.

"Ah, I don't think he's going to come down and help," I pointed out. "He likes that spot *way* too much to leave it."

"Guys, Sprocket was talking about Brian, remember Wes told us to grab him if we needed to deal with something," Eagle explained, thrusting his chin over at the base of the stairs. "Void you're with me, we'll take the right side, Sprocket you take Cognac to the left, and Picasso head up the center to the front lines."

We all nodded in agreement and dispersed, wading into the crowd. In the scheme of things, having the five of us against a room of well over a hundred people was pointless, but it was better than nothing. Glancing up at Dax I saw she was now sitting on the railing one leg crossed over and let out a shrill whistle when everyone started to get wild. The atmosphere in the room shifted and I couldn't place my finger on it but as she was talking about how the Empire would live on as it has, not letting fear rule, I couldn't help but be proud. Then in a daring move she stood up, hands thrust into the air screaming her battle cry.

Then I heard it.

"No!" I shouted as I saw her starting to fall.

Wes shot forward to try and grab her, but more shots rang through the air, causing Wes to dodge for cover then dive for the railing but it was too late, Dax had fallen. Sprocket elbowed me in the ribs, trying to get my attention and signaled that we needed to move low and fast. I drew my gun and headed to where I'd seen Dax fall. The crowd didn't know what to do, everyone had guns or knives drawn shooting at the hint of someone trying to attack them. I couldn't tell if it was only one person who started this chain reaction, but it was full-fledged panic. It was then I noticed men dressed in black leather. They didn't have cuts that were marked with a club but I knew it had to be the Mad Dogs. Did that mean Mastiff had given up on taking Dax alive?

"Sprocket, it's the Mad Dogs!" I yelled and pointed over at one of the men in question.

Without hesitation, Sprocket aimed and took him out. "They knew the deal. Come back on our turf and you're dead, no second chances."

As we worked our way forward, we took out men left and right, but I didn't take the shot unless I knew I could pull off a one shot kill. I didn't want to waste ammo or hit an ally. Finally, we made it to the front just in time to see Dax save Eagle and take out a Dog, shooting until her clip was out, but not before the fucker got a shot off. It hit her in the neck right below the ear, knocking her back to the ground. I caught sight of two more Dogs trying to make a play for her and Eagle, but Picasso and Wes took them out as we all raced over to Dax. Her eyes were open for a moment and a small smile was on her face as she took us all in before fainting.

"Dax!" Void roared at her, his shirt staunching the blood coming from her neck. "Someone better get a motherfucking ambulance here, now!"

"Already called for help, they should be here any second, I was worried something might happen so I had someone I could trust nearby," Weston explained, as he kneeled by her head.

He opened her eyes and checked for something, but I didn't have any medical background to even try and guess.

"Her lung got hit, she was coughing blood," Void stated. "If we don't get her some help *right now*, we are going to lose her. I'm going to lift her and carry her outside so they can get to her without dealing with all of this."

The sound of gun fire kept going off behind us but I couldn't pull my gaze from my *loba*. I never thought I would find someone I would trust to even think about giving my heart to after losing my family. That first time I laid eyes on her at Gabby's party though, I knew she was something special. She didn't take my shit and somehow knew the moment I was being fake with her, drawing out the real me. I hid behind flirting and my good looks because most women just took me at face value, but not Dax, no my *loba* demanded the truth. Picasso grabbed me and pulled me to the left, breaking my line of sight to Dax.

"Pull it together man or we're never going to get out of this," he snapped. "What's your ammo status?"

It took me more time than it should have to understand what he was asking me. I pulled out my gun, dropped the mag and found I had two bullets left out of sixteen. "Almost out, you got back up?"

"Dax does," Weston answered, holding out a handful of mags. "She never carries without at least two extras per gun."

"You sure they'll work?" I asked as I grabbed one and slid it into place and it locked in.

Wes met my gaze, his eyes full of conflicting emotions. "She always makes sure they fit most guns. Glock is useful that way. Now we need to cover them and then end this before we can leave."

"What do you mean, who's gonna take her to the hospital?" I demanded, panic beginning to set in.

"Void is going with her, the rest of us are going to settle matters here. They will need to operate and there's nothing we can do but wait. On the other hand, if she finds out we let things go to hell, she'll shoot us," Wes justified.

In my gut, I knew he was right, but I didn't want to admit it, there was no way that we could just send her off and stay behind.

"We've got to go now!" Void bellowed. as he started to charge toward the back exit.

Sliding a round into the chamber, I was locked and loaded. We burst out behind the warehouse and the ambulance was there, their door open, and two men waving us over frantically. The sound of bike engines roared in the night, and I spotted the headlights as more Mad Dogs rolled up. We were so fucked.

Void leaped into the ambulance, and they slammed the doors closed, taking off like a bat out of hell, and leaving us to make sure they had a clean getaway. I spotted a forklift, and I ran toward it while thanking whatever gods that were listening that the keys were in it. I started her up, lifted the blades so they would be about the height of a motorcycle and took off, aiming right for the group of them. Wes blew past me on his bike, gun at the ready, shots sounding off, sparks bursting into sight as he missed a few. Then a bike blew up, and I had to wonder if he really did miss or learned that trick from Dax. The forklift was nowhere near as fast, but it had a metal cage around it for safety, making it much harder for them to hit me. When I crashed right into the first bike, it caused the whole thing to shudder, but it kept right on moving as the screech of metal grated on my ears. I lifted the forks and raised the bike and rider that I'd speared until I could scrape it off into the dumpster. Backing up, I swooped around and aimed for the next group—this time I took out three at once that were all side by side.

I lost track of how many riders there were or where the others of my crew had gone, but eventually the back lot was quiet. I slowed to a halt and tossed open the door to look around. The destruction and bodies that were laid out on the pavement was like something out of a war movie. Slowly, I stepped out of the cab, pulling out my gun and making my way back to the warehouse. Out of the corner of my eye, I saw movement almost a second too late, but I dropped and rolled so I was facing my attacker and shot, hitting him twice in the chest. My heart pounded against my ribs as I flopped onto my back and looked up at the night sky. It was harder to see the stars this close to LA, but it still was a sight to see, and one I wanted to share with Dax someday. That thought alone spurred me back to my feet and had me walking toward the back entrance. When I re-entered the place more dead bodies littered the floor. Almost all of them were the Dogs, but there were a few of Dax's people scattered throughout. It hit me then what it meant to be at war, the tactics that were being used didn't follow the guidelines, but neither would we when we planned our retaliation. The Mad Dogs had now written themselves a death sentence, and I aimed to make sure it happened.

"We need to clear the bodies to make room for the medical staff coming to deal with the wounded," Weston announced. "I'll open the back garage door and we'll dump them out there, I don't give a rats ass what the cops have to say, we need them gone."

Those unharmed got to work dragging bodies toward the large doors and I saw where the controls were, so I jogged over and hit the green button. The doors rumbled up, and I kept my eyes peeled for anyone that I might have missed. It didn't take long for the warehouse to be cleared but I stood guard, nonetheless, wanting to be able to tell Dax that I'd looked out for her people. I knew Eagle was looking through a tinted lens when he said she didn't care about her people, she just didn't do it the same way he did. She might not call them family or want to have a cookout with everyone, having them all live in the same plot of land, but she would fight like hell to keep them safe in her own way. This attack will have sealed the fate of who was truly behind all of this, because I firmly believe that the Mad Dogs were promised far more than just Dax and control over the West Coast.

"There you are, man, that was some crazy stunt you pulled using that forklift." Sprocket grinned, walking up to me.

I noticed he had more damage to him than what happened between him and Eagle. "You good, man?"

"Yeah, just didn't get out of the way of a bike fast enough. I got clipped, but I also pulled that bastard right off his ride," Sprocket assured me. "There had to have been fifty of them, Cognac. How the fuck did no one notice that when they were gathering? I mean, the guy at the door clocked us right away."

"That just proves that there's someone on the inside that's turned against her," I muttered.

Seeing that everyone was back in, I closed the door and slid home the lock, wanting to make sure there were no more surprises coming in that way. Sprocket and I wandered our way back over to where cots were getting set up and I noticed Picasso sitting on one, his arm hanging in a funny direction.

"Fuck, bro, what happened to you?" I asked, face scrunching up at the pain I imagined him in.

With his working arm he flipped me off but groaned at the movement. "I joined Wes on my bike and chased down some of the guys that went running after you went crazy on the forklift. No way we would have made it out of that alive if you didn't pull that stunt. Well, I didn't see the trip wire they set up, and I got clotheslined right off my bike and hit a shipping container."

Sprocket and I both hissed at the sound of that. "Damn, that is just wrong. You waiting for someone to check you out?"

"No, I'm holding off until we get to the hospital they took Dax to. I'm not in any life-threatening danger and the medics need to look after others. Speaking of which, we need to go. I can't take sitting here anymore, not knowing what's going on. Void's not answering his phone either—it's driving me fucking crazy." Picasso grunted as he got to his feet, clutching his arm to his body. "Let's grab Eagle and Wes then we're out."

Seems they were on the same wavelength since an SUV was sitting outside with Eagle at the wheel and Wes walking toward us. "Let's go, guys, our girl needs us."

We put Picasso in the front seat to be safe and the rest of us climbed in. From the glance I got, Wes and Eagle both looked relatively unharmed, which was good because I can only imagine the hell on wheels that Dax is going to be when she wakes up.

Chapter Twenty-One

Dax

THE FIRST THOUGHT THAT entered my head was why the fuck was I in so much goddamn pain? My body felt like it had gotten flattened by a steam roller and then the devil danced on it as he laughed in my face, sending me back to the world of the living as punishment. For what, I didn't have a fucking clue. Once I got past the wall of pain, I was able to hear machines humming, someone or more than one person snoring, and the soft clacking of someone typing on a computer. I wanted to open my eyes, but it just seemed like so much work, so instead I tried to shift my body to see if that would make things more comfortable. A wave of pain flooded my body causing a whimper to pass my lips.

The sound of typing stopped, and I heard footsteps heading in my direction. "Dax, can you hear me? I'm Dani, your nurse and you're at the hospital. Can you open your eyes for me?"

I tried to turn my head toward her voice but it hurt too much, and I felt a tear trickle down my cheek.

"Can't you see how much pain she's in, put her back under, this is torture," a voice, that sounded a lot like Eagle's, snarled.

"We've been over this already. I have to be able to check and see if she has any brain damage. She lost a lot of blood and her heart stopped twice during surgery. There is no way to tell what ramifications there are from that and the only way to test is to lower the pain meds," the nurse, Dani, snapped, making me want to grin.

"Look, she's grinning at the fact you just scolded me, is that good enough for you?" Eagle pointed out. "Trust me when I tell you that is the most normal thing for her to be happy about."

Dani sighed and I felt two fingers slip into each of my hands. "Try and grab my fingers as hard as you can Dax."

I could do that easily with my right, but when it came to my left, I grunted in pain and broke out into a sweat. "That's very good, now can you wiggle your toes? Excellent!"

"Has she done enough tricks for you, lady?" Void growled.

"You know, you really should be nicer to me. I don't have to allow you to be in here, you're not family and there are six of you that keep coming in and out of this room when it should only be two at the most. This is the ICU, you know."

I was liking Nurse Dani more and more.

"Alright, Dax, I'm going to turn your pain meds back up and I'll check back in with you later, sleep now."

"We have to move her, *now*!" Weston bellowed, pulling me out of the darkness. "I don't care what I have to sign. I'm her medical proxy and her power of attorney. She *cannot* stay here or they will kill her. Do you get that?"

"Sir, I understand your concern, seeing as your companions apprehended an impostor of our staff, but this patient is still critical. It's only been three days since her surgery and it's much too soon to try and transport her anywhere," a voice I didn't know answered in a snooty tone.

"This is where I'm telling you I don't give a *fuck* what you think. Your hospital failed to keep her safe, so we are going to take her where we know she will get the best care and security. Now sign the goddamn papers or I will destroy you and this hospital," Wes threatened.

What did it say about me, that in my twisted little heart, that was the most romantic thing I'd ever heard in my life?

"Give me a few moments and I'll get things pulled together. Do you have a destination you wish me to send her paperwork to?"

"No need," Sprocket interjected. "Print off everything you have, and we'll hand it over to those that need it. And be quick about it."

The need to know what was going on made me restless and my right arm shifted toward the voices, as if I could reach out to them.

"Easy there, little rebel," Sprocket whispered, his lips brushing my forehead. "We're going to get you out of here and somewhere safe, I promise. You just keep fighting to get better. We have everything else handled."

With an epic amount of effort, I was able to open my eyes and took in a blurry vision of Sprocket's face. It took blinking a few times, but I was finally able to get them clearly and I noticed his battered face. I tried to lift my hand, but it felt like it weighed the same as a ton of bricks. He saw what I was doing and took my hand in his, lifting it to his face. I was able to stroke my thumb against his cheek but that was about it.

"I'm fine, nothing to worry yourself about." He smiled and kissed the back of my hand. "You have no idea how good it is to see those beautiful eyes of yours. Now be good and go back to sleep, it's the best thing to get you better."

Licking my lips, I felt how cracked they were and how chalky my mouth felt, like the Sahara Desert had relocated without me knowing.

"Hey, Wes, can you grab the ice chips?" Sprocket asked.

"Fuck, they all melted. I'll be right back," Wes said, followed by quickly moving footsteps.

I'd never heard Wes so stressed before. We'd been through a hell of a lot in our lives, but I'd never heard that tone before. Sprocket reached out and smoothed my forehead where it had furrowed.

"You scared the shit out of us, little rebel, and some are dealing with it better than others. That is nothing for you to worry about though, we're handling things, and once we get you to the private medical care that we have lined up, things will be even better. They only let two of us stay in here after six and then let them back in at seven in the morning. At this new place, we will all be able to stay with you around the clock and I know that will help soothe some ruffled feathers," Sprocket chattered.

It was comforting to have him here and so relaxed about everything that's going on. Weston's face appeared behind Sprocket, and it immediately set me on guard. It looked like he hadn't shaved in days, his hair was all over the place, and his shirt had seen better days. Then his eyes locked onto mine and they had a viciousness that I'd never seen before in them.

"Welcome back, my heart, you had us a little worried there," Wes murmured, as he held out an ice chip and let it melt on my lips a minute before slipping it onto my tongue.

I couldn't help but hum at how wonderful it felt to have that cold water slide down my throat. He gave me a few more the next time, and I savored them like they were the best candy I'd ever had in my life.

"Thank you," I rasped, but it was cut short when I tried to take a deep breath in and groaned. "What—happened?" This time I took shorter breaths and that seemed to go better.

Sprocket and Wes looked at each other, then back at me. They better not fucking lie to me, half dead or not, I would whoop their asses.

"Calm down, Dax," Wes warned, looking at something over my head. "We need you to stay calm. Stress isn't good for you right now. So as long as you can keep your cool, we'll give you the Cliff Notes version."

I glared at him but nodded.

"The Mad Dogs hit us, somehow they got inside information about the location, and they had help getting smuggled into the meeting. You were shot in the shoulder, the back on your right side so it missed your heart, and then got nicked by a bullet on your neck when saving Eagle's life," Sprocket explained. "We dealt with the matter while Void got you to the hospital. Then last night there was another assassination attempt, but your boy, Wes, here handled it before anything could happen. It seems they want to take out Two Tricks while you're still laid up."

"How many losses?" I asked.

Wes's shoulders slumped. "We lost five, mostly underlings, except for Oscar. We did however take out about fifty of the Mad Dogs' crew and with a surprise attack like that, I'd say we did pretty well."

Shifting my eyes back to the ceiling I closed them, taking in everything that they told me. I'd been reckless in being so open about the meeting. I should have done it at a different location that could have been guarded better. Hell, what I really should have done was just had a small meeting with the underbosses and people who really needed to know and let it leak out to the rest of the Empire. This was my fault—four good men and a friend died from my mistake. I knew better than that, but I was pissed and let it rule my judgment.

A hand cupped my cheek, causing me to open my eyes and meet Sprocket's gaze. "Don't. I can feel you beating yourself up and I won't allow you to do that. It happened, learn from it and do better. Everyone makes choices day in and day out, some work—some don't. Is it tragic that we lost good people—yes. Just don't turn your back on them or their families. This won't go away just because you feel bad about it or want to run away, you need to get better and show those fuckers that they messed with the wrong woman."

"Don't go soft on us now, little demon," Void added, coming to stand on the left side of my bed. "It's time to go, they're going to knock you out again so you're not in too much pain during transport. We'll all be there when you wake up again, alright?"

"Okay," I answered, giving him a weak smile.

Void leaned down and brushed his lips to mine before he stepped back for a nurse to inject something into my IV.

"You know this is a terrible idea, right?" she asked me.

"I trust them with my life. They won't let anything bad happen to me," I stated, and the moment I said it, I knew it was true.

The last thing I saw was the nurse looking at the wall of men staring her down and I smirked as I slipped back into unconsciousness.

"*Loba*, are you with us, *loba*?" Cognac whispered, his lips brushing my ear.

My eyes fluttered open and I started to turn my head, but the pull of the bandage and the stitches reminded me to be careful.

"It's alright, you can move without pulling the stitches, you just need to be gentle," Cognac assured me as I shifted to meet his gaze.

It would appear that wherever we ended up, I was now in a bed big enough to have them lay beside me like Cognac was doing now. He grinned at me, excitement shining in his eyes as he ran a finger lightly along my cheek.

"What are you so happy about?" I asked, my voice still a little husky.

"Just this, that I get to be right next to you without anyone yelling at me or telling me that I couldn't fit in your bed. I made sure that we never have that problem again—isn't that right, Sprocket," Cognac called over my shoulder.

The bed shifted, and I felt a hand settle tentatively on my left arm. "Yup, big enough the three of us can fit and not run into you while we sleep."

I wanted to shift my head to look at him, but the effort just seemed so monumental, so instead I slowly opened my hand and wiggled my fingers for his hand. Quickly, his fingers interlaced with mine and with Cognac's help I shifted myself to sit up a little higher with a pillow, while the whole back of the bed lifted as well.

"We got all the bells and whistles for this, since you'll be stuck here for a bit longer," Cognac explained.

"You guys didn't have to do all this," I muttered, glad to finally be able to see my surroundings.

The room looked like any old bedroom but was full of the medical supplies needed, along with two futons and some recliners. They were all filled with sleeping men at the moment, and it put a smile on my face. Then a woman walked into the room wearing scrubs, long blond hair up in a ponytail swinging behind her, with an IV bag in her hand.

"Oh, look at you," she greeted with a bright smile. "We haven't officially met yet but I'm Dani, your nurse. I took care of you on the day shift and the guys hired me to stay on with you here since I knew the case."

"Eagle was convinced that you would like her, for some reason," Cognac added.

She gave him a scolding look and shooed him out of the way as she hooked up the new bag and came to check my vitals. "How is your pain level? I backed off the meds to try and keep you a little more coherent, but if it's too soon, you let me know. Your body took quite the beating."

"It's nothing I can't handle," I said with a shrug, letting out a cry, forgetting all about my shoulder. "Fuck."

The guys who were sleeping sat bolt upright and were out of their chairs in seconds, rushing over to me.

"What's wrong, what did she do?" Eagle demanded.

Dani huffed and narrowed her gaze at Eagle. "I didn't do anything. She just shrugged, forgetting about her shoulder. This is the most alert she's been since the trauma happened. It's bound to take her a little time to wrap her head around what's going on in her body."

Ah this is why Eagle thought I would like her... he was right.

"Everyone take it easy," I wheezed and then coughed, which I tried to fight, and led me to cough even more.

A dense heart shaped pillow was pressed into my arms. "Hug this as you cough, it will help the pain from your lungs and shoulder. The more stable your body is, the less it will pull at the injuries."

Tears streamed down my face at the stabbing pain, some of the worst I'd ever experienced. This was going to be such a bitch to heal, and I was notoriously a terrible patient, it made me super crabby. Eagle reached out to rest his hand on my knee and I knocked his hand away with my good arm, careful not to knock the IV loose.

"What the fuck are you doing here, anyway?" I snapped. "Didn't you decide that *Nelly* was a more important part of your 'family' than me? Or did you promise her that you were all-in for having a relationship and back out already?"

Regret flashed over his face, but I didn't want to hear it, so I turned to Dani instead.

"I think I'd like something for the pain now."

Dani looked at me with understanding and nodded. "Alright, I'll be back with the medicine."

It didn't take her long to grab the meds from the other room and return. Hands on her hips, she gave the guys a stern look. "I think it's best if you gave her some space, gentlemen."

"Except Wes," I called, watching him walk away.

He paused and then crawled into bed with me, as Dani injected the pain meds into my IV port. "Stay with me... please."

Chapter Twenty-Two

Weston

I WATCHED HER SLEEP for a good hour or two, then shifted off the bed and headed out into the living room of the house we rented. It had taken a lot of favors and cash to make sure we had everything we needed, but both Dax and I were well enough off that it wasn't a problem. The simple ranch house was about two hours outside the city, where none of us knew anyone or had connections, in an effort to keep her safe. I thought about her apartment, but I wanted to keep it safe if we ever needed it again, and I didn't put it past them to blow up the building. Dax was proving to the world something I always knew was true... she didn't go down easy.

The guys sat around the kitchen table, coffee mugs in front of them, looking half-dead but they snapped to attention when I entered.

"She okay?" Picasso ventured.

"Yeah, Dani said she'd be out for another few hours." I yawned, pouring myself some coffee.

In the past four days, none of us had gotten much sleep, fear keeping us all on high alert even before the assassination attempt. Things in the Empire were volatile at best, everyone wanted retribution for what happened to Dax and word had gotten out it was the Mad Dogs. It made our alliance with the Phantom Saints all that more precarious, because in their eyes it was further proof that MCs shouldn't be trusted, like Tricks always said.

"How the fuck are we supposed to fix this if she won't even hear me out?" Eagle muttered, slamming his fist down on the table. He looked up at me with fear and regret in his eyes. "Did I do the one thing she won't forgive?"

It was clear to me that any doubt these men had about Dax had been washed away with her blood on the concrete. Seeing her holding on to life by a thread of sheer willpower had fucked with all our heads. Never had I so badly wanted to go back in time and strangle myself for letting her pull a stunt like that without proper protection. She should have been wearing a vest or had more than just me up there to keep an eye on what the hell was going on. If we'd had a bigger security presence, then things might have been different. Shoulda, woulda, coulda, isn't going to change the fact that we almost lost her, now we needed to handle the fall out.

"Dax will never be a woman who forgives easily—even with me at times," I cautioned. "The trick is not to let her win, you can't give up, no matter what she says. The whole thing is to see if you're really going to stay with her even if she's cruel to you. She'll do everything to make you walk away again, just to prove that she was right all along to be mad at you. But, if you don't back down, then the level of trust will grow and grow."

Picasso shoved back his chair so it was balancing on two legs, chewing on his bottom lip. "I don't get it, she's fine with the others, just not Eagle. How does that work?"

"As much as I know that woman, she's still a mystery. It could be as simple as she believes that they were being good soldiers and backed up their president. You haven't really spoken to her yet, I'm not sure you're in her good graces after that crack about her brother," I couldn't help but point out.

Most of the guys had begrudgingly accepted the fact that I was now part of the deal—everyone but Picasso. I have no idea what fucking chip on his shoulder he had about me but getting the chance to get a rise out of him was just too good to pass up.

"Fucking hell," he swore as his chair came slamming down on all four legs. "Clearly, I screwed up. We all know that her brother is the biggest trigger for her, isn't it?"

"Yup," I answered with a barely concealed smirk. "I would definitely expect some retaliation for that."

"As much fun as this is to point out all the ways we've fucked up, I'd rather talk about how we can keep my little demon safe," Void interjected. "Do we know where the hit came from?"

"The Wright brothers are still radio silent, but as soon as they get my message, they should get back in touch with me," I shared. "That and I have to make sure I tell Harper what happened, she'll be furious with me if she finds out after all this is over and done with."

"That doesn't really help us, now does it?" Picasso snapped.

And that was the last strand of my tolerance for this asshole snapping.

"What the fuck is your problem?" I demanded, stepping up to tower over him. "Ever since you came back from saving Harper, you've been a dick."

"Actually, that's nothing new," Cognac interjected.

Picasso just glared at him then turned his attention back to me. "You've had her all to yourself for how long and the moment someone else has a chance with her, you pull out all the stops. Why the fuck do you get to be the golden child when you've fucked up worse than us, allowing her to almost get killed multiple times?"

"Are we really back to this?" I bit out, fists clenching. "You've known her for all of two weeks and most of that has been with her pissed or unconscious. When you've known her for twenty years, then you can come at me with shit like that. I've earned my place next to her, going to hell and back to make sure she was safe."

"From where I'm sitting, all I see is Dax doing all the work," Picasso huffed, crossing his arms. "Every story I hear is Dax going in with guns blazing but where are you?"

"Right behind her watching her motherfucking back!" I roared. "In the early days, she didn't have bodyguards or other people to back her up. When she started the Hidden Empire and created Two Tricks, she worked from a grunt on up to make sure no one knew she was the mastermind behind it all. Yeah, I was placed up in the top ranks faster because of my skills, and it let me watch over her better, but I used to go on every job I could."

"When did it change?" Sprocket asked.

"What?" I questioned not following his train of thought.

"When did it change? When did she lock you away in your tech tower?" He rephrased.

I blinked at him a few times as I thought back to when she'd stopped letting me go with her. "Just after we moved in together. She rose in the ranks and became an underling to the lead enforcer at that time. Dax pointed out that it didn't make sense for one of the most valuable people to go with her to get the money we were owed and shit like that."

"Hmm," Sprocket mused, nodding his head. "Seems to me, from your expression, that's when a lot of things between you changed."

"What does that have to do with anything?" Picasso butted in. "It doesn't change the fact that he let her walk into those jobs without backup."

"Did Eagle go with you everywhere as you guys worked through the ranks?" Sprocket challenged. "I don't recall you getting special treatment at all from anyone, least of all your big brother."

Picasso opened his mouth to argue but shut it again, scowling.

"We're missing something..." Eagle announced, catching all of us off guard. He looked around at all of us and rolled his eyes. "The attacks, we have to be missing something that connects all of this. Why Dax? Why the Mad Dogs? Why the cartel? She's been running the show for a decade, and no one has made a move this big before."

"Dax said the same thing before she went out to give her announcement. She'd had a meeting with one of our arms suppliers and he gave her a tip that someone international was coming after her, but no one knows who," I mused, tapping my chin with a finger. "It would have to be one hell of a threat to make moves this big and no one really knows who was going after her."

"Do you have a list of people the Empire has taken down? There might be a connection to all of that you didn't see at the time," Cognac suggested, surprising me.

I walked over to the counter, grabbed my laptop, and sat down at the table. "It's something to look into, that's for sure. It'll take me awhile, but it would be a good place to start."

"Mr. Weston," Dani called from Dax's room. "She's getting restless, like she's having nightmares again."

Since they'd lightened up her pain meds the last two days, she'd started having these nightmares. Normally just having someone in the bed seemed to help, but it seemed to be getting worse and only Void or I could get her to calm down. Scooping up the laptop and my coffee, I headed back to do the work in bed. We needed a break in this, because I wasn't sure how many more hits like the one we'd just survived we could take. The guys couldn't stay here with us for much longer, they had a whole club to deal with and protect. If the Empire got hit, who's to say they weren't next, thinking we'd hide out there. I pulled up the security system of the compound and took a look around as I did most days to keep Eagle from losing his mind. Things look normal, but didn't they always before it was too late?

Dax started to toss and turn her head, flail her right arm and kick out with her legs as if she was fighting someone off. Quickly, I set my computer aside and reached out to comb my fingers through her hair.

"You're safe, my heart, I'm here with you watching your back like the good shadow I am," I whispered, placing a kiss on her forehead. "I promise, I'm doing everything that I can to find out who is behind this."

Her arms shot out and clutched my arm, her nails digging into my skin but I ignored it. Instead, I shifted closer, so my body was aligned with hers. It seemed to calm her a bit, but it wasn't enough. She needed someone else to make her feel protected on both sides.

"Dani, can you grab Void? I think she's gonna need more than just me this time," I said, my gaze never leaving Dax's face.

A few seconds later, Void was pulling off his t-shirt and climbing in on her other side. He tucked in as close as she could without messing with her shoulder and put his arms around her waist. "Be a good little demon and rest now," he murmured into her ear.

A frown appeared on her face at his words. "Don't pout, my heart, we just need you to get better."

Now that she knew that we were both here, it seemed to set her at ease, and she took as deep a breath as she could and finally relaxed.

"Do you think the nightmares will keep happening after the pain meds wear off?" Void asked Dani, who watched with a worried expression.

"Hard to say." She sighed. "It could be a side effect of the meds, or it could be PTSD from everything that happened. The fact that she doesn't have any other issues from what we can tell so far is a miracle."

"That's our girl—always defying the odds," I whispered, placing a soft kiss on her lips.

Chapter Twenty-Three

Dax

"**B**ACK THE FUCK OFF or I swear I will find a way to stab you," I growled as Cognac hovered around me while I shuffled to the bathroom.

"*Loba*, it's only been six days since your surgery, and they just okayed you to get out of bed. I don't believe that was approval to go wandering all over the house," Cognac scolded, as he followed me into the bathroom.

I paused and looked at him. "Can I get a minute?"

"No."

"Dude, I need to pee, we are so not at the level where you can be here for that," I grumbled.

"Sorry, *loba*, if you want to do it on your own, I'm going to be right here to pick you up off your throne when you can't stand up."

"When did you turn into such a mother hen? God, all of you are smothering me and it's driving me insane," I yelled, so the others in the house could hear me.

Cognac didn't budge from where he leaned on the wall with a raised brow. "You gonna pee or not?"

"Fuck it," I muttered and used the IV pole to balance as I plopped unceremoniously onto the toilet.

Being able to pee like a normal person was magical, I would never take it for granted again after this. In all the years that I've been Two Tricks, this was the worst shape I'd ever been in. Yeah, I'd gotten shot, stabbed, or beat up, but this—this was different. Dani told me that I coded twice during surgery, and they weren't sure I was going to make it, then somehow, I turned a corner, and they were able to fix me up. With one arm in a sling, it made getting to the toilet paper a little tricky, but I managed, even if I had to grit my teeth in pain. Something about feeling this weak just pissed me off, I hated that I wasn't able to just bounce back from this, that I had to rely on others for almost everything. Well, I was sure as fuck going to wipe my own ass, that's where I drew the line.

Finished, I gripped the IV pole and pushed up with my legs, but my whole body started to shake with the effort. Just as I was halfway up, the pole rolled forward and it sent me chasing right after it. My body tried to put both arms out to save myself, but the left was trapped, and the right side screamed at the strain on my back wound, letting me know I was fucked. Next thing I knew, Cognac was swooping in and catching me against his chest as he wrapped his arms gingerly around me, keeping me from toppling to either side.

"Now who could have predicted that this would happen," he teased, as he scooped me up bridal style and waited for me to grab the IV.

I glared up at him, sticking my tongue out as we exited the bathroom. Thankfully, he didn't put me back in bed but brought me out into the living room where everyone else was lounging about.

"Well, look who's making an escape?" Sprocket grinned when he saw me. "Come to see what's happening out in the real world?"

"The warden finally said it was time for me to get some privileges," I answered, returning his grin.

As if her ears were burning, Dani walked back into the house after taking the morning off. "Ah, looks like you decided to take advantage of your new freedom."

"I would have done it sooner, but they didn't tell me I was free to leave the bed until ten minutes ago," I shared, glowering at Cognac. "Some seemed to believe I couldn't be trusted with that information."

Dani just laughed and headed into the bedroom, only to return with everything she needed to change the bandages. This was my least favorite part of the whole thing. My skin was all but raw from the tape they've been using to hold the gauze in place. It was unfortunate that all of my wounds were in areas that moved a lot and tended to weep more than others.

"Seeing as the first thing you did was get up and walk to the bathroom, trying to do it all yourself, I think we made the right call. Then she almost wiped out getting off the toilet," Cognac informed Dani.

My jaw dropped at the fact that he had just thrown me under the bus. "Whose side are you on?!"

"Yours always, *loba*, even if that means I have to piss you off to take care of you," Cognac stated, with a shrug.

I didn't really have anything to respond to that, so I just huffed and shifted away from him so Dani could get to the dressing on my back.

"Dax, I can tell you're going to be *that* patient but please understand that if you push your body too far too fast, it will only make things worse. Getting up and moving around will help, not to mention physical therapy for your shoulder, it took a lot of damage. The bone was shattered and cut up a lot of your muscle. It's a miracle that it hit your non-dominant arm but it's going to limit you for a while," Dani explained as she worked. "You also seem to have the benefit of six men who want to take care of you, and that doesn't happen. Teach me your secret," she whispered that last part, making me smirk.

Then the reality of what she said sank in. My left arm was going to be jacked for a long time, the undercurrent of what she was saying is that I should count myself lucky to eventually have full use of it again. If I didn't fuck it up before I got to that point. I wanted to scream at the world. Hadn't I been through enough?

Void's imposing shadow crossed over me as he sank to be at eye level. "You're strong, little demon, this isn't anything you can't handle. Like Dani said, we aren't going anywhere, whether you like it or not."

My gaze flickered over to Eagle and Picasso, who sat next to each other on the couch, watching me intently. "You sure about that?"

"All set here, I'm gonna deal with things in the bedroom if you need me," Dani said as she made a quick exit.

I couldn't blame her. I wouldn't want to be involved in another person's drama if I could help it. Hell, I didn't want to deal with my own drama.

"Dax, I owe you an apology—no, more than that—I rightly deserve for you to make my life hell until I prove to you that what I did was wrong, and you didn't deserve it," Eagle voiced, getting up from his spot and sitting on the coffee table in front of the lazy boy I was sitting in. "I would like to explain to you why I reacted as I did, not as an excuse, not to guilt you or to make what I did right in any way—because it wasn't. Hearing this might just help you understand what triggered me into being a bigger asshole than usual."

Did I care enough to listen? Was there a chance he could ever redeem himself to me? Did I want him to?

"Just because I listen to this doesn't mean it will change things between us right now," I warned. "You fucked up in epic proportion and I demand penance from those who have wronged me."

"Understood." Eagle nodded.

"Fine, I'll listen."

"Did you ever hear of an MC called the Devils Spawn?" Eagle asked.

Now he had my attention. The bust of that MC had been all over the news. They had been caught smuggling and trafficking people in and out of the US.

"Yeah, I remember watching the take down on the news," I answered.

Eagle caught my gaze as he spoke. "My uncle was the leader of that crew, and I was a part of it when I graduated from high school. He went by Hannibal, but his real name was Enzo—that's the reason I don't let anyone use my birth name anymore. When Picasso and I were younger, we looked up to Hannibal and would do anything to be like him. When I was old enough to prospect, I found out what really happened behind closed doors, but it was too late. I couldn't just walk away. I lasted as part of his crew for about two years before I got up the balls to turn him in to the FBI."

"You blew the whistle?" I gasped.

"Yeah, I was forced to help out behind the scenes at the auctions where they drugged them and raped those who didn't need to stay pure. It was one way they made it so we couldn't snitch on them, since we would go down with them. Since Hannibal wanted me to run the Devils with him, he kept me doing other jobs until others complained that I was getting special treatment. I knew my time was running out, and I had to do something, so I turned myself in and flipped on my uncle. Since it was such a big hit, I was able to deal immunity from being prosecuted for those crimes and got off scot-free..." Eagle paused and ran his hands through his hair. "When they raided the place, they were able to get everyone *but* Hannibal. A week or so later he grabbed Picasso and nearly beat him to death and sent me pictures of what he'd done and what he'd do if I didn't give myself up to him. My uncle was a psychopath, but he'd been able to hide it well enough that no one in my family had a clue but my other uncle who ran the Blackjax. I turned to him for help and we went together to get Picasso. I ended up killing Hannibal—point-blank shot to the skull. He'd lost his mind completely at that point and when I shot him, I knew that I had the same fucked-up genes he did buried deep inside me."

Eagle reached out slowly and grabbed my hand, giving me all the time in the world to jerk back from him but something stopped me. I looked deep into his eyes, and I saw his pain and fear as clearly as if it was my own.

"Dax, you scare the fuck out of me."

I went to pull my hand back, but he held on tightly, dropping to kneel before me with both hands clutching mine, his gaze piercing with its intensity. "You scare me, little hellcat, because I would let that crazy out to burn down the world if you asked me to. I chased you away any way I could, to make you hate me so I wouldn't have to admit to myself how I'm already yours. Which means that no matter how much I have to grovel and beg for you to let me stay by your side, I'll do it. Even if you never end up forgiving me or letting me into your heart, I won't fail you again. Just let me stay by your side."

Out of all the things I expected to come out of Eagle's mouth, this was not it. One of the proudest, controlling, confident men I'd ever known was now on his knees begging for me to not send him away. Most girls at this point would burst into tears and sob their forgiveness and undying love—but I'd never been like most girls. This terrified the *fuck* out of me. Yeah, I'd taken big steps and admitted that I loved Weston but that was a long time coming. This... this was something uncharted that I didn't know how to handle. I looked up, searching for Wes and we locked eyes as I pleaded for his help. He gave me a small smile and shook his head no... I had to do this on my own.

Double Fuck, fuckity, fuck, fuck.

Then out of nowhere a thought struck me. There was a second reason I knew about the Devils Spawn.

"Eagle, didn't the Devils work with the De León Cartel?" I demanded.

He blinked at me, taking a moment to catch up to what I was asking. "Yes..."

"Wes, were they still trafficking when we kicked them out of the West Coast?"

Wes frowned, grabbed his computer, fingers flying over the keyboard. He paused to read something then looked up at me. "Yeah, but they were the middleman at that point. Losing the Devils all but killed their business for years, then they joined up with a major cartel in Mexico and started to supply them with the flesh they needed."

"What cartel?" Cognac asked.

"The Tesoro Cartel," Wes answered as we all watched Cognac lose his shit.

In the blink of an eye, the carefree man I'd come to know was raging, punching holes into the wall and yelling and screaming in Spanish. From what I could pick up with how fast he was talking, it would seem that the Tesoro Cartel was the one he lost his family to and now they were after me... but why?

Chapter Twenty-Four

Dax

"Dax," Eagle ventured, pulling me from my thoughts.

"Hmm?"

Eagle's brow furrowed in confusion as he watched me. "Do you have anything to say about what I told you?"

I knew blowing him off right now was somewhat cruel, but I'd only promised to listen—giving an answer was not part of the bargain.

"Nope, not really, but I might later," I answered, yawning. "Right now, I could go for a nap and food doesn't sound all that bad."

As the magical medical fairy that she is, Dani reappeared. "I think it's time that we can get some food in you, but sadly it needs to be boring and simple. You've been on tube feeding the last few days, so your stomach isn't gonna be thrilled with you throwing just anything at it. Why don't you take a nap and I'll work with the guys to figure out something to eat for when you wake up."

"Any chance I can ditch the IV too?" I begged, glaring at the contraption still attached to me.

"I think that might be arranged," Dani shared, as she helped me to my feet and followed after me as I headed back to the bedroom.

She had me sit on the edge of the bed as she shut off the flow of the IV bags. "Now you know that this means we'll have to go to oral pain management."

"Would it surprise you to know that I'm far more willing to deal with that then to drag it around with me?" I smirked as she shook her head at me.

"No not really, guess it's like waving a white flag, proving that you're not well."

"I knew you would get me, Dani."

Now with my good arm free of all things medical, I could finally curl up on my side, even if it did pull at my back stitches. All things considered, it was the least painful thing happening with my body.

"How long until I'm able to manage real life again? This whole invalid thing is not really my cup of tea," I grumbled as I forced my eyes to stay open.

"Woman, you need to give yourself a break." Dani huffed. "Give it time and it will happen faster than you realize."

When I woke from my nap, the smell of something delicious made my mouth water and my stomach growl with excitement. Tossing back the covers, I trudged my way out of the bedroom to find that the living room was empty. There was not a sound to be heard anywhere in the small house as I entered the kitchen. The stove had a large pot on it that the source of the yummy smell came from, with the burner on low. I flipped it off, not wanting to worry about the house catching on fire or ruining the food I hoped for. Scanning the room, I looked for some note or reason that everyone was gone but nothing was out of place.

"Okay, guys, like this is getting fucking freaky what the hell is going on?" I called out, hoping that this was just some elaborate joke.

Getting no answer, my hand twitched for a gun, but I had no idea where mine ended up after everything. So I grabbed a kitchen knife from the block—hey it was better than nothing. Hugging the wall, I slowly made my way down the hall on the long side of this ranch house, where I assumed the other bedrooms would be. All the doors were closed, and I battled with myself on if it was smart to bother opening them or if I should just get the fuck out of the house.

What if they are tied up and can't answer me?

I thumped my head against the wall, frustrated on what the best move would be. Normally this wouldn't be a question, I would fend for myself and GTFO. Damn these men for making me sit here like a fucking deer in headlights deciding what to do. Growling, I moved to the first door and crouched low, facing the wall since I only had one good arm. Most people would assume that you're standing when you open a door, so keeping low made you less of a target. Add in the fact that I'm short as shit, and I was even harder to hit. I shoved the door open, waited a moment, then peaked ever so slightly around the corner finding the bedroom empty. Signs of someone staying in it were clear, but there were no obvious markers of a struggle. Slinking down the hall, I got to the next door and repeated the process, finding it once again empty. One more room left and this one was facing down the hall so I couldn't approach it the same way. Tucking myself into the corner, I reached over with my right hand and opened the door just enough so it wouldn't catch on the latch then kicked it in with my heel. It bounced off the wall but nothing else followed, so I ventured a look and found Eagle and Picasso sprawled out on the floor face down and the room was a wreck.

"Shit!"

I glanced around the room but didn't see anything that would indicate someone else was in the room so I stepped in further. I went to the closet door that was shut and instead of opening it I shoved the dresser in front of it. If someone was in there, then they weren't going to get out. Darting over to the two idiots, I checked their pulses and found them still alive, and I was oddly relieved. Both of these douche canoes didn't really deserve my help after what they did and said, but I knew I couldn't leave them like this. This room was a second master bedroom with a sliding glass door out to the yard. It was slightly open, as if they didn't get a chance to leave or that's how whoever did this got in. Now the question was—what the fuck do I do? There was no way that I could drag these fuckers out with only one good arm and going after whoever did this was just as much of a risk.

"Goddamn it, where is everyone else?!" I snapped, running my hand through my hair. "Okay, calm the fuck down, Dax. This is not the worst spot you've been in, so figure your shit out."

Moving over to the sliding glass door, I opened it and stepped out onto the grass making sure that the backyard was empty. None of this was making sense. If they wanted to fuck with us, they would have killed those two and come after me, but they didn't. Not to mention, there is no way that Wes would have left me without giving me a note of some kind. Leaving the two sleeping beauties, I headed back to my bedroom and checked there to see if I could find anything. Sure enough, I'd missed a note on the nightstand from Wes telling me that they were going on a food run and checking in on things, leaving the two idiots with me. A sneaking suspicion of what might be going on rolled around in my brain.

Back in the kitchen, I found a large bowl, filled it with ice from the fridge, added some water for good measure along with some chili oil I found in the pantry. Lugging the large bowl, I had to take a few breaks now that my adrenaline was wearing off reminding me that I was busted up, as I made my way back down to the room the brothers were lying in. I dumped the water right on their faces.

"Holy fucking shit!" Picasso screamed rolling around on the floor. "Why is it burning the fuck out of my eyes?"

"Goddamn you, woman, what the hell did you do to us?" Eagle snarled, as he clutched his face.

I dropped the bowl on the floor and watched them writhe around in pain for a few minutes before I left the room. Grabbing a bowl, I took the lid off the pot and found vegetable soup that smelled orgasmic. Filling my bowl, I sat down at the table and started to eat, grinning at the sound of the brothers swearing and moaning about my retaliation. They needed to learn real fast not to fuck with me if they couldn't take the consequences of their actions. This little game had done nothing but piss me off at them even more. *What had they hoped to gain from this?*

"What on earth is going on back there?" Dani asked, as she walked into the kitchen with a bag of groceries.

Grinning at her, I sipped another spoonful of soup as the sound of someone crashing into something followed by a string of curse words echoed down the hall. "They're just learning they can't play with the big dogs."

"Do I need to go check on them?" she ventured, as she flinched at another burst of swearing.

"Would chili oil in the eyes cause permanent damage?" I inquired, while resting my chin on my hand.

"Oh God, well, they'll have to use milk to get it to stop burning. They can't just wash their faces," Dani informed me.

I laughed so hard I started to cry. "That idea just keeps getting better and better. I need to remember that trick the next time I need to get someone to talk."

"I think I better go deal with that." Dani sighed and headed down the hall.

Seeing both Eagle and Picasso walking behind Dani holding her hands, since their eyes were red and swollen shut with tears streaming down their faces was just priceless. She guided them to a chair and got them each a milk-soaked paper towel.

"Now don't rub, just gently blot them and let the milk counteract the heat and oil, alright," Dani instructed.

Both of them sat there with their heads tilted back, crying milky tears.

"Either of you care to share what the fuck you were thinking?" I asked.

"Spitfire, you are pure evil. I respect the fuck out of you, but goddamn," Picasso muttered.

Eagle dropped his milky towel and cracked an eye open to look at me. "Do you really hate me that much?"

His question caught me off guard. "Really, that's what you think this is about?"

"Why else you would try and fucking blind me?"

"Eagle, do you know what you just did with this little stunt? There are people actively trying to kill me, and by association you. In what universe did you think it was a good idea to fake an attack when I'm the weakest I've ever been in my life? That doesn't instill trust in the slightest," I explained.

Hearing what I said, Eagle deflated and dropped his face back onto his milk. "I thought it would be a good way to see if you really didn't care about me. If you left me there and saved yourself, I would know for sure if I had a chance or not."

"What about you, Rembrandt? How did he talk you into participating?"

Picasso let out a heavy sigh. "Weston said you were probably majorly pissed at me for the stupid shit I said, throwing your brother in your face."

"Wow, guys, just wow," I muttered, rubbing my forehead. "I don't even know where to begin with how fucked up all of that logic was. Picasso, was I upset you pulled the brother card on me—yeah. Not enough to leave you for dead, asshole, but don't ever do it again or I might. You also need to work on your brother complex a bit, because it's getting you in lots of trouble with me, just saying. As for you, Eagle, I really don't know what you want from me. Yeah, you told me your whole story—you think you have pure evil living inside you and I'm going to set it free, causing you to set the world on fire. Thing is, I don't really need you to do that for me, I'm very capable of doing that all on my own if I want to. You need to slow your fucking roll a second and give me a chance to build some trust. This bullshit—not a good move."

Taking a deep breath, I walked over and sat right on Eagle's lap, grabbed his face and peeled back the paper towel. "Did it ever cross your mind that I wouldn't have taken a bullet for you if I hated you? If I thought you were completely written off, no chance in hell of getting back in my good graces, I'd have let you get shot. Stop trying to fix things and force it to work when all you have to do is be you. The Eagle who's President of the Phantom Saints, the guy I was willing to consider moving in with that's a neat freak and cooks amazing food. Remember him? The dick who always wants to make me submit and challenges me in the sexiest ways possible... that's the Eagle I'm willing to give a chance to redeem himself. Whoever this whiny insecure dude is, I don't like him—at all. Stop asking me to forgive you and make me forgive you, just like you've always done things with me."

As if he finally was hearing me, he grabbed the back of my neck and slammed his lips down on mine, devouring me. We fought for control of the kiss, but it just made it all the better. His hand shifted to get a fist full of my hair and shifted the angle of the kiss, deepening it so it felt like he was tongue fucking my tonsils.

"Okay, you two, easy there, she does still have stitches in her neck, and we don't want them to tear," Dani called out, breaking the two of us apart.

I couldn't help but grin at Eagle as his eyes, still swollen and red, finally had that commanding fire back in them. "Well, would you look at that, the president is back in business and ready to play."

"I'm gonna stop you right there, Dax," Dani cut in once again. "No sex until we get the stitches out. It's been six days, so you have another week to go, missy."

Shifting so I could glower at my nurse I whined, "What the hell Dani? Here I thought you were cool but all I'm hearing right now is that you're cockblocking me!"

Dani gave me a smile and a wink. "Sorry, girl, but I'm a nurse first and this is what you're paying me for, so deal with it."

I tried to stand up, but Eagle yanked me back down. "Nope, sorry, little hellcat, but I've gone too long without my fix, and I believe you told me to take what I want."

"Don't get too full of yourself, bub, you're still in time out," I informed him.

"I can deal with that, but personally, I think chili oil to the face earns me some cuddles at least," Eagle countered.

"What the fuck about me?" Picasso blurted. "I didn't even fuck up as bad as he did."

"Yeah, this is punishment for letting him talk you into pulling that stunt." I smirked as he started to cuss under his breath.

I caught Dani watching the whole event, leaning on the counter with raised eyebrows. "Is it always like this between you guys?"

"Some days are better than others." I shrugged.

"Yeah, some days she asks me if she can give my dick a mouth hug," Eagle chimed in.

"Once... that happened once... when I was drunk."

"Still happened."

Chapter Twenty-Five

Dax

"WHAT DO YOU MEAN you're not coming back tonight?" I demanded.

"My heart, you know I would be back there if I could, but without you or I around the last few days, there's way more to handle here," Weston explained. "This is one of the problems with keeping this whole thing running around the two of us. If we had another person under me who you trusted to keep things going, it wouldn't have been such a big deal."

"Whoa, are you putting this on me right now? I'm the one who got shot!" I snapped.

Wes let out a heavy sigh. "No, I'm not blaming you, Dax, I just am seeing the downside to how we decided to do things. This is keeping me from being with you, which is where I want to be. Now I have to be here dealing with everyone wanting to chase down any biker they see in the street for retaliation. Brian has been helping to keep things in order, but they really need to hear from you and I'm not willing to risk you again so soon."

"Could we do a video call or something with the underbosses? Or are things still too volatile for that?" I asked.

"It couldn't hurt," Wes agreed. "This might be a good time to let them know about the Phantom Saints as well, so we can have them around without worrying they'll get shot."

I growled at this, thinking of any of my men in danger from my own people. "We need to make this happen now, Wes, I won't risk any of them just because people are trigger happy."

"Alright, I'll see what I can do from my end and let you know. It will have to be tomorrow though, since it's nearly midnight," Wes countered. "You managing with Eagle and Picasso around? I didn't like the idea, but the others overruled me."

I glanced over at Eagle who was now passed out on the couch, while Picasso watched *Top Gear* on the television, giving me space to talk to Wes. "Let's just say that they learned the hard way not to play games with me. When they lose, it never goes well for them."

"Dax... what did you do?"

"Hey, they deserved it for the stunt they pulled, not to mention the other stuff. Now we are closer to being even—if that's even possible," I defended. "Do you know if the others will be back tonight?"

"I touched base with Sprocket, and they had a few deals to handle that were going down tomorrow and didn't think it was smart to come back only to leave again."

"Humph, they couldn't bother to call and tell *me* that?"

Wes paused a moment at my response. "I'm sorry, I think I must be hearing this wrong... do you miss them?"

"I have no idea what you're talking about."

"Nope, I hit the nail right on the head, you miss all of us not being there with you," Wes stated.

"Westie, you know I love you, but don't push your luck on this," I grumbled. "Just because I don't want to be alone in a house, in an unknown location, doesn't mean anything more than I want back up."

Before I could do anything about it, the cell was yanked out of my hand and Picasso wrapped his arm around my waist, sitting me on his lap to keep me from going after the phone. "Okay, now I need to know what you said to get her all riled up. You should see the look on her face right now."

"You better not tell him a damn word, Weston!" I yelled, waking Eagle up.

"What the fuck is going on now?" he muttered as he sat up eyeing the two of us. "Something I should know about?"

Picasso then hit the speaker button on the burner phone. "Say that again for me, Wes, so the room can hear."

"Dax is getting pissy because she misses the rest of us and is mad we won't be home tonight," Wes proclaimed loudly.

"You're dead to me, Weston Price!" I announced. "I don't want to see you back at this place ever again, you hear me?"

"Oh well, that got her going." Eagle chuckled. "Everything okay on your end there, Westy-boy?"

"Nothing I can't handle, just need to be around to do it though, think you can deal with her alone for another day?"

Picasso and Eagle looked at each other and grinned. "Oh, I'm sure we can come up with something to do."

Something about their look made me pause. The two of them combining forces against me might not be the best idea, I've seen the trouble they can get into alone, but together—that was a scary thought.

"I'll make sure to come back with some art supplies just in case things need to be smoothed over," Wes offered.

"You're still on speaker, I can still hear you," I retorted.

"Yeah, shortcake, I know."

I gaped at the phone, suddenly deciding that these men all coming to an agreement was not good for me. Six against one was not odds that I like to deal with very often... unless it was naked. That I could get behind.

"Whatever you're thinking, it's making you wiggle your ass on my dick, if you don't want to wake the snake, I wouldn't continue to do that," Picasso whispered into my ear.

"I'm sorry, did you just say wake the snake?" I asked, trying to hold back my laughter as I looked over my shoulder at him. Sadly, it was a losing battle and I burst out laughing and slumped back against his chest. "Oh my God. Oh my God. Oh my God, that was hilarious."

"Did she get pain meds recently?" Wes asked.

I grabbed Picasso's arm and pulled it down so I could get closer to the phone. "Did you hear what he said?"

"Ah... nothing that would cause you to start cackling like this," Wes said, confusion in his voice.

"He was worried I might wake the *snake* with my ass wiggles," I shared, falling into another fit of laughter.

Picasso stood up, dumping me back into the chair and glared down at me. "It wasn't that funny, Dax."

"Oh shit. I think I might have hurt his feelings," I called after him. "I'm sorry, I didn't mean to anger the python!"

"I think now might be a good time for me to hang up," Wes ventured. "Dax, I'll talk to you tomorrow about the video call. Guys, if you need help with anything I'm around."

"Night, Westie!" I shouted as Picasso hung up.

The room fell into an awkward silence as Eagle kept looking from his brother back to me. I had my eyes locked on Picasso, trying to figure out what exactly it was that I did to piss him off, because I didn't think it was the snake thing—it had to be something else. I got up and padded over to him, where he now sat next to Eagle on the couch and sat right in front of him on the coffee table. My gaze caught his eyes, but they were guarded, more so than I'd ever seen.

"What's up, Van Gogh?" I inquired, perching my chin on my good hand.

"Why do you always do that?"

My eyebrows shot up at this left turn of a question. "You might want to narrow that down for me just a bit."

"Look, I thought you and I had a breakthrough back at your house after I saw your art. I know I've said some stupid shit and I am happy to pay penance for that, but don't give me a glimpse of the real Dax and then shut me out. That woman who told me she wanted to travel the world and paint is the core of who you are. I'm not saying that this bad ass bitch persona isn't you as well, but there are so many more layers to you than you let anyone see. Hell, I think Weston and Harper might be the only people who know that side of you exists," Picasso vented. "We are here alone, in this house, safe as we can be for the time being, why can't you let your guard down for a little while? You don't need to use sass and humor to cover up how you're feeling."

I sat back, a little stunned that this was his outburst. It would seem that I keep forgetting that he is a sensitive soul under all that gruff and anger. Knowing what his childhood was like, it made more sense, he wanted to see the good in the world, so he didn't lose hope in all of humanity—I was someone he saw the same thing in.

"Picasso, it's not that I don't know how to relax, or I don't feel safe—it's that I can't," I paused trying my best to explain this. "What happened at that meeting was my fault. I wasn't on my A-game, and it cost me good people, as well as putting myself in the hospital. If I let that part of me out right now, I'm going to be too soft to see this through. In war you need to be ruthless and do whatever it takes to see the job done. Artist Dax wants nothing to do with that, she would want to find a way to save the world instead of burning it to the ground if it meant ending this whole thing. Does that make any sense?"

Eagle reached out and tucked my hair behind an ear, letting his thumb caress my cheek. "I understand that more than you know."

I leaned into his hold, feeling his support and acceptance.

"I'm sorry I don't get that at all," Picasso muttered, rubbing his hands over his face. "I get that we are at war but why do you have to sacrifice part of you for it?"

This time I reached out and grabbed Picasso's chin, forcing him to look at me. "So you don't have to."

Realization shows in his eyes at that, and the next thing I knew his lips were on mine, his hand cupping the back of my head to hold me steady. I allowed myself to let him take charge, bending to his needs, knowing that this was an important moment for us. Fumbling, he tried to pull me into his lap but with an arm in a sling it set me off balance. Eagle was there to scoop me up and plop me on his brother. In an oddly normal way, Eagle let his hands rest on my hips, holding me steady as his brother slipped his hands under my shirt going right for my handfuls of boobs. I moaned as Picasso rolled my nipples between his fingers before giving them a slight tug.

"Dani said no sex, but she didn't say anything about foreplay," Eagle whispered into my ear, his lips brushing against it, sending shivers down my spine.

Pulling back from Picasso, I gasped as Eagle gently nipped at my throat. "Help me get this shirt off."

Carefully, they maneuvered my arm out of the sling, then Eagle took a knife and cut up the back of the shirt so I could slip it off without raising my arms. Between the two of them, they laid me out on the couch, making sure I was comfortable and supported by pillows, before they slipped my leggings off. I hadn't bothered to put on underwear, thinking it was just another hassle when I needed to pee, now I was even more grateful to have forgone the layer.

"Look at that perfect pussy," Picasso purred, running his hands down my legs. "No wonder you fell for her so fast, Eagle."

"I haven't even gotten to taste it yet, but Cognac assures me it's addictive." Eagle grinned.

I shoved myself up on one arm glaring. "You guys share notes about your sexual experiences with me?"

"How else are we supposed to know what you like and don't like? Play smarter not harder," Picasso teased as he massaged my inner thigh muscles, moving nearer to the promised land.

"That is hot as fuck and a little creepy." I chuckled, falling back onto the couch when Eagle wrapped his big hands around my breasts.

Within seconds, I was lost in the feeling of both of them stroking, kissing, licking, and nipping at my skin. Just as Eagle wrapped his lips around my nipple, Picasso ran his tongue from ass to clit. I wanted to rocket off the couch, but they held me steady.

"Easy there, little hellcat, we can't get in trouble with Dani, or she'll change the rules. We wouldn't want that now, would we?"

I groaned as his lips moved against the tip of my nipple, making them harden even more than they already were. Those bitches could cut glass right now. Picasso spread me open and let his finger wander around my clit in a slow circular motion.

What is with these men and torturing me? Guess they did take notes...

"Hmm, seems Weston wasn't holding out on us either," Picasso said as he slipped one finger inside, putting my G-spot. "Right where he said it would be."

"Oh fuck!" I blurted, kicking out with my legs as he put in a second finger.

"Sorry, spitfire, that's not on the menu tonight, but don't worry we'll make sure you come. Three times was the goal, right?" Picasso asked.

"He said he only got three out of her, so we should shoot for at least four," Eagle corrected.

"Oh, thank God, I didn't die," I murmured, my eyes rolling into the back of my head as Picasso latched onto my clit and sucked.

With my right arm, I reached out toward Eagle and blindly felt for his pants, needing to give myself something to do.

"What are you after, little hellcat?"

"You wanted a mouth hug, didn't you?" I smirked, looking up at him from hooded eyes.

Possessive fire blazed in Eagle's eyes, but he shook his head. "Not tonight. This is about you and making damn sure you know exactly how I feel about you. Once Picasso's had a chance to make his case, it's my turn."

Just as I was about to argue, Picasso dropped the teasing act and got down to business. His fingers thrusting in and out of me, all the while rubbing along the money spot, as his tongue lapped at my clit. No longer could I keep a coherent thought in my head, I was now in the clouds, floating outside of my body. Eagle started his work on my breasts and kissing up along my neck then capturing my lips with his own. My orgasm came crashing into me and if they hadn't held me down, I would have done a crunch and latched onto Picasso's hair. Once it subsided and I stopped seeing stars, I pulled Picasso up so I could show him just how much I enjoyed what he did.

"Now it's my turn," Eagle announced and shoved his brother off me and out of the way.

Eagle pulled me up, so I was sitting on his face with my thighs clamped around his head. Picasso came to stand in front of me, so I didn't tumble off the end of the couch onto the floor.

Eagle, true to form, didn't waste time; he shoved his tongue right up inside, giving his best effort to see how many licks it would take to get to the center of a tootsie pop. I latched onto Picasso and rested my head on his chest panting like a bitch in heat. Then Eagle caught me off guard when he slipped a finger in and then pulled it out, heading right for the back door. He swirled his finger a few times before testing the entrance, which made me cry out in pleasure.

"Holy fucking shit, I'm gonna kill Wes," I babbled as Eagle now worked both holes.

Eagle chuckled at my response, which vibrated against my clit sending me into another orgasm, but Eagle didn't stop, instead he picked up the pace as I rocked on his face, chasing after that third cliff to fall off of. It didn't take long before I was a quivering mess clinging to Picasso as my body refused to offer any support.

"No more, please I don't think I could handle another one right now," I pleaded as Eagle slid out from under me.

"She is still recovering... guess we should take pity on her," Picasso suggested. "I think some cuddles might be just what the doctor ordered, don't you?"

Eagle scooped me up, and I lay there boneless and sated. "I think I'll keep you guys around for a bit longer."

"Does that mean we're forgiven?" Picasso ventured.

"I'm not that sex drunk, but you're working off your debt rather quickly if you keep that shit up."

"Works for me, little hellcat, I like to make my pussy purr."

"I think you should stop talking before I add on more time to your sentence," I mumbled, glaring up at Eagle who just laughed.

Chapter Twenty-Six

Dax

"YOUR NECK IS HEALING really well, Dax, I think I can take the stitches out today along with the ones on your back. We'll have to keep Steri-strips on them just because they are in high movement areas, but this means you get to shower. After we cover your shoulder wound that is, but that is easier to do and the shower has one of those detachable heads and all," Dani chatted as she worked on my back stitches.

"Think you could take out the ones in my leg too? I feel like they are long overdue to come out," I asked, trying not to shift as she worked. The skin was itchy as all hell and being that it was in an area I couldn't get to, it was pure torture.

Dani leaned to the side to look at my thigh where Sprocket had sewn me up what seemed like months ago, when it had only been two weeks. "How often do you get shot?"

"This is more than usual, typically it's only a once-a-year thing but I seem to be trying to outdo myself," I joked.

Unamused, Dani finished on my back then moved to my left and swiftly took those out, before venturing to my neck. "You might need to put me on full-time staff if you're going for gold. Who else is going to patch you up and keep you alive without taking you to the hospital?"

"If that is a genuine request, I won't say no, I've been looking for some medical professionals that I can trust. We had a doc at one point, but he got hooked on Oxy and made one too many mistakes taking care of my people, so I had to remove him from his position," I shared. If she wanted to join the Empire, I wasn't going to stop her, but I wanted her to know the reality of it.

"Alright, so I get paid better than I've ever been paid, deal with calls at random times of the day or night, and have one or two patients to care for? Yeah, I'm not seeing the downside to this..."

I grinned at her, pleased that she was taking this all in stride. "You're forgetting that you'll also have our protection so if anyone tries to mess with you all you need to do is let me know and it's handled. We also have a great dental plan if you need that."

Dani laughed at that as she finished with my neck. "Damn, Dax, where has this job been all my life? Now I just need to find me a nice man or two to keep my bed warm at night. Working the late shift in the hospital doesn't give you much of a social life, but with this new gig I feel like my prospects are looking up."

Our laughter was interrupted when someone knocked, before Eagle walked into the bedroom, his face telling me what he had to say was not going to be good.

"What's wrong?" I demanded shooting to my feet.

"It's Wes... the feds got him and took him into custody about thirty minutes ago," Eagle explained.

The moment his words made any sense to me, I saw red, fury burning through my body. As I made for the door, but Eagle wrapped his arms around my waist and held me back.

"Wait there's more," Eagle bit out as I tried to kick him in the balls. "Just give me a minute and listen to me, little hellcat."

Shooting pain from my left shoulder set my teeth on edge as I fought against Eagle's hold, making me cry out in pain.

"Motherfuckers, how dare they take him—*he's mine*!" I growled as tears from my pain and anger pricked at my eyes.

Eagle hoisted me up so my feet couldn't touch the ground and sat us both down in one of the armchairs in my room. He didn't say anything but just put his head in the crook of my neck and waited out my anger as I beat and kicked at him. At some point, Picasso entered the room and tried to talk to me as well, but I wasn't hearing any of it. This had always been my worst nightmare. The FBI was one organization that was hard to crack and I didn't have an inside man anymore. They'd found my mole years ago, and I hadn't been able to turn anyone since. Weston had always kept an eye on things but what happened at the warehouse was way too big to just keep to the local police. If they were at all suspicious of a turf war between me and one of the other gangs or cartels in the area, feds were bound to be called in. The sting of someone slapping me across the cheek shocked me into silence. I blinked up at Picasso standing before me, his chest heaving as he looked down at his bright red hand that matched the heat I felt on my own skin.

"What the fuck was *that*?!" I snapped, glaring at Picasso.

"You needed to calm down, and I didn't know what else to do. I thought about a bucket of cold water, but I wasn't sure if you could get your wounds wet..."

Okay, the fact that he thought it through did make this a little better—but only slightly.

"Clearly, you have my attention now, what could possibly be more important than the fact that the FBI took Weston?"

"Does the name Cameron Black mean anything to you?" Picasso asked, crossing his arms. "He seemed to know who you were on a fairly intimate level."

My jaw dropped upon hearing the name of a person I didn't think would ever be in my life again. "What did he say?"

"The only chance Weston has is if you turn yourself in to him," Eagle murmured from behind me. "The FBI is more interested in you than Weston but if they can't get you, they'll take what they can get."

I relaxed back against Eagle as I dissected the bomb they just dropped in my lap. Cameron was working for the FBI now? I guess I shouldn't be surprised, since he was studying criminal justice back in college. Did he know who and what I was, or is this another case of using me to get to Tricks? How fast had word spread that I was Two Tricks? From what the guys told me, we didn't get all the Mad Dogs who'd come to attack us that night. They could be spreading it around like wildfire.

"So do I have any real clothes around here?" I asked as I pulled out of Eagle's hold.

"You can't seriously plan to go turn yourself in?" Picasso demanded taking my face in his hands. "Look, I know this is bad, but we can find some other way to handle this. Don't you have a lawyer that can get Wes out of there?"

"Not if Cameron has him." I sighed. "He knows that I will do anything for Wes, so he took him to get to me."

"How do you know this guy? Had a run-in with him before?" Eagle questioned, scowling at me.

I could see the possessive male coming out in him at the mere thought of another man making a move on me. "I guess you could say that. He was my boyfriend for a year, back in college."

This caught them both off guard, giving me the chance to get out of their grasp and root around the room for some clothes that weren't oversized t-shirts and leggings. I would also need to take a shower but Dani had said I could do that so that was good, now where would I find underwear?

A door banged open, alerting me that someone was home, so I peeked out of the bedroom and saw Void charging his way over to me. His face was a mask of anger and determination and once he met my gaze, I knew I was in trouble.

"Hey, big guy... oomph," I grunted as he all but tackled me, putting his shoulder in my ribs and hoisting me up so I was hanging over his back. He'd managed to do all this without causing much trauma to my shoulder, which was impressive. "Where are we going?"

"Far away from here. You are not going to turn yourself in to the feds," Void stated, as he carried me out of the house to the SUV that was idling in the drive. "Weston and I were on the phone together when it happened, and he made me promise that I would put you first. He's calling your lawyer and is going to handle things, but we can't risk you getting trapped there with them. You know that when they want something, they'll do whatever it takes to make it happen. They could lock you up in some secret location and never let you go. Not to mention if the CIA gets wind of this and they want a piece of the action. You do have some friends in high places that they've been looking to take down for years."

Gently as he could, Void set me down in the back, where Dani was already waiting for us, a concerned look creasing her brow. I reached over and took her hand in mine, giving it a squeeze. "You sure you still want the job? We can let you out right now and you don't have to be a part of this at all."

Dani squared her shoulders and shook her head. "No, I can handle this, I always wanted to work in the military or doctors without borders. This is just the urban version of that right?"

"We'll keep you safe I promise, the one they are after is me," I assured her.

Void got into the driver's seat and Eagle hopped in the passenger side as Picasso tossed all our bags into the back. Once we were all in the vehicle, Void shot out of the driveway and roared down the street like a bat out of hell.

"Hey, big guy, do you think we can do this without adding more injuries to my list?" I suggested, as we took a corner on two wheels.

Void just glanced at me in the rearview mirror and winked, making me grin. He knew exactly what he was doing and now that I got the memo I relaxed, clicking my seatbelt into place and watched the world fly by. I didn't bother to ask where we were going, because I knew that we would never make it there. If Void had been on the phone when Cameron showed up, it wouldn't take him long to find out who was on the other line. It was times like this that I wonder if I was always meant for this lifestyle. I'd never dated all that seriously even before Devin died, but I never went for the good guys or the golden boys who were looking to change the world for the better. No, I always seemed drawn to the dark and brooding men, who under the surface, were far more dangerous than you would ever know.

We hit the highway and headed north, I wondered how long it was going to take before they headed us off. They took Wes about an hour ago at this point, so I was giving it another fifteen twenty minutes if they stopped at the house first. Who would have known that they would let someone like Cameron Black into the FBI? It must have been a deal.

"Where are the other two?" I asked, trying to break the tension in the car.

"Sprocket and Cognac are in the middle of a deal right now. I was back at the compound, so I was able to get to you faster," Void explained. "They would be here too if they could, you know that right?"

In all honesty, it was a good thing that we weren't all together. I wasn't sure what they would do finding me with a group of known one-percenter bikers, but I was hoping they would just take me if I went willingly. The trick was going to be getting the guys to agree.

"Business is business, I wouldn't ask you guys to drop everything to keep your crew running. You have a lot of people to support, it's no big deal," I said with a half shrug. "It might be better to have people out of this situation as it is."

"What does that mean?" Picasso demanded from the back seat. "You make it sound like we're already fucked."

"That's because we are." I pointed to the cops blocking the on and off ramps so that no other traffic could join us on the freeway. "We are about to get caught in his net and when he sets a trap, no one gets out of it. When we get detained, I need you to let me go with them, don't fight this or else you'll be thrown in prison. It's going to be much easier for me to get myself and Wes out of this without you guys causing a scene."

"The fuck, Dax?" Eagle growled, twisting so he can look at me. "What are you talking about?"

"Cameron is not your average FBI agent," I informed them, unwilling to share more than that until I knew it really was him we were dealing with.

Two black SUVs went flying past us with their lights on, followed by a truck with a guy in the back of it tossing out a spike strip.

"Everybody, hold on!" Void roared as he slammed on the breaks and tossed the car into reverse.

Flooring it, he wrapped an arm around Eagle's seat as he drove us away from the cops, before spinning us back around so we were driving the opposite way in the oncoming traffic. Thankfully, it was all but nonexistent with the cops blocking people from entering, but there were still people that hadn't gotten off. Void was an incredibly skilled driver as he maneuvered our way out of this, but none of us saw the truck coming out of the ditch to hit us in the back panel of the SUV, sending us spinning like a dreidel. I was slammed into the car door, a scream escaping my lips as the impact landed mostly on my shoulder. I saw stars as the car came to a standstill with a swarm of cops and FBI agents in their navy jackets with the yellow lettering on the back announcing who they were.

It took a few moments to catch my breath. "Everyone, okay? Dani, Picasso?"

"Ugh, yeah I'm good, just slammed my head into the window," Picasso groaned.

"I'm fine, you alright Dax?" Dani asked unbuckling to crawl over to check on me. "Nothing looks worse for wear, you hit your shoulder?"

"Yeah, that fucking hurt," I bit out as she probed around to make sure I didn't do major damage. "Void... Eagle you good?"

"Other than the red laser on my chest, yeah we're both fine," Eagle growled.

"Step out of the vehicle with your hands up behind your head and lay on the ground!" someone shouted over the loudspeaker.

"Remember what I said, guys, just be cool," I warned, as I unbuckled and kicked open the door.

Sliding out of the SUV, I stood blinking at the bright midday sun before I raised my right hand. Clearly my left was in a sling so I hoped they would figure out that I couldn't do as they requested. I waited until all of us were out of the car before we dropped to our knees. It was harder for me to get on the ground with my arm throwing me off balance, but the cops had other plans. They swarmed on us, getting the guys in handcuffs, none too kindly I might add. Then a cop came up to me and shoved me down on the asphalt so my face slammed onto the hot surface, getting road rash on my chin and cheek.

"You fucking leave her alone!" Void bellowed.

I could hear fighting as he struggled to get to me, a second later the telltale sound of a taser went off, followed by more swearing and grunting.

"Guys, knock it off!" I yelled, trying to keep my own anger in check.

The cop yanked off my sling and jerked my arm around my back as I let out a blood curdling scream at the pain. Then the pressure on my back was gone and someone carefully rolled me onto my back and helped me to sit up. I was staring into golden brown eyes that I never thought would look at me with concern again.

"Hello again, beautiful."

Chapter Twenty-Seven

Dax

EVEN THOUGH IT HAD been almost eight years since I saw Cameron Black, he was as handsome as I remembered, if not more with a dark gray suit, fifties style haircut and scruff on his face. When I'd dated him, he had more of a skater boy look but this right here looking down at me was a man. Before I could even respond to what he said to me, the cool metal off the cuffs went around my right wrist and the sound of the other side closing told me that he just tied the two of us together.

"Hmm, like old times I see. Always trying to tie me down," I mused.

"Aw come on now, beautiful, we both know that you didn't really mean it when you broke up with me. It was the grief talking. But I think I've given you enough time now to yourself. It's only right we get back to how things should be."

"Yup, still the same cocky son of a bitch I remember." I smirk.

Cameron chuckled as he helped me to my feet and grasped my face gingerly with his fingers. "Sorry about that, they got a little hyped up with the whole cat-and-mouse game. You know how those things go."

"Actually, seeing as I'm usually the cat, being the mouse is a whole new experience and I gotta say—not a fan," I muttered, shoving his hand away. "Think they'll let me have my sling back now that they know I don't have any tricks up my sleeve?"

"Bakersfield, would you mind bringing me that sling you so rudely ripped off Miss Blackmore?" Cameron called over my shoulder. "So that's why you've been hiding out, you got shot in the whole warehouse debacle."

"Three times to be exact, let's just say it was a rough night… Is that what this is all about?" I ventured, watching as the cops dragged my guys away. "Do you want me to help with that? I could get my boys to go easier if you give me a clue as to what's going on."

Cameron tilted his head a little as he glanced between me and the guys. "I have to say, you being buddy-buddy with the Phantom Saints is not what I expected, but since I need Eagle and Cognac's help, it might be good to calm things down."

"If you put us all in the same car, it will help. Oh, and let Dani go. She's just my nurse. We've kept her in the dark about everything," I added, crossing my fingers and hoping he would listen.

Shocking the hell out of me, Cameron kissed me on the cheek and intertwined our fingers before heading over to the guys. "Hold up there."

Void looked like he was ready to murder Cameron when he saw us cuffed together, holding hands. "What the fuck you playing at, fed? Get your fucking hands off my little demon!"

Yup, there is definitely something wrong with me because that right there was sexy as fuck.

"Lachlan, that is a conversation we will need to have later. For now, I'm willing to play nice if you do the same in return. Get in the SUV willingly and I will make sure that Dax is in there too." Cameron paused to see the guys' response to this, and they relaxed slightly. "Great, now Dani, is it?"

"Yes well—Danielle Oberwise is my full name," Dani answered.

"Lovely name. I'm sorry you got caught up in all this and one of these nice officers will take you home now," Cameron instructed, waving a cop over.

"What, I can't leave Dax, she's in my care. Do you even know what she's been through? That stunt you pulled could have caused internal bleeding if you ruptured any of her internal stitches," Dani challenged.

Cameron glanced down at me then back at her. "I see why she likes you, Dani. What if I promise to have her checked out by our medical staff the moment we get to where I'm taking them? Will that set your mind at ease? After all, it is our responsibility for causing the trauma in the first place."

I could see Dani ready to fight him, but I gave a subtle shake of my head to let it go. "I'll be fine, Dani, I promise, if those bullets didn't take me down the first time, I'm not gonna let them do it a second time."

"You'll reach out when you can once all this is over?" she asked.

"For sure, now go home and be ready to start your new job next week, alright?" I suggested.

She nodded and followed the cop that was going to take her home, letting her slide into the back seat then drove off. Now that she was gone, I turned on Cameron and looked him dead in the eye. "Where the fuck is Wes?"

"Ah there she is. I was wondering when the possessive lioness was going to come out and protect her cub." Cameron grinned. "You'll just have to wait and see, now won't you? Come on let's not keep everyone waiting. There is so much to catch up on—I mean it's been like eight years."

"Is that all?" I grumbled.

"All right, Saints, pile on into the car and we'll get this show on the road," Cameron announced.

Picasso glared, looking him up and down. "What the fuck's wrong with this guy?"

"Did you want that in alphabetical order or more to less irritating?" I chirped.

"Nope, I don't like this at all," Void rumbled, as he ducked into the SUV.

Eagle puffed out his chest and took a step closer to Cameron trying to intimidate him, but Cam wasn't one to be pushed around that easily. "Don't get comfortable with that hand of hers G-man, she's already spoken for."

"I look forward to hearing all about it once we get out of the middle of the freeway and let the normal people return to their lives. Ladies first," Cameron answered, giving Eagle a beaming smile.

It took everything within me not to snort at the face of pure hatred that Eagle had going on right now. That was Cam for you. He knew just how to get under your skin in the most irritating ways. Except for me, it was his biggest challenge to get a rise out of me, but I just shot it right back at him. I think that's actually how we ended up dating, because neither of us planned that when I caught him breaking into the computer lab to steal the tests for the chem students' midterms.

"Just ignore him and he'll eventually give it a rest," I told Eagle. "The sooner we go the sooner we can get the fuck out of there."

Eagle dipped his head down, giving me a searing kiss before he joined the others in the car. I couldn't help but hum my pleasure at the fact he was staking a claim in front of Cam. It just did my little broken heart good.

"Oh, this is just going to be so much fun. I can't wait to see how the others will react when they join us," Cam shared, as he slid in first and helped me up beside him.

"Wait what?! What do you mean the others? What others?" I demanded a tingle going down my spine, telling me I was not going to like this.

"The other two of your men of course. I told you that I needed Juan and Enzo's help. Oh, I'm sorry Cognac and Eagle, as I'm sure they prefer to be called," Cameron corrected but not before Eagle was growling in the back seat. "Eagle, you should relax, it's not like it's the first time you've dealt with the FBI. If I read correctly, you came to us for help with your uncle, right?"

Now it was my turn to step in. I twisted my hold on Cameron's hand so if I kept bending it, I would snap his wrist. "That's enough, Cam."

"So that's where you've been hiding Two Tricks, bubbling right under the surface. Big fan of yours I must say, totally had me fooled for years. I thought it was Weston," Cameron chatted, not at all concerned that I was willing to hurt him... or did he think he was safe from me? Guess I'll have to test that out later when it would really do me some good.

The car fell silent as we drove, navigating through the roadblocks until we headed toward downtown. I leaned my head against the window, trying to block out the pain that was still throbbing down my arm from the cop trying to arm wrestle me. Although I knew the silence in the car wouldn't last that much longer, knowing my guys.

"You okay, little demon?" Void asked from right behind me.

I shifted to look over at him and gave him a small smile. "Nothing I can't handle, big guy."

"I'll make sure we get you some pain meds when we get back to the office, I promised after all," Cam said, running his thumb over the back of my hand.

It was strange how oddly comforting it was to have him around again, I didn't trust him as far as I could throw him, but still it felt... right. I had no idea what to tell the guys if they asked me about him, it wasn't my story to share, and I didn't know how much the FBI really knew about his upbringing. In an effort to keep my mind off my arm I went through the top reasons why they would need me as well as Eagle and Cognac, for something. We didn't really have a connection other than three weeks ago when they kidnapped me, before that I wouldn't be able to pick them out of a crowd.

"When we get there, I'm calling Gabby," Eagle stated. "No way I'm saying anything without a lawyer present."

Ah that's right, I almost forgot about their sister being a lawyer, although I didn't think she was the right kind to help them with this problem. "Don't waste your time. I'm sure if they gave him a chance, Wes already called our lawyer, and he's the best at dealing with this kind of shit." I sighed.

"Who Manshooly? Yeah, those guys are pretty good if you can afford him," Cam agreed.

"He's been on retainer for the past few years, just for a situation like this." I smiled, winking at Cam. "Hope you weren't counting on me sticking around."

"See, here's the thing, beautiful, that would help you if you were being charged with something. I'm actually here to make a deal with you and the boys," Cam confessed.

"What the fuck, man? Why the takedown if you need our help?" Picasso snapped.

"You could have killed us with the stunts you were pulling back on the highway," Void pointed out.

Eagle just glared at Cam, not willing to voice his thoughts just yet.

"Give me a chance to get you guys safe, Dax looked at, and I'll explain everything," Cam coaxed.

"Don't bother trying to get anything else out of him, he's fucking Fort Knox when he wants to be. Oddly endearing as it is irritating, trust me," I said, rolling my eyes at the mock look of horror Cam gave me.

Finally, we pulled into the underground parking for the Federal Building and were escorted in a side entrance where they patted us down. The guys got their knives taken that the cops hadn't found when they patted them down the first time, making me feel a little proud of them. You can't teach shit like that, you either have the gift or you don't. I of course was packing nothing, seeing as I didn't have the chance to get ready like I wanted to.

"You three go with Agent Todd while I take Dax to the doctors. We'll be with you as soon as we're done," Cam instructed.

"Not a fucking chance feeb, no way you are taking her somewhere that I can't keep an eye on her," Void threatened, dropping the pretense of "playing nice."

"Why can't you have the doc come to us, hmm?" Eagle challenged.

Cameron looked at them with raised eyebrows. "Wow, you guys have zero faith in me to make sure she stays safe do you? Guys look, I was taking care of her long before you even knew she existed, let the OG boyfriend deal with things, okay?"

I choked on my own spit as he called himself my boyfriend. "Excuse me? My what?"

"Details, but it's bound to be true soon enough, I know you still have a thing for me, and you've always been the only woman for me so..." He shrugs. "Either let me take care of her while you hang out with Weston, or I have to put you guys in holding cells until we're done. You pick."

"You guys do remember I know how to take care of myself, right? Yeah, I'm a little gimpy, but that won't stop me from chopping his dick off if I have to," I reminded them. "Go tell Wes what's been going on and I'll see you guys in a bit. Don't burn the building down with me in it, okay?"

They all muttered their agreement and walked off with Agent Todd.

"You are one hard lady to get alone, you know that?" Cam sighed.

I turned to tell him off, but his hand slipped around the back of my head pulling me to his lips. It was just as intoxicating as I remembered, like smooth whiskey on my tongue, lighting a fire as it made its way down to my stomach. Then I remembered who I was, where I was, and who he worked for. I jammed my knee into his balls, catching him totally off guard as he crumpled to the ground clutching himself with his free arm, so he didn't pull me down with him.

Guess he did think he was safe with me...

Chapter Twenty-Eight

Dax

"OKAY, WELL PLAYED," CAM wheezed out as he slowly stood.

The security guards came rushing over to help him and the lady at the lobby desk looked horrified at what I'd done. Cameron waved off the help, assuring them it was all fine. It took him a few minutes to pull himself together, but I waited, basking in the glow of watching a man get knocked down a peg. It dimmed slightly as he grabbed my hand once again and led me out of the lobby to the doctor he'd been alluding to.

"You know I'm not going to be able to live that down, right? The whole office is going to know that I got kneed in the balls for kissing the woman I'm handcuffed to," Cam pointed out.

I just shrugged and grinned at him. "Who's to say that wasn't my plan all along? Someone was feeling a little too sure of themselves and I needed to prove a point... did it work?"

"Not in the way you're hoping, it's just gonna make me work all that much harder to get back in your good graces," Cam informed me, as he swiped his keycard and pushed the door open for me.

This hall reminded me of a hospital, all white and sterile with that scent of disinfectant. I trailed after him as he led me into a room and hit the intercom on the wall.

"Can I get a doctor to exam room three? I have an undercover operative that needs to be looked at," he said.

"Someone will be with you shortly," a woman on the other side answered.

Cam took out a key from his pocket and unlocked the cuffs. "Now I know you could have gotten out of these at any point, but I appreciate you complying."

"I only did it so that the guys wouldn't get crazy by trying to cause a distraction to let me slip away. There was no way I was gonna leave them behind to deal with you," I shared, hopping up on the exam table. "Care to fill me in a little more on why I'm here?"

"No, I don't think so. I would prefer to only have to go through this once, because we have a lot to do and not a lot of time to do it in. But... I will once again reassure you that you are not officially under arrest. There is plenty I could detain you for but that would ruin the whole plan, so that's lucky for you, now isn't it?"

"It's amazing, grown-up appearance, big boy job, but still the same petty punk I remember with the skater boy hair and baggy jeans," I mused, shaking my head. "How's your old man?"

Cam's face fell into a scowl for a brief moment, letting me know I still knew how to get under his skin, even if he could never figure out how to get under mine.

"We haven't talked in about five years. The bureau doesn't look kindly on fraternizing with criminals, even if they are family," Cam retorted.

"Then it could never work out for us to get back together, now could it?" I countered.

Cam opened his mouth to say something but a woman in a white lab coat entered the room. "Hello, I'm Doctor Matthews. I was told someone needed to be looked over?"

I raised my hand. "That would be me, Doc. I was shot in the shoulder on the left side and the back on the right with a bullet graze on my left side as well. To keep my cover, they had to do a hostile takedown where I was in a slight car accident and then almost had my arm pulled out of my socket when they tried to cuff me. Since the bullet went through my lung and I had surgery for it, they just want to make sure they didn't cause any internal bleeding since it happened about a week ago."

Doctor Matthews just blinked at me once I was done speaking. "Goodness."

"My arm hurts like a bitch, but I don't think they caused any internal damage," I offered.

This seemed to snap her out of her shock. "Well, I'll be the judge of that. If I could have you put on a gown so I can look at your wounds that would be helpful."

"No need, I'm not shy," I said as I pulled the shift off my right side to slip it down the left arm.

I, of course, wasn't wearing a bra since the straps and band would hit me in all the wrong places, meaning Cameron got a full-on reminder of what he'd once enjoyed. He had to stifle a groan when he took in the sight of me now covered in tattoos and way more toned than I was back in college. I was curious to know if Cam had the same sexual preferences as he did back in college or if he grew out of those kinks? Something in the way he looked at me told me he hadn't or that he very much would like to dabble in old habits.

"Looks like a few of the stitches in your shoulder got pulled out, I'm guessing with the black shirt you didn't notice," Doc Matthews stated. "I'll have to take the others out and see what I can do about fixing it. Unfortunately, it will set you back another week before they can be removed. If I could, I'd like to do an ultrasound on your chest to check your lung, just to be sure but I don't see any signs of trauma to the area."

Glancing at my shoulder, I noticed it was weeping blood. "Huh, is that why it's been hurting like a son of a bitch? Do whatever you need to, Doc. I won't fight you on it."

"I'll inject a local then we'll see what we can do to help manage the pain..." she paused and looked over at Cameron. "Does she still have work to do today?"

"Yes, we need to have a debriefing but then she can rest," Cam answered.

"Alright, so I'll have to give you something milder and send you with another dose to take when you can sleep because it will knock you out," Doc Matthews explained.

Shrugging my one shoulder I gave her a small smile. "I'd prefer that, I don't like taking narcotics if I don't have to, but I know this is going to hurt a lot more tomorrow."

"Smart girl, a lot of undercovers get into trouble pretending to live darker lives." She tutted as she worked on cleaning up my shoulder.

I looked over at Cameron as I spoke, "Some can handle the darkness and tame it to their will. While others fear it. The problem is when you fear it and run from it... it likes to chase you down."

"Sure you don't want the cuffs back on me?" I teased as we exited the elevator onto the tenth floor. "Or are you saving those for later?"

Cam turned on his heel to face me and backed me up against the wall, caging me in with his arms on either side of my head. "Beautiful, I would suggest you stop playing with me if you don't intend for me to act on it. I'll give you a pass on the nut shot back there, it was wrong of me to think I still had the right to do that. But don't mistake that moment to mean that I'm not the man who I've always been with you, my little one."

His voice sent shivers up my spine, and I knew instantly that I was in big fucking trouble. Cameron had always been able to turn me on in a flash and our combined darkness loved to come out and play, feeding off each other. He was deliciously dangerous, and in some ways, it was very bad for us to be together, but no one could deny our chemistry.

"Duly noted, Cam," I answered, trying to keep the need out of my voice. "Just know that if you ever want a shot with me, you have to convince *all* of them before I will ever touch you. Not too long ago I almost shot a woman for getting too handsy. I can't even imagine what six pissed off guys will do if they found out you kissed me."

A flash of excitement shone in his amber eyes, as he grinned at me. "Like I said earlier—this is going to be so much fun."

Pushing away from the wall, he ushered me down the hall until we reached a set of glass doors. Once again swiping his card, he pushed them open, and I found myself in the middle of a command center of sorts, with people hovering around computer stations. They all looked up when we entered and many of them stopped what they were doing to gawk at me, while others looked none to pleased with my presence.

"What the fuck is going on?" I whispered harshly at Cam. "Why do I feel like I'm the shark in the aquarium everyone wants to stare at?"

"Hmm, that's actually a fairly good analogy there, beautiful." Cam smiled as he guided me through the workstations to a conference room in the back.

The blinds had been closed but the moment my guys saw me enter the room, I was swarmed by them. Eagle looked me over before hugging me to his chest and kissing me soundly on the mouth, then I was yanked away by Picasso. He looked me in the eye, silently asking if I was okay. Once I nodded, he kissed me on the forehead. Wes stepped up next, creasing his brow as he looked over my shoulder at Cam then back down to me.

"I heard they were rough with you, shortcake," he murmured, running his fingers along my cheek. "Everything okay?"

"Had to get my shoulder stitches redone but nothing too major," I assured him, as I tilted my head back.

He responded right away, taking his time with his kiss, marking his claim on me in front of Cam. These two had never gotten along, always trying to cut the other out of my life, saying they weren't good for me. Now I know it was because they both wanted to have me for themselves. Good thing Wes learned to share.

I pulled back first, knowing he would keep going just to push Cam's buttons. "The other two here yet?"

"I just got a text that they arrived and will be up shortly, it seems the take down with them didn't go as smoothly as yours did," Cam shared. "Why don't we all take a seat and once they get here, I'll explain why you're here."

Cam made a move to reach out and grab my hand again, but Void scooped me up bridal style and headed for a seat at the opposite end from him. Void set me in his lap and wrapped his arms around me like I was his favorite stuffed animal. The guys filled in seats on either side of us, so Cam didn't have a chance of getting to me. In true Cameron fashion, he just observed with a slight smirk on his lips, enjoying the show of dominance they were putting on.

"Would anyone care for something to drink? We'll be in here for a bit," Cam offered.

The guys shook their heads, but I raised my hand. "I'd kill for a cup of coffee."

"Still drink it black?"

"Like my soul," I answered.

Cam stuck his head out the door and asked someone to bring him a mug of coffee, it seems he didn't trust to leave us all alone. My coffee and the last two of my guys arrived at the same time, but Void refused to let me up, so Sprocket and Cognac had to come greet me where I was. It was a good thing too because these two looked like they put up one hell of a fight—shirts ripped, hair disheveled, and Cognac had a fat lip to boot.

"*Loba*, what happened to your face?" Cognac asked, letting his finger ghost over my skin. "Did they do this to you?"

I grabbed a hand with my own and pulled it to my lips. "I'm alright, they even had a doc check me out."

"Little rebel, were you causing trouble again?" Sprocket questioned, giving me a knowing look, as he handed me my coffee.

"It wasn't my fault this time, promise." I grinned.

"Alright," Cameron announced, drawing our attention. "Shall we finally get down to business?"

"Who's the fucking suit?" Cognac asked me in a loud whisper.

"You don't want to know. I know, and I wish I didn't know," Void stated, narrowing his eyes at Cam.

Sprocket's eyebrows raised as he looked between the two men, but he didn't comment.

"I am Agent Cameron Black, head of a taskforce that is specifically targeting the major crime lords in our surrounding area. One of which is none other than Two Tricks herself—although for the longest time I thought it was dear old Westly."

Wes didn't fall for his bait and just crossed his arms and relaxed back into his chair. "That still doesn't tell us why we're here, Camster."

Everyone grinned at Weston's not-so-subtle dis, but Cam took it in stride.

"Fine, we'll get down to the root of it. I know that Dax and Two Tricks are being targeted by the Tesoro Cartel that is now being run by a new leader. They want to take back the West Coast that they lost after the Devils Spawn got disbanded and when Dax pushed out the last of the De León Cartel. Both of these parties fed the Tesoro Cartel their biggest amount of skin, but it was too hot for them to try and fight back without any help. This brings us to the Mad Dogs, one of the largest MC's, spanning over many different states, being held back by both parties sitting here. The Phantom Saints and the Hidden Empire might not have planned to work in tandem on this matter, but you did. Once both of you got your footing, human trafficking in the West Coast dropped to the lowest it's ever been—thanks to you both. Problem is, that other than Texas, you're blocking the easiest way to move bodies in and out of the States," Cam informed us.

With this last piece of information everything started to fall into place. "Who is Kimber working for?"

"That would be the Mad Dogs of course, but since you slipped through their fingers and killed Mastiff's enforcer, he's not too happy with her."

"So that's why she bailed, but who helped her?" I pressed, knowing that wasn't everything.

"It would seem that she is now an official bed warmer to one of the top members in the Tesoro Cartel—"

That fucking bitch sold me out for the last time. When I get my hands on her, I will wring the life out of her and smile while doing it.

Chapter Twenty-Nine

Dax

"YEAH, I'M STILL NOT putting together why we're all here though?" Picasso interjected. "If you guys know all this, why aren't you doing anything about it?"

Cameron gave Picasso a pitying look. "Not the brightest crayon in the box, are you?"

"What the fuck does that mean?" Picasso snarled, shoving out of his chair. "You got something to say to me?"

"Not particularly no, but if there is any hope of getting back into Dax's good graces, I'll have to play nice," Cam sighed.

"The problem that we have is that their base of operations is in Mexico and their government is bought and owned by the cartel. They won't let us in to deal with it or arrest them and hand them over."

"So you expect us to do the job for you?" Sprocket asked, cocking his head to the side.

I could see Sprocket trying to follow the logic of what Cam wanted us to do but couldn't quite seem to connect the dots together. The problem was he thought Cam would stay within the line, like most FBI agents would, but that wasn't really Cam's style in life.

"Yes and no, I'll get to that in a moment," Cam said as he dimmed the lights in the room and clicked on a projector.

A vaguely familiar face popped up on the screen that seemed to set the others off.

"What the fuck does he got to do with anything—he's dead!" Picasso blurted, slamming his fist on the table. "Hannibal has been gone for over twenty years now."

Ah, so it was the family resemblance that I was seeing in this man's photo. Their uncle had the same dark brown hair and jawline, but Eagle took after him more than Picasso did. I suppose that is why his mother named him after her brother.

"We are well aware of the fact that he is dead, but members of his crew are not. Some of them have gotten out of prison and joined the Mad Dogs, since they are similar minded in lifestyle choices as the Devils Spawn was. Mastiff is just as cruel as Hannibal was, if our information on this man is accurate. I want to offer you all a deal of full immunity from crimes you've committed and might still commit while working on this case with us. Our goal is to take down the Mad Dogs and the De León Cartel, cutting off the Tesoro Cartel's legs, before we wipe them out too. This is why we had to take you in the way we did, so that the criminal world wouldn't think you came in willingly. I will be your handler and for the next two days you'll be under our protection as we make plans on how to take this trafficking ring down," Cam proclaimed, a pleased smile on his lips.

Wes shifted in his chair to look over at me with a raised brow. "You dated this prick for how long?"

"Whoa, rewind. What did you just say, Wes?" Cognac spluttered, before turning to me. "You dated a fed, *loba*?"

Rolling my eyes, I gulped down the last of my coffee and set the mug on the table. "Cameron and I dated for about a year back in college, the year Devin died. Once my twin passed, I broke things off, and well you all know the rest of the history on that. I haven't seen or heard from him in eight years, I had no idea he'd turned to the dark side."

"Very funny, beautiful, you know that we dated for over a year, and you didn't dump me, you vanished into thin air with a note telling me it was over," Cam corrected. "Full disclosure, I was recruited from the police academy once you made your rise, Dax, or should I say, Two Tricks. I've been watching you for six years, protecting you from the eye of the FBI, since I believed that Westly was the man behind the curtain. The two of you together created this taskforce and gave me the job I have now. So imagine my surprise when our informant told me that—*you*—the pink-haired sprite, was none other than the illustrious Two Tricks the whole time."

"What can I say, I've always been an overachiever," I shrugged. "So, what is this, some kind of *Blacklist* deal where I get a tracker and you as my handler allowing me to carry on with my life of crime so I can bring down the big baddy you want? Where does it end after we've accomplished this whole thing?"

Cam hit a button on the remote, causing a string of names and faces to get tossed up on the screen in some crazy interconnecting pattern. "Funny you should mention the *Blacklist*, only this time I'm Redington, with the list of names, and you're going to lead me to them."

As I take in the hundreds of people, I notice that they are mostly people that I deal with, or clients of mine. "You expect me to give them all up? I'd have nothing left, there's no way that they wouldn't figure out it was me. Some of these people don't interact with anyone outside of a small circle of trusted sources." Shaking my head, I pushed out of Void's lap to stand. "No. Arrest me, throw me in jail for the rest of my life, but I'm not doing that. The Hidden Empire is mine, created with my blood, sweat, and tears. I won't betray it or my friends to get out of jail."

Cam caught my gaze and held it, searching my expression as if trying to determine just how serious I was. The answer to that question is deadly—deadly serious.

"You would let all of your lovers take the fall and end up locked away for years, if not a life sentence, because of your pride?" Cam challenged. "That's asinine even for you, Dax. What happened to the woman I knew that wanted to be an artist that traveled the world, drifting from one place to another? I can set you free from this life of crime, just like I was able to do with your help, all those years ago."

So this was his plan all along, he wanted to save me from this version of myself. Well, guess what motherfucker, this is who I've always been lurking deep down. It was way too easy to become Two Tricks, it felt natural, like a part of me that I'd always denied myself.

"You, Cameron Able Black, can fuck all the way off. I don't need your goddamn help or for you to save me from this 'dark' world that I motherfucking created!" I fumed. "I'm out, I want nothing to do with any of this. Just know that if you lock me away, then no one will be left to fight this battle for you, because it's clear you can't do it on your own or why else would you have come to us? Either let me go and I'll deal with this problem my way, or you put me in a cell, because there is no fucking chance in hell I'm going to play this game with you. The Dax you dated is gone, she was burned in a fire of loss and pain and was reborn as this—and it's never gonna change."

The room fell silent at my declaration, but when I quickly glanced around the room, admiration with a mixture of heat flickered in my men's eyes. They saw the real me, even if Picasso felt like I was hiding things from him sometimes. I didn't want to go back to the rose-colored glasses life, this new version took the world by storm and that's how I wanted to keep it. Cam, on the other hand, looked like I'd just thrust a knife through his gut, eyes wide with shock at my challenge.

"I think it might be best if we all took some time to wrap our heads around this," Sprocket suggested. I started to speak, but he cut me off with a look. "It seems that there might need to be some adjustment to the plan and Dax is still recovering from surgery. Stress isn't really the best thing for her right now, you did say you wanted us to stick around for a few days, yes?"

Cameron shook himself out of his funk and seemed to bring himself back to center. "Yes, today has been full of unexpected turns of events for both parties. I'll escort you to where we have you set up in protective custody."

Void picked me up and set me on his hip like a little kid, but I just wrapped my legs around his waist and let him hold me. Out of all the guys, Sprocket and Void seemed to just understand what I needed without having to voice it—just like Wes. Dropping my head to his shoulder, I closed my eyes and just took a few deep breaths to calm myself down from the fury that still flickered under my skin. No one really talked as we piled into a blacked out fifteen passenger van. Cam stayed behind and two other agents drove us a few blocks away to an apartment building. It was nothing special and reminded me where I used to live before Wes and I bought our house... but much cleaner.

When we walked into the apartment, it was a simply furnished three bedroom, with a fully stocked kitchen. Eagle headed there right away and started to pull things out to make us some dinner. I hadn't realized how late it had gotten, being inside a building that didn't let in a whole lot of light. I settled on the brown corduroy couch that looked like it came out of the eighties, but it was comfortable, and flipped on the television. There splashed across the seven-o'clock news was our arrest with cellphone images of us getting put in the SUV.

"So much for keeping this low profile," I muttered, as Sprocket came to sit next to me.

He uncurled me from my ball, setting my feet in his lap and started to massage them gently. "You want to talk about what happened back there?"

"Do you?" I shot back, knowing I was taking out my anger on the wrong person.

Sprocket just gave me a look and turned back to the television. "All you had to say was no, little rebel, I'm not gonna force it out of you."

True to his word, we sat in a comfortable silence as the others drifted in around us. I noticed Wes wasn't here in the living room, so I glanced around the space spotting him working side by side with Eagle. They were talking in low voices as they worked, like it was the most normal thing in the world for them to do this. Letting my head fall back against the arm rest, I let my mind wander. Somehow, in a way I never saw coming, I now had a family again. Yeah, we were still new to this and each other, but somehow it just seemed to... work. Wes fit in with this group of guys easily, even if Picasso gave him a hard time and called him stupid nicknames, but it was almost like they acted like brothers. Sprocket seemed to have found a solid friendship with Wes, which made sense to me; their brains worked in a similar way. Void could deal with anyone as long as they didn't stand in his way, same with Cognac, who was more than happy to have another bro to hang out with.

This moment right here made me feel safe, warm, and dare I say... happy. So why do I feel so bothered that Cameron pulled the shit that he did back in the conference room? Was it my need to screw things up when they become too good to be true? Harper always warned me that I seemed to blow something up when it looked like it might be more than skin deep. Well, these assholes, as much as I didn't want to admit it, were way more than fucking skin deep. They were well and truly under my guard and it was amazing as much as it was terrifying.

Chapter Thirty

Picasso

I WATCHED HER AS she sat there on the couch lost in deep thought, her brow wrinkled with tension around her eyes. The past few weeks with her had been a rollercoaster from hell but there was no way I wanted off the ride. As much as I hated to admit it, Eagle had been right all along about her. Dax was a woman unlike any other, more layers to her than an onion, but it's what makes her who she is. I wasn't Sprocket or Wes, who seemed to be able to get her to open up with the right probing question, but I did know one thing that might help. I got up from my seat in the lumpy armchair and headed into the kitchen.

"Hey, Wes, any chance you can work your cyber voodoo and get some stuff delivered here? Or maybe find a way to get me out for a bit to get it myself?" I whispered.

Wes looked at me with a skeptical brow. Okay sure, I'd been a dick to him since he showed up, but I was more of the 'no new friends' kind of guy. I didn't trust or let people into my family without proving they would keep it safe like any of us else would. My own flesh and blood that I looked up to all my life almost killed me using his bare hands, I still have nightmares. Which is why I had converted the garage back at the house to my room and studio space. It was insulated enough that you couldn't hear it when they got bad, and too proud to admit it still haunted me.

"What do you need that badly?" Eagle questioned, staring up to me.

People think that I was the one with the brother complex, but Eagle was just as bad, he just hid it better than I did most of the time. "It's not for me, it's for Dax. A lot has happened, and I know she tells us she's fine but none of us have told her about the nightmares she can't wake up from. I think it might be a good idea to get some simple art supplies for her to mess around with. If she's anything like me, talking doesn't always help but art never fails you."

Both of them glance over to where Dax is snuggled up and I know I'll have their help.

"There's someone else who can get that stuff without us having to cause a whole scene. I'm also betting he would love to have an olive branch right now," Wes muttered. "The bastard doesn't deserve any help from me, but I love her too much not to do something I know will help her. Smart thinking Norman Rockwell, you might have just redeemed yourself."

Wes pulled out a simple black burner flip phone and hit the call button. *When had he been slipped that, and why didn't he say anything about it?* No, no, it was time to put my suspicions to rest about Weston Price. Dax loved him, and frankly, she needed him in her life to keep her grounded in a way none of us ever could.

"Shut up and listen because I'm only going to say this once, you hear me, Cammybear?" Wes growled into the phone. "You want to help her then send over art supplies, nothing too crazy. A sketch pad, chalk, charcoal, pencils, shit like that for her to use while she processes everything you just dumped on her. God, do you even know how bad you fucked up?"

As I listened in, I couldn't hear a response, which told me he might have a clue. I didn't envy that man, having spent some time in his shoes. Thankfully my fuckup wasn't as catastrophic as his was. I'll take chili oil to the eyes and get told off any day if it meant she would forgive me. Wait... why was I worried about this guy being forgiven? I saw the spark between them. This dude was someone who could go toe to toe with Dax and challenge her mentally, in a way I haven't seen anyone come close to, but Sprocket. Cameron also had a darkness to him that I didn't like one bit, there was something about him that we were all missing. My money was on the fact that Dax knew what it was, but she hasn't decided to share it with us just yet.

"I'm sure you expected things to go differently because you always have the upper hand, right? Did you forget that didn't apply to her? For Christ's sake, you idiot, just because you watched her all these years from a distance, doesn't mean you still know her... yeah, is that what you think? This is why you should have stayed the fuck away, Cameron. You can't handle a woman as strong as Dax who's just like your father."

Now I could hear yelling and swearing coming from the phone, which Wes proceeded to snap closed, cutting off the tirade.

"You gonna fill us in on him?" Eagle asked as he pulled stuff off the stove. "You know Dax doesn't like to talk about pre-Tricks life, but I feel like we're flying blind on this, and I don't like it."

Wes rubbed his forehead, letting out a heavy sigh. "I can't tell you the whole story, but he was the first guy she'd ever truly dated and seemed happy with. When Devin died, he was there, supporting her, alongside me and Harper. When she graduated, he asked her to move in with him, but Dax had already decided on taking down the Blackjax and knew Cameron wouldn't support her in that. He was going for a criminal justice degree and already had too much going against him in that area. If she'd been honest about her plans, he would have done everything in his power to stop her from turning into who she is today. So, with my help, she cut ties, we scrubbed her from social media and anything else that would connect the two of them and she vanished into the darkness. Harper has been her only connection, but even then, not many people took notice of her in the fashion world that Harper surrounded herself with."

Wes paused and looked in her direction with sadness in his eyes. "I had to talk her out of doing the same thing to Harper, but I knew she needed someone who knew Dax Blackmore and not just Two Tricks. I believe that Harper kept her alive, since it was because of her that Dax refused to let the world know that Dax and Tricks were one and the same."

I sank into one of the kitchen table chairs. "Damn, has that woman ever been able to catch a break?"

"Not so far, and doesn't look like it's coming anytime soon," Wes grumbled, as he chopped up stuff for the salad he was making.

"What are all of you muttering about in here?" Dax asked, causing us all to freeze as she snuck up on us. "Whatever it is seems to be rather interesting."

As if it was the most normal thing ever, Dax sat her perfect round ass on my lap as she waited for her answer. Instantly, my dick hardened as she shifted to look at me, like I would have a brain cell left to say anything right now. I flicked my gaze up at the others and Eagle gave me a knowing look and grinned, silently laughing at my situation.

"Just going over what happened back at the FBI building," Wes said, drawing her gray-blue eyes away from me. "At least we know the whole picture now with what's going on."

"I guess, but I don't think that's all of it. Cameron told us the plan he needed our help with, yet I have a feeling that there are more layers to this. How in the hell did the FBI find out everyone I might be working with and the clients I might have? Doesn't it seem odd to you, when I know how careful we are to keep that shit under lock and key?"

Like a lightbulb turning on in my head I understood what she'd really just said and started laughing. "Holy shit, spitfire, you played him like a dealer in Vegas. Oh, I believe everything else you said in there, but that wasn't the *real* reason you told him no, was it?"

Dax grinned at me and winked. "Look at you, catching on before the others did."

My laughter brought the others into the kitchen with questioning looks.

"What's going on?" Cognac asked, as I continued to chuckle to myself.

Eagle scowled at me and crossed his arms. "Well Einstein, you gonna tell us your great revelation?"

"They don't have a fucking clue who your clients and connections are, there is no confirmed list. My guess is they picked out every big baddie out there in the hopes that you would believe them and take the deal, confirming which ones you do have a connection with," I shared, looking back at her to see if I was right.

Her answer was to kiss me like I'd been wanting to since the moment she sat down on my lap. It didn't help with my raging boner, but I would just have to take a shower to deal with that later. I've gotten used to rubbing one out at least once a day since she popped into our lives. Finally being able to eat her like a fat kid at a buffet was everything I'd hoped it would be, and more. Now, I was just waiting for the all clear and I would tie her up to a bed for at least twenty-four hours to truly show her how sorry I was. One of the guys let out an obnoxiously loud cough, telling us to break it up.

"Well fuck, now all of us are going to try and be the smart one if that's the reward we get," Cognac smirked.

"You might as well sit at the table, dinner's ready," Eagle said, waving them over. The table only had six chairs, so I kept Dax right where she was, no sense in moving her, if there wasn't a chair.

Eagle made stir-fry and my guess is that he did it so Dax could eat it with one hand. Void stood and dished up a plate before any of us could even make for the platters of food, then set it down in front of Dax. "What do you want to drink, little demon?"

"Water's fine, thanks, big guy," she answered with a soft smile.

Within a few minutes, we all had full plates and fell into silence as we stuffed our faces.

"Okay so explain this to me again?" Sprocket asked first. "The people they put up on the screen weren't your clients and connections?"

"A lot of them were but others weren't. That's what tipped me off. A few were dealers and transporters that I would never work with because they tend to stab you in the back... literally. Then there were others I had never heard of or seen before. It was like Picasso said, they collected every known criminal and put them up on the screen. What stood out to me was the fact that they hadn't missed any of my people. They were all there. Many of them connect to each other too, so I couldn't even give up the ones I hate to work with but can get me what I need where I need it," Dax explained.

"Is this the type of thing you alert your people to?" Void questioned.

"God no, they know that someone is watching them from some government group, but to tell them which one would make them crazy paranoid. Add on that, I'm American, it would cause them to cut me off for sure, might even put me on the blacklist."

"What's our alternative? Can you smuggle us out of the States?" I asked.

This question seemed to shock her. "You would up and leave everything behind, just like that?"

"Over jail, hell yeah, no question. If we end up locked up for the next twenty to thirty years, what's left for us? The Phantom Saints would pick new leadership and carry on, we couldn't manage things from inside the clink. Maybe if it was just one or two of us, but not all five," I answered. "Besides, it means we all get to stick together—better to have five people watching your back than none. Well, and the fact that we're family Dax. You belong to us, we belong to you, simple as that."

The others all nodded their agreement.

"The only way you'll be rid of us, little hellcat, is if we're dead, otherwise we'll do whatever it takes to stay together and free," Eagle affirmed.

Dax just sat there for a moment and stared at us all. "If I was any other woman, I would be crying right now, that was way too fucking sweet for you guys to say."

I couldn't help but laugh at that and the others joined in, giving us a moment to forget what might happen in the future. With all our brains combined I had to believe we could figure a way out of this, I just hoped it didn't force us to abandon everything, even though we would, without question, if it came down to it.

Chapter Thirty-One

Dax

I was still snuggled up in bed with Sprocket and Cognac when a knock sounded from the front door. Refusing to be bothered, I burrowed deeper into Cognac's chest as Sprocket pulled my ass tighter against his morning wood. Unable to help myself, I wiggled and gasped when he pinched my nipple in retaliation.

"Little rebel, don't make me break the rules and take you right here right now," he warned, his voice rough with sleep.

My little tryst with Eagle and Picasso had helped to stem my libido, but it was not typically my nature to go this long without sex. Sadly, his threat did the complete opposite of what he wanted as I arched back into him, grabbing my tank top and lifting it so now his hand was holding my bare breast. Cognac shifted back slightly, giving me a sleepy yet lustful look.

"Oh, *loba*, are you sure you want to play this game right now, because I'm not very good at being the bigger person when it comes to you?" Cognac asked as he trailed a finger across my lips.

I opened my mouth quickly, biting onto the tip of his finger, holding it still as I sucked it into my mouth, running my tongue along its length.

Drawing back, I released it with a pop and grinned up at him. "Who says I'm playing? I know my body and I'll be able to manage the two of you just fine. Now, are you going to fuck me, or do I have to go find one of the others to do the job?"

Both Sprocket and Cognac growled, their grips on me tightening, telling me that I was totally going to get what I wanted. Sprocket started kissing up my neck as he massaged my breast, sliding his other arm under me to get ahold of the other one. Cognac moved lower, kissing down my stomach as he pulled down my panties and tossing them across the room. The bed was a queen, so with three of us in it left little room to maneuver, but that wasn't going to stop either of them. Cognac lifted my leg and hooked it over Sprocket's hip, leaving me open to him. Slowly, he ran a finger through my pussy and pulled it away, showing me how wet it was.

"Goddamn, *loba*, did you have naughty dreams about us, or have we left you unfucked for too long?" Cognac purred, as he lifted the finger and sucked it clean. "It seems that this is going to take the two of us to catch up on things, now isn't it."

Sprocket humped against my ass slowly, letting me feel his hard cock covered in a pair of gym shorts slide between my cheeks. "How do you feel about taking both of us, little rebel? Or would that be too much for you to handle?"

I shivered, feeding off all their dirty talk and teasing touches. "God yes, I want... no... need you both to fuck me until I can't remember my own name."

Sprocket smiled against my skin before he nipped it, pulling me on his chest as he rolled onto his back. Grabbing both of my legs, he pulled them back and wide, so I was on display to Cognac. "Would you do the honors of getting her ready for me?"

"Oh, an honor it will be to feast on this first thing in the morning. Today is going to be a great damn day," Cognac muttered, as he slid in between Sprocket's legs and cupped my ass to lift me to a better angle.

He proceeded to start with my pussy, lapping at it like a cat with a bowl of cream before sliding in two fingers and scooping out some of my natural lube and smearing my asshole with it. Keeping his attention on my clit, he massaged my backdoor, gently pressing his finger against it. Sprocket went back to playing with my nipples, turning my head so he could plunder my mouth at the same time. Cognac made a steady rhythm of working both holes until two fingers easily fit in both and I was a shivering mess of need, resting on the edge of an orgasm.

"In my expert opinion, I would say our girl is ready," Cognac proclaimed, as he pinched my clit, sending me soaring right off the cliff and let out a cry of pleasure.

"You two better fucking stuff me full of cock or I'm going to lose my mind," I panted, as they maneuvered me back on my side, leg tossed over Cognac as they lined up.

Sprocket bit the shell of my ear as I felt him run his dick along my pussy, lubing it up for the real action. "We can't have that now can we, your mind is too beautiful to be lost over such a thing."

With that, he fisted his cock and guided it into my ass as I pressed against him, encouraging him in faster. Now that my ass was claimed, I looked up at Cognac who cupped the side of my face, pulling me to him and kissing me like I was the air he breathed. In the chaos of our kiss, he slid home, making me moan with the sense of fullness that never ceases to blow my mind. The feeling of being so full to the point you weren't sure you could handle it, was unlike any other. They slowly started to work in and out of me, alternating as I adjusted to them both being in my body and relaxing into it. Their hands were everywhere all at once, rubbing my clit, tweaking my nipples, clutching me tighter, making it impossible to find where I ended, and they started.

Their speed picked up, and I fell into the motion as well, rocking to deepen their thrusts. The room filled with heavy breathing, moaning, and the slap of skin on skin, but something caused me to take in my surroundings. There in the doorway was Cameron, casually leaning against the door jamb watching us with hunger clear in his gaze. The bastard always loved to watch or be watched by others, figures that didn't change over the years. I held his gaze as Sprocket grabbed a fist full of my hair and pulled, arching me so he could get a better angle, followed by his teeth gripping my shoulder as he pounded frantically into me. Cognac kissed and licked up my neck freely as it was now on display to him. I could feel them both nearing their finish, so I clenched, causing them both to grunt and groan their pleasure as I milked them, sending me into my own orgasmic bliss.

We laid there for a few minutes, catching our breath as they placed gentle loving kisses over whatever skin they could reach. I let my hands trail over their bodies, now covered in a sheen of sweat from our activities. These were moments I never let myself indulge in before all of them. I was a hit it and quit it girl, I didn't let myself become attached and enjoy the afterglow. Now that I was giving it a chance, I discovered that I quite liked this blissed-out haze as we each tried to bring our souls back to our body.

"I didn't think it was possible, but I think you've actually gotten sexier over the years, beautiful," Cam said alerting the others to his presence.

Cognac sprang to his feet, causing me to moan at the loss of him, but there he stood proudly ready to defend me. The view of his perfect bronze ass didn't hurt the situation at all either. Sprocket grabbed the sheet and pulled it over us, as he carefully pulled out, tucking the sheet around me as he got out of bed.

"Ah, why are we getting up? There's not going to be a round two?" I asked, stacking some pillows behind me so I could sit against the headboard. Both Sprocket and Cognac looked at me a little surprised. "Oh, don't worry about him, he likes to watch, not to mention the whole exhibitionist thing. Hey, you still into blood play and 'marking' your women with your teeth?"

"What the fuck?" Cognac blurted, rushing at Cam, slamming him against the wall, holding him by his throat. "You fucking cut her up? What kind of man does that to a woman he's in love with?"

Sprocket reached out and grabbed Cognac's shoulder. "He might be able to answer you if you let him breathe."

Releasing his hold on Cam, Cognac took a half step back, still within his personal bubble. I just grinned, watching Cameron glare at me for calling him out on his hidden kinks, that I know he only shared with me because I was just as freaky as he was. Cam didn't like others to know about the darkness he hid from everyone, but I'd always seen through his façade.

"You know for a fact that you're the only woman I've ever marked as mine," Cam snarled possessively. "I told you before there will never be another woman for me but you."

Tossing back the covers I scooted out of bed, feeling cum leak out of me, making me shiver with an echo of our pleasure together. I walked over to Cam, nudging Cognac out of the way so I could look my ex in the face as I said what I needed to.

"Here's the thing, Alpha," I paused for dramatic effect, using his primal name watching his eyes dilate at it. "I don't trust you enough to look after a house plant, what in the fuck makes you think I would trust you to take you back after what you said to me yesterday? No, see we don't know each other anymore—not really. So, if you want to somehow find yourself back in my good graces, stop lying to me and be honest. Trust that I know more than you about everything when it comes to the criminal world. I'd already figured out it was the Tesoro Cartel after me, I just didn't have the full picture, which you've now given me. With that last part of the puzzle, I'll be more than capable of dealing with matters."

"You can't do it on your own, Dax, it's too big," Cam challenged.

I bopped him on the nose and winked. "See that's the thing, I'm not doing it on my own. I have the Phantom Saints, and the rest of the Hidden Empire to back me up. We both know you have no idea how far my control goes and I'm not going to tell you. Who knows, I might even reach out to your father and see if he wants to come and play. It would be fun to reconnect with Dante Black. His mind is almost as brilliant as yours is for finding things."

"Have you lost all your humanity that you would stoop that low to hurt me?" Cam asked, pain and sadness filling his amber eyes. "You know that all I've ever wanted was to be free of him and his black shadow, to be my own person. You encouraged me to do it, helped me stay on the straight and narrow instead of falling into his world. A world that you seem to have jumped into with both feet and now rule, I might add."

Letting out a huff, I turned and sat on the bed, crossing my arms and legs, needing to control my frustration. "Cameron, do you understand that I am one of the monsters that goes bump in the night? Your father, he is a con artist and a thief, granted he's the fucking best, but on a scale of evil he's right up there next to the people who run chop shops. Then there's me, yeah, I don't deal in flesh, but that's about all I don't take part in. If they pay me enough, I'll get whatever someone needs to where they need it. If you can't handle the fact that your dad is a career criminal and trained you to follow in his footsteps, then any chance you think you have of being with me is zero."

Cam took a deep breath and walked out of the room, leaving me there gutted at once again having to push him out of my life. Before the guys, he was the closest I ever allowed myself to thinking I could be happy with someone for the rest of my life. Why the fuck did I pick the damaged bad boy that only ever dreamed of being the white knight in the fairy tale? Sprocket stepped up and wrapped his arm around me, followed by Cognac sliding in behind me, making a cocoon of protection. I couldn't remember the last time I cried over something emotional, it was dumb and didn't do a goddamn thing to fix things, but here I was, hot tears rolling down my cheeks over a stupid boy.

They held me for a while, but then Sprocket pulled me up and hustled me into the shower. It couldn't fit all three of us, so Cognac left to use the other bathroom while Sprocket took care of me. I remembered back to that second day I'd been kidnapped with a raging hangover, and he showered me just like this, without needing anything in return. There was something magical about a shower, it had the power to wash away so much more than just your outer dirt and grime. By the time we were both clean and dressed, I was back to normal and ready to find a way to get the hell out of this place. Being under the thumb of the FBI was never part of my life plan, and it was holding me back from getting my revenge for all the shit these assholes have been putting me through.

Chapter Thirty-Two

Dax

Much to my surprise, I found Cam sitting in the kitchen drinking coffee while the others ate and gave him scathing looks.

"What do you know, I figured you would have run with your tail between your legs," I huffed, as I poured myself coffee and filled my plate.

"If I'm going to prove that you can trust me, it would only make sense for me to not run the first time I get bit," Cam answered, flashing me his signature smile.

Frowning, I padded over to Eagle and kissed him soundly on the mouth. "Boss man, if you keep making meals like this, I'm gonna get fat."

"More of you to love is all, little hellcat." Eagle grinned, as he pulled me down to his lap. "Sounds like you've had a busy morning, I thought Dani said no roughhousing?"

I grinned down at him. "Trust me there was no roughhousing. I was very well protected from both sides."

He just laughed and nuzzled the side of my neck, kissing me behind my ear. "Angel boy didn't upset you, did he? We all told him to leave it alone, but he said you wouldn't mind..."

"Now, Eagle, are you asking me if you can watch the next time I get fucked?" I teased. "If that's the case, then no I don't mind at all, as long as everyone else is fine with it."

"God, you are the perfect woman, aren't you," Eagle praised as he drew me into a kiss.

I had to hand it to the guys. They were taking this all in stride, utterly ignoring Cam where he sat quietly watching us as we ate and chatted.

"What are the chances I get my bike back?" Eagle asked, giving me the bacon off his plate.

"Are you trying to bribe me?"

"Would it work?"

"Not a chance, but I suppose you've paid enough penance to get your bike back. I was gonna have to replace the handlebars on it anyway, I've never been a fan of those stupid things." I grimaced thinking of the ride back to the city.

Eagle just shrugged. "To each their own I suppose, just like those pink nine mils you had on you the other night. Never pegged you for such a girly accessory."

"I bought them for her as a birthday present. It was the first time she wore them out in public," Wes interjected.

"Damn man." Void chuckled. "How did you not get shot with them pulling a stunt like that?"

"Because they happened to be my favorite guns to shoot, even if they were an obnoxious color," I added.

Cam took that moment to set his mug down forcefully on the table and stood up, his gaze locked on me, bringing us all to attention. I could feel the guys tense, ready to move if they needed to defend me in any way, while Eagle got a better grip on me in case he needed to bail out of the chair.

"This whole thing has been a setup. I talked my boss into letting me bring you in, telling him you would give up your client list to me. They sent every assassin they could after you because of how big of a threat you are if you join with the Phantom Saints. How could I let you go through that without protection? You are the reason I created this taskforce so that I could keep an eye on you, be the knight coming in to save you from the dangers of the world you got sucked into. I now understand that you left me all those years ago because you *chose* to live this life and you're damn good at it." He paused to take a deep breath as if whatever he said next would change everything.

"Dax, I can't arrest you, it would kill me to see you behind bars because I put you there. I'm going to get you out of this, even if that means I have to become what I've always been running from. If we're going to do this though, you have to play along to some extent so I can get you out of protective custody and back home. You were right when you said the FBI couldn't do this without you. We don't have the right people in place, and we can't get them there. You already have the network established and I don't want to stand in your way any longer—I love you too much to do that to you."

The guys and I exchanged looks, unsure of what to do with this declaration.

"Cameron, what is it exactly that you're saying?" Wes ventured.

"I am going to lie to my superiors and tell them you agreed to the plan, but you refuse to give us the list of clients until your life is no longer in danger. As a show of good faith between you and the FBI, we will let you return to normal life, along with myself as a new associate, to take down the Tesoro Cartel. Once that is done, I'll help you get out of the deal or get you out of the country if I can't," Cam explained.

"Just like that... you want us to believe you've had a full one-eighty, just like that?" Sprocket questioned. "I was present for what you said to her back in the bedroom. There's no way you could have a change of heart that fast, I'm sorry."

Cam didn't back down though, he straightened his shoulders and shifted his gaze to Sprocket. "Name your price. What do I have to do for you to believe that I'm trying to make an effort here?"

"Leave the FBI right now. Call them up and tell them that you resign," Picasso interjected.

"No, we still need him to have access to their databases," I argued. "You joked about your offer being like the TV show *Blacklist*, well, maybe we can take a note from them. Let us put a tracking chip on you so we can monitor your whereabouts, allow Wes to clone your phone and computer so we can see everything you're doing."

"You want me to become a double agent?" Cam confirmed.

"Basically, we need to know that all this isn't just to sell us out to your bosses later. I agree you will stick with us, but in no way are you to be involved in Empire or Phantom business. We will tell you what you need to know and compare notes when needed," I explained.

Cam sat down, folding his hands on the table, eyes searching my face for something. "Tell me there is hope to get you to trust me again, Dax. To me this isn't a game. Ever since I've met you, I've done all that I can to keep you out of jail or noticed by the FBI more than you already were. All this might sound like lip service and Sprocket it right not to trust me, I know I have to earn that, but only if there's hope."

"I don't get it Cam, you've spent all this time watching me from the shadows, why didn't you approach me before all this?" I pressed, knowing that if I gave him a glimmer of hope and he betrayed me, it would crush the part of my heart he held and I tried to keep safe.

"Deep down, even though I didn't want to admit it, you were destined for this kind of life. Two Tricks might have been born out of pain, but it was always inside you, it's what drew me to you all those years ago. You don't need a white knight to save you, no you need dark knights to support you as you rule. The bureau wants me for my knowledge of being a criminal, and I've had to deny what I'm really good at so they don't see me as a threat." Cam dropped his gaze, pulled off his tie and unbuttoned his shirt to show a tattoo of my calling card on his chest over his heart. "What if I've been a double agent for you all along, but I needed to test you to see you're really the queen I've been looking to serve?"

Stunned, I sat there in Eagle's lap, knowing that Cameron Albert Black had just played the longest con of his life, and he did it for me. "Cam, hand me your phone."

Without hesitation, he pulled it out of his pocket and slid it over to me. I placed my thumb on the sensor and of course it was already programmed in, being the cocky son of a bitch that he is. Clicking on his contacts I scrolled down until I reached the name we always used as a joke for his father, Thomas Crown. I hit the call button and waited as it started to ring.

"Is this my idiot son having failed in his conquest of love, or is this my dear sweet Dax who thinks he's full of shit?" Dante's silky southern voice answered.

The man, the legend, the myth himself, who'd stolen millions in his career and never got caught, sounding far too pleased with himself. "You came up with this plan for him, didn't you?"

"What would you do if your one and only child is devastated when the love of his life leaves him in the middle of the night? It took me a year or so to figure you and that operation of yours out, but soon enough it became clear that once again, you should never doubt a woman scorned. I have to commend you on pulling off one of the best cons I've seen in the criminal world, showing me yet again, that you are the perfect woman for my son. Would you mind if we switched this to speakerphone so all those around you can hear me?" Dante requested.

Blowing out an exasperated sigh, I hit the speaker button and set it on the table.

"Hello, boys," Dante purred. "I would suggest a video call to see all you lovely men, but I'm in my dressing gown still, and well, that's just not proper."

The guys all looked at the phone then to me and Cam, clearly not understanding what was going on and who the manly southern bell was on the phone. "Guys, this is Cameron's father, Dante Black. The mastermind behind Cam's master plan to become the best inside man we could ever ask for in the FBI."

"Wait, hold up!" Cognac sputtered, as he stood and started pacing. "Look, I know I'm not the level of smart that Sprocket and Wes are, but what the actual fuck is going on right now?"

"Settle down now, we're getting to all that, it's why I had her put me on speaker," Dante admonished. "I'm assuming everyone knows that Dax and Cameron dated?" They all muttered yes. "Good, well when she left, leaving him with only a letter and a broken heart, I knew it had to be for a good reason. See, these two are meant for each other and you can't find a love like that just anywhere, let me tell you."

"Dad," Cameron growled.

"Fine, take all my fun away from me, why don't you." Dante huffed. "As a father, I knew I needed to do something to help him, but first I had to figure out what Rainbow Bright was up to. It didn't take much more than six months to find out about her brother and what really happened and not what they put in the papers. As I told her, it did take me a while longer to figure out the long game and the fact that she was Two Tricks, and baby, that stand in you had in the early years was awful. I'm glad you got rid of him before he ruined the whole thing. Now, knowing the criminal world like I do and what it takes to survive, I might have suggested a way that Cameron could be of help to you and when the time was right, swoop in and save the princess from getting locked away forever!" Dante proclaimed.

"Are you trying to tell us he's been watching Dax's back this whole time? He joined the FBI to be her double agent when the time came and that he isn't trying to fuck her over?" Picasso asked, breaking it down to bare bones.

"Child, isn't that what I just said? You need to listen better," Dante tutted. "When I scraped my son off the floor of the house he bought for the two of them, I brought him home for a spell. That's when I did my research and figured everything out, during that time he stopped trying to fight who I raised him to be and what he was born to do and accepted it wholeheartedly. When he went back to school, he did everything he could to catch the eye of the FBI and it worked. He got recruited and used the whole 'my father's a criminal and I want to be the good guy' bit to reel them in. Once they were on the hook and the Hidden Empire was well underway, he was the ever-loyal knight working in the shadows. We both agreed that now was the time to pull back the curtain and let Dorothy meet the wizard, because you've had too many close calls, young lady, getting shot like that."

All my guys looked completely blown away by what they were hearing right now. "Welcome to the mind of the master con artist, guys."

"So, we just believe that and forget everything that's happened so far?" Wes argued.

"Weston Price is that you?" Dante cooed. "Son, I know you aren't fixin' to slight her against my boy now. He's grown up and learned a lot over the past eight years. He hasn't even slept with another woman since Dax, so you can take the mother hen act and stuff it."

"Wes, you know his father?" Void asked.

"Yeah, I know that man, and this type of fucked-up crazy-ass mental twister is right up his alley," Wes grumbled.

"You say the nicest things, Weston," Dante preened. "Now I'm gonna hang up, but if you need anything, Dax darling, you just let me know."

Picasso flopped onto the table and banged his head against it twice. "How did this shit get even more confusing? Is he good or is he bad? Do we believe him and his weird ass southern bell of a father or not?"

I stood and walked into the kitchen grabbing one of the knives from the block on the counter and meandered over to where Cam was sitting. My gaze flicked to Void and gave a slight nod when I saw he knew exactly what I was going to do. Fast as lightning, Void struck, slamming Cam's head into the table, stunning him before locking him into a choke hold. I used the knife to cut away all his clothes, leaving him naked, making my search for any kind of tracker or listening device on him easier. I knew on the black market there were adhesive listening patches that could record sound and be played back later. Scouring every inch of him, I didn't find anything that would lead me to believe he was playing us. I tossed the clothes to Sprocket who started to look over them for the same thing.

Taking Cam's dick and balls in hand, I tucked the knife right up under them where they connected to his body. Looking him right in those amber eyes that I thought I could read so well, I demanded answers.

"Are you loyal to the FBI?"

"No. I'm loyal to you and you alone."

"What about your father? Are you loyal to him, hmm, would you turn me over if he asked you too?"

"Never, I'm grateful to him for everything, but I would sooner let you cut off my balls than give you up to anyone."

"Do you believe that if I discover you're lying to me about anything I will kill you without hesitation?"

"Yes, I would expect nothing less from Two Tricks, Queen of the Hidden Empire."

I glanced at the others over my shoulder. "Anyone else have a question?"

"Yeah, I got one," Eagle said, standing up and walking up behind me, hands on my hips. "Are you expecting to become one of her men? By that, I mean those of us who are in a committed relationship and would die to protect her, whether she wants you to or not?"

"If she granted me that honor... yes. I pray to one day be counted as one of her men," Cam answered, looking down at me, no longer hiding behind any walls or charade, just revealing his pure longing and need for me.

Pulling the knife away from his jewels, I gripped the handle so I could cut my name into his flesh right under the tattoo. "Your life is mine, Cameron, whether you get to keep living it is up to you and your actions. Now I want to go home, make it happen."

Chapter Thirty-Three

Dax

An hour after our heart-to-heart, Cam made good on my request and all of us got in the van and headed to the Phantom's compound. I'm sure Cam already knew where I lived, but I felt better heading back there where more eye-witnesses were around, just in case. I believed that this could be a whole set up and Cam wanted to help me, but I still didn't trust the man himself. If he could pull something like that off without the FBI noticing, then he's stepped up his game since I knew him last. What else could he be hiding in plain sight?

We all piled out of the van in the center of the compound, triggering a surge of bikers to come pouring out of the clubhouse.

Some gave bro hugs to the guys, while others asked questions about what happened, but Eagle took charge right away.

"Hey! Meeting in the clubhouse in an hour, spread the word. I want everyone there, including the old ladies!" Eagle announced.

This seemed to settle everyone down for a bit as they scattered to let the others know what was going on. Ah, small town living, where everyone needs to know your business—well I guess when it's broadcast on the evening news it might make some waves. The guys and I headed into their house and oddly it was nice to be back here, it was familiar and felt like my men. I headed right for Eagle's room where I'd last seen my bag of clothes that Tilly got me, but as I scrounged around, I couldn't find it.

"What are you getting into now, little hellcat?" Eagle asked, watching me with a smirk.

"Looking for my clothes, you didn't throw them out in a fit of rage, did you?" I countered.

Pushing off the wall he was leaning against, he walked over to his dresser and pulled open the middle drawer. "Figured this would be easier for you to get to since you're so short and all, but it's yours to keep whatever you want here."

"You gave me a drawer of my own? Even after our whole fight?" I hedged, walking over and peeking at the clothes that were all neatly folded and clean.

Eagle wrapped his arms around me, resting his chin on the top of my head. "I told you that fight wasn't really about me being upset with you, that was all about me and my own personal demons. When I said I wanted you to move in with us I meant it in every sense. I even got you your own toothbrush so you don't have to use mine."

I couldn't help but laugh at that. "Wow, the boss man is ready to share his personal sanctuary with me? I feel so honored."

"As you should, I don't let just anyone live after using my bathtub—that should have been your first clue as to how I felt about you," Eagle teased, before slapping me on my ass and stepping back. "Now get changed, we've got a lot of ground to cover with the crew."

Grabbing clothes, I managed to get them on without too much trouble and situated my sling before peeking in the bathroom to see the neon pink toothbrush with cheetah print on the handle. Rolling my eyes, I let it go, because for some reason the fact he put that much effort into picking it out made me smile. Even though it was getting close to lunch time, I could smell fresh coffee coming from the kitchen and I let my nose lead to the source.

I was about to make a joke, thinking it was one of the guys but there was Cameron wearing borrowed jeans with no shirt on and bandaging the mark I gave him. I know I shouldn't be so thrown off by this. I mean, I held the man's dick and balls at knife point not too long ago, but I wasn't in the mood to acknowledge how good he looked. Not that I was in the *mood*, but it was hard to deny that he was a shirtless buff gorgeous man standing in the afternoon light doctoring a wound that some crazy chick gave him. Add on the fact that he knew I was watching but didn't bother to call me on it, allowing me to gawk my fill.

"Did someone make coffee?" Sprocket asked, coming down the stairs.

I looked over my shoulder and just pointed, still not able to speak coherent words.

Sprocket kissed me on the forehead and headed over to the cabinet with the mugs. "You want some, little rebel? Sorry, that was a dumb question, of course you do, let me guess you just got a little distracted?"

"Fuck you, Sprocket," I snapped not liking being called out like that.

Grinning, he winked and handed me a mug. "Anytime, anywhere, just say the word."

"Oh eww, you did not just pull a Cognac." I scowled.

"What about me?" Cognac asked, sliding up behind me. "Is someone getting you all hot 'n bothered and I'm missing it?"

I stomped on his foot, getting a satisfying *oomph* out of him, before walking away out onto the porch. I spotted a porch swing that hadn't been there before and settled on to the soft seat cushion, pushing off with one of my legs to get it going. After a few moments, Void came to join me, taking my empty coffee cup out of my hand, before picking me up and setting me on his lap straddling his thighs, so we were face to face.

"What's up, big guy?"

He brushed his fingers along my jaw, tucking some hair behind my ear just watching me for a few minutes before speaking.

"You don't have to keep him, you know. If it's too much or too painful, I'll take care of it. You just give me a nod."

Smiling at him, I leaned into his touch, loving that he was so ready to do what was needed to take care of me. "Have I ever told you how amazing you are, Void? I don't think I've met another person who understands my level of stabbyness the way you do. Like back with Cameron, I didn't have to say a word, and you just knew what I was planning on doing with him, that kind of bond is rare."

"That's because you are my soulmate," Void stated, as if it was the most obvious thing in the world. "You are the other half of my soul and no one is ever going to take you away from me—not even death."

"You would fight death for me?" I giggled.

"Yes, or I would join you in the afterlife. One does not keep living life without their soulmate once they are found, little demon," Void explained.

I blinked at him, shocked by how serious he was being about this. "You're not kidding about this, are you?"

Void shifted his hand so it was now cupping the back of my head as he drew me to him and showed me just how serious he was being about all this. It was not hurried or frenzied, no it was slow and sensual, making me curl my toes with pleasure. I wrapped my arm around his neck and leaned in so our bodies were melded together, while his other hand sat on my ass pulling me tight against him. I could feel his dick hardening under me and I let out a moan, biting on his lower lip before we came up for air.

"I've never been more serious about something in my entire life as I am about you, Dax," Void whispered, resting his forehead against mine.

"Um... I can come back, if now isn't a good time," Tilly's voice said from over to the left.

Lifting my head I grinned at her, and Void helped me off his lap so I could go greet her. "Aw, you can't be embarrassed by stuff like that, you've got two husbands after all."

"Embarrassed please, that shit was hot as fuck." Tilly grinned and she gave me a side hug. "I heard you got shot. What the hell, man? I can't have my new best friend dying off on me so fast. What will the next one think when she asks what happened to my old BFF?"

I hugged her back one more time, having truly missed her. "God, I've been surrounded by so much dick it's nice to have some estrogen in the air."

Void just grunted and headed off to the clubhouse with a wink. I waved Tilly over to the swing and sat down, ready to catch up on what's been going on here the past week.

"To be honest, things have been really boring with you gone, the guys were a hot mess for a few days. I could tell there was something going on but no matter how I tried to ask, they just ignored me. I even talked Mutt into asking Void what was up, since they're friends, but all he got was, and I quote: 'Our President is an idiot.' Which we all know every man can be at some point, so that was no help," Tilly shared, grinning. "Gator is convinced that you are going to be more trouble than you're worth as a friend, but I think that's just your charm."

"Hmm, seems like I need to butter Gator up, so he'll let you come out and play when I ask," I teased.

Tilly just tossed her head back and laughed. "That man knows better than to tell me I can't hang out with someone, how do you think Mutt entered the picture?"

The sound of a phone ringing paused our conversation as Tilly answered her phone. "Hello this is Tilly... yes she's here... who is this?" Tilly pulled the phone away and muted it. "They won't say who they are but they're asking for you—he sounds Hispanic."

My stomach dropped into the pit of my stomach. I'd gotten one friend to safety but now another was in danger. "Hand it over and go find Wes please, he should be still in the house. Tell him we need to trace a call from a friend south of the border."

Taking a deep breath, I unmuted the phone and lifted it to my ear. "Who the fuck is this and why the hell are you calling on this phone?"

"*Hola, senorita,* it is nice to finally speak with you," the man on the other end greeted. "As for who I am, I'm Marco Tesoro."

Motherfucking son of a bitch, this guy was no longer playing in the shadows, he was stepping up his game.

"To what do I owe this pleasure? It's not every day that you get to speak to the man who's trying to kill you," I mused as Wes appeared with his computer and plugged a cable into the phone.

Wes's fingers flew over the keyboard as he pulled up whatever he needed and got to work.

"*Si*, it is most unfortunate that we must chat under such circumstances, but you see I promised my father on his deathbed that I would bring our family name back to the glory it once was. My father was a great man who built an amazing empire, such as yourself, but he became ill and refused to fight to take back what we'd lost over the years. Now that he is gone, I plan to do what he could not and you, *senorita*, stand between me and that goal. People are drawn to you and support you. I've tried many ways to unseat you but their loyalty is to be commended. So, what is left for me to do other than take out the queen, clearing the field for me to move in as king," Marco shared, speaking as if I was some ignorant child.

"That still doesn't explain this phone call," I snarked back.

Marco let out a sigh. "It is so tragic to lose such a strong woman as yourself in this day and age. Tell me, has your lover traced my call yet? If he has, there should be a very panicked look on his face..."

Glancing at Wes, he met my eyes and flipped the computer around and pointed to a building on a map that looked just like my house.

"Keep watching, you don't want to miss this," Marco goaded. "Three... two... one."

There before my eyes, my house exploded, sending shrapnel everywhere, blowing out the windows of the houses beside us. The video feed went dark after I assumed the surveillance that Wes put up was damaged in the blast.

"You fucking bastard! Do you know what you've just done?!" I snarled into the phone.

"I most certainly do. Now stop ignoring me and fight me like the demon that everyone tells me that you are!" With that, he cut off the call.

Chucking the phone and letting out a roar of anger, I started to punch whoever it was that walked up to me. I was dragged off the porch and out into the yard where I tore off my sling and went full out. I couldn't think, I couldn't see, all I could do was fight, landing punches and kicks left and right. I took a hit to the ribs, but I knew they were holding back, which pissed me off even more. This proved that nothing was safe in my world. Anything could be taken from me, and I was done playing defense.

I am Dax motherfucking Blackmore, also known as Two Tricks, and I was out for blood.

The end

About Author

Elizabeth is an International Best Seller, originally from Illinois but now living in sunny Phoenix, AZ. Elizabeth has been writing for nine years and started out in YA Fiction but recently found herself loving the Reverse Harem genre. Like her favorite books, Elizabeth loves to write about strong women of all varieties. Not all strength is flashy or apparent at first glance—some lies just under the surface.

Don't Miss Out!

Be the first to know what is coming next by following Elizabeth's social media! You never know when or what will be coming next!

Website: ElizabethKnightBooks.com

Facebook: Elizabeth Knight's Unicorn Queens

Instagram: elizabethknightauthor

TikTok: elizabethknightauthor

Newsletter: sign up here

Also By

<u>Omegaverse</u>

Knot All Is Lost: Part 1

Knot All Is Lost: Part 2

Knot All Is Ruined (January 2023)

<u>Caprioni Queen</u>

Book 1 – Glitter & Guns

Book 2 – Blood & Heartache (February 2023)

<u>Found by Monsters</u>

Book 1 – A Siren of Beasts

Book 2 – Tamer of Beasts (April 2023)

<u>Hidden Empire Series – Complete series</u>

Book 1 - Two Tricks

Book 2 - Three Tricks

Book 3 - Four Tricks

Book 4 - More Tricks

Book 5 - Our Tricks

Hidden Empire Novel
Harper's Renegades

Omega Assassin - Complete series
Book 1 - Dual Nature

Book 2 - Hidden Nature

Book 3 - Perfect Nature

Hope Series - Complete series
Book 1 – Hidden Hope

Book 2 – Claiming Hope

Book 3 – Defending Hope

Book 4 - Obtaining Hope

Mercenary Queen Series - Complete series
Book 1 – Birthright

Book 2 - Dragon Queen

Book 3 - Forgotten Throne

Book 4 - The Final Battle

<u>Elementi Series - Complete series</u>
Book 1 - Discovering Synergy

Book 2 – Refining Earth

Book 3 – Liberating Water

Book 4 - Taming Fire

Book 5 - Rescuing Air

Printed in Great Britain
by Amazon